INDIAN LEAP

INDIAN LEAP

SETH KANOR

 Heliotrope Books

New York

Cover design by Heather Seksinsky

Typeset by Naomi Rosenblatt

To the most beautiful boy in the world

I'd like to get away from Earth awhile
And then come back to it and begin all over.
—Robert Frost, "Birches"

PART ONE

PART ONE

128th and Convent

Because I am a lifelong insomniac and because my apartment—like so many New York City apartments in winter—was hotter than a Turkish sauna, I couldn't sleep, and the air conditioner would be no help. Pulled from the window for winter, it had been pushed to the back of my closet, where it was now hibernating under a pile of dirty clothes, and my rotating fan, a mechanical thing with a mind of its own, skipped and juddered whenever its arc drew near. Desperate for air, I rolled off my low bed, stumbled toward the window, and raised the shade.

The building across the courtyard, if you could call it a courtyard—and you couldn't—was abandoned. Splatters, splotches, and squiggles of white-gray and blue-gray paint ran down the crumbling brick, and most of the windows were boarded with plywood and two-by-fours. A pink barbell, the only remaining sign of the former inhabitants, lay on the rusted fire escape. Above, a fat pigeon was croaking his strange song; below, chained in the narrow passageway, the super's pit bull had begun barking.

It was hard to know which would be worse: the window open and the croaking and barking, or the window closed and the stifling heat.

I cracked the window and went back to bed.

It was now both too noisy and too hot.

Soon, the rest of the city would wake and the noise would be unbearable. Soon, the issues of my insomnia, the heat, the hibernating air conditioner, the broken fan, the croaking pigeon, and the super's pit bull would be rendered moot. Soon—in a matter of minutes or maybe an hour at most—Cesar would be returning.

Cesar lived next door, Cesar was a teenage timbale player, and Cesar, entitled little prick that he was, felt that it was his God-given right to practice his timbales whenever-the-fuck and wherever-the-fuck he felt like it.

Apparently, he was a virtuoso. A Tito Puente in the making. Or so his mother believed.

She was a part-time medical receptionist and a full-time priestess in the Church of Santería. On Sundays she sanctified chickens by decapitating them and pouring their blood into brightly colored receptacles. Santería required this. It also required that icons be kept in the house. Lots of icons. When she ran out of space, the drywall was ripped from the studs and the rapidly multiplying miniature saints were placed on the exposed, one-by-three horizontal slats. This addition-by-subtraction shelving meant that all that separated my bedroom from Cesar's rehearsal room was a single sheet of drywall.

One day I spotted her coming out of her apartment and managed to corner her near the mailboxes. She was wearing a low-cut, white spandex blouse, a black bra, and a tight, white miniskirt that clung to the magnificent imperfection of her legs. She was at least twenty pounds overweight and, in my opinion, twenty more would have looked good on her. Barely suppressing the desire to beg for sex, I complained meekly about the noise. Could she control her son, I asked? Get him to stop playing so late at night?

"I'll try, papi," she said, "but you know how hard boys are."

It was ridiculous. Out of a cheap porno. But she had me in the palm of her hand.

This was not good.

This was not good because Cesar, like his namesake, intended to conquer—if not militarily, then certainly, sonically.

In his hands, the timbales—with their gunshot rims and tightly tuned heads—were weapons; and his stereo system—the electronic equivalent of a small thermonuclear device—was no less destructive. Some nights, I could see the three-quarter-inch plaster pulsing while the floorboards rattled in time with the pounding bass lines that rolled relentlessly from the powerful subwoofers. It was torture.

At 6:38 a.m.—just around the time I'd expected it—it started.

Lying in bed, I could more or less imagine the scene.

Cesar—flying high on a mixture of Hawaiian Punch, vodka, and crack cocaine—had just returned with a gaggle of groupies. The red power light had been turned on, and the subwoofers were warming, rattling the speaker cabinets. Approaching the timbales as if preparing for a ritual sacrifice, Cesar was warming up with a rudimentary series of cross-rhythms. It sounded like someone was shooting an AK-47. The groupies responded with frenzied, high-pitched Spanish yodels: modern mating calls that pinged sharply from pinched nasal cavities. I imagined their hips shimmying and shaking as they cried out. Then I heard the sound of cans of beer being popped.

I was powerless. As a middle-aged white man in a mostly black and Latino neighborhood, calling the police would only mark me as a target—if not of violence, certainly of ridicule. Briefly, I considered homicide, but I was outnumbered and had no suitable weapon. Spotting an exposed pipe overhead and noting the length of the sheet that covered my already corpse-like body, it occurred to me that suicide might be my best and only course of action. Meanwhile, Cesar had slipped one of his mother's records onto the turntable, had dropped the diamond needle onto the disc, and Willie Colón's horn section—a trumpet, a trombone, and two saxophones—was now blasting through the drywall and into my room.

"Who is that, papi?" a kid screamed.

"*El Malo!*" shouted Cesar.

"*El Malo!*?" the kid asked.

"Willie Colón, you motherfucking *puta madre!*" said Cesar, picking up his sticks and striking the taut skin of the timbales with another martial roll.

As it happened, my aunt had taken me to see Willie Colón and Celia Cruz when I was just a kid, and I'd loved the music. But at 6:46 in the morning it was a total fucking nightmare: the blare from the horn section, like a matador's red cape, making me murderous with rage; the bass rumbling around in my innards and roiling my guts; and each sharp crack from the timbales shocking my nervous system. I couldn't breathe. I felt nauseous. I felt like I was going to have diarrhea. Or a heart attack. Or both.

The stereo was turned up another notch.

And then—breaking under the pressure of the sonic bombardment and lack of sleep—I started feeling paranoid.

It occurred to me that I was being watched.

Barbaro, the superintendent—a heavily tattooed Dominican fireplug of a man—had cameras everywhere. He'd told me that he had only placed them where they were needed for security, but the involuntary smirk that appeared on the man's face whenever our paths crossed led me to suspect that he had me under total surveillance.

I recalled feeling strangely uneasy in my bathroom. On the toilet, I liked to read, which I realize is rather typical toilet behavior; but after I finished, I often lingered in front of the mirror, improvising nonsensical poems that integrated strings of obscenity with long clusters of closely rhymed gibberish. Typically these filthy flights of invention were sung or chanted, with repetitive, rhythmic grunts and a series of spastic facial expressions marking the ends of each stanza. Why I did this, I don't know. Maybe it was a touch of Tourette's.

And there was more: I sometimes masturbated in front of the mirror like a lonely monkey in a zoo.

No wonder the super smirked.

Convinced that there was a camera concealed somewhere in my bathroom, I remembered earlier humiliations.

At the age of four, a European friend of the family—Swiss, I think—had walked in on me while I was on the toilet. Still new at the technicalities of the thing, I had screamed at her to let me be, but she had been totally unable to understand my upset. Then, just a few years later, my father had taken me to a public swimming pool in the Bronx. As soon as I jumped in, three girls, all black and in their early teens, surrounded me in the water, teasing me and tugging at my swimsuit. For most of the afternoon, I'd managed to squirm away, but one girl—a teenaged Captain Ahab but with two good legs—had relentlessly pursued me until I was cornered and clinging to the lone ladder that lay at the farthest reaches of the deep end.

Suddenly, her hands were everywhere, scratching my little lily-white belly and clawing at my little lily-white legs. The other girls swarmed alongside. After a protracted struggle the mad little Ahab dove beneath the churning maelstrom of bodies and in one quick motion, pulled my swimming trunks down past my ankles.

Triumphant, she surfaced, screaming and pointing at me.

"What is it?" cried her friends. "What? What?"

"Dive back under and look," she cried. "Look! Look!"

"What is it? What is it?"

"His thing is hard!"

Terrified, I'd pulled the swim trunks back up and had scrambled up the ladder and out of the pool.

Yes. I was a classic Freudian case. I had toilet issues and sexual issues. I was a walking cliché. Even a bad analyst could figure me out. In fact, I had a bad analyst, and the analyst *had* figured me out.

I had not "individuated." I had no "sense of self." I had no "boundaries."

Barbaro could film me. Cesar's mother, by virtue of her tight clothing and abundant flesh, could sexually dominate me. Cesar himself, though only a teenager, could torture me. Even the Chinese woman who ran the Laundromat down on 125th unsettled me. Often my clothing came back dirtier than when I had dropped it off, but I said nothing. These newer immigrants. They had force. Vitality. I was a member of a species that was dying.

Oh God! The noise. The fucking noise!

Still lying in bed—but face down and with a pillow over my head for protection—I continued to turn on myself. I was a failure, and the fact that I lived in a shithole was only proof positive.

Why had I left my Central Park West apartment?

The divorce had been Lily's idea. Why was I the one who had been pushed out?

Then, a reprieve. A divine intervention. Maybe, mercifully, a fuse had blown. Or maybe there had been an argument. I wasn't sure. But the stereo was suddenly off, and through the thin sheet of drywall, I could hear muffled cries of *"Puta Madre!"* and *"Que mala suerte,"* and *"fucking Maricon!"* Then the sound of feet shuffling out of the apartment, and then, silence. Elusive, momentary silence.

But it was too late.

The city was awake.

The subways were rumbling; the taxis swerving; the workmen shouting; the passing sirens crying. And underneath the rumble, swerve, shout, and cry, the never-ending hum of the grid was humming its never-ending hum. And then the sun, shaking off the salt and brine of the Long Island Sound, climbed like a goat up the steeply stepped buildings, its lengthening rays flooding the cross streets. The metal behemoths were now done. Brimming with the plastic waste of modern man, they lumbered toward the landscaped mounds of landfill that lay along the edges of the outer boroughs. Overhead, the sun was still climbing, lifting the curtain on the city at work. Jackhammers were jack-hammering; erectors were erecting erector-set scaffolding—the endlessly multiplying crisscrosses of pipe chasing after the rising sun.

The sun climbed higher.

Horns honked, bus brakes squealed, trains rumbled like timpani.

The urban orchestra was tuning.

On the avenues, quickening currents of cars, cabs, trucks, and carts clogged the crosswalks and log-jammed the lanes. The chained pit bull had started barking again; more pigeons had joined the lone, fat croaking one; the pink barbell had not moved; and Barbaro, the superintendent, was standing in the hallway, shouting into a multifunctional mobile telephone in machine-gun bursts of blasphemous Spanglish.

The plaster of Paris offered little defense.

Then Barbaro finally wandered off, and I fell for a blissful moment into a brief sleep and had a dream concerning the moon.

And then the phone rang.

The Call

And there she was. Lily. My ex-wife. In my room. Her voice in my room. Her voice but barking mad and unglued with grief—the long, animal howls punctuated by choked syllables devoid of sense.

And these howls—further distorted as they passed through my answering machine—seemed not to come from a modern woman suffering in a modern apartment built by modern men in a modern city but seemed, instead, to come from a madwoman manacled to the walls of a cave.

I didn't pick up the phone. I wanted to but couldn't.

Eventually, she managed to form words, to speak.

Having no one else to call, she had called me. In three long messages, she told me what had happened.

It was her brother, Orin. He'd been in a bar. Drinking. In Indian Leap.

Sometime during the night, or maybe it was early in the morning—she didn't know when—he'd lost control of his car. It had gone off the road and into the woods.

Her beautiful brother, Orin, lying dead in the snow. Covered in twigs and dirt. Covered in gravel and blood.

Gone, she cried, gone. All she had left. All she had in this world.

Yes, he drank, she admitted—as if pleading his case to an invisible inquisitor. He drank because people used him and hurt him; he drank because people had taken advantage of him; he drank because nobody ever gave him anything or did anything for him; he drank because he was surrounded by ignorance and stupidity; he drank because nobody understood him; he drank because there was nobody for him to talk to. Nobody.

Not in Indian Leap.

What was he doing there? Why was he in that place? That horrible place.

The machine cut her off. The phone rang. The machine answered.

"Oh God," she cried, "I knew it. I knew something would happen. Fucking devil!" she cried.

The devil in question was Lily's father, whom she felt was at the root of her brother's sadness.

His name was Hamish, and he was a poet: a writer of sonnets who viewed family as an albatross. Suspicious of his wife's possible infidelity and possessed of a morbid sense of humor, he had named Orin after the avenging son in a Eugene O'Neill play based on the Oresteia. Still unable to shake his suspicions, he'd abandoned the family when Orin was twelve years old.

But who, Lily had asked, names a boy after a figure in a Greek tragedy?

Who would want to bring such a curse down on his own paltry house?

And how could a man who had no soul dare to call himself a poet?

All Orin had *wanted*—all her brother had *needed*—was a father. But this devil-father had feared the beauty and brilliance of his son. Had come to view his son as a rival. A year after the abandonment, Orin had shown up on the devil's doorstep.

The devil had denied him.

And now Lily's last and most important link to the living was gone.

I tried to force myself to reach for the phone but couldn't.

Her voice, having exhausted itself, turned hollow. She was still talking, but it seemed as if her voice was coming from a distant dying star…or from a black hole.…

"Are you there…are you there…?" she kept asking.

And then the machine reached its limit and silenced her.

I was staring at the blinking red light. My body was shaking badly. In my head I could still hear her howling.

I had heard her howl like that before. It was after a visit to the dentist. Disengaged and disapproving, the dentist had poked and prodded her gums. They were tender and bled easily. In all four quadrants he had found problems. Some of the pockets in the tissue around the teeth were three-millimeters deep;

some were five millimeters, or more. Shaking his head, and barely able to hide what seemed like repulsion, he read the numbers to an assistant—a sympathetic Haitian woman who tried to smile throughout the procedure.

The dentist delivered his verdict. The gums were in bad shape. There was also significant bone loss in two premolars in the upper left quadrant, and he'd found an abscess that had formed around one of the canines on the lower right. He'd caught the abscess early, but the two premolars would probably have to be pulled.

Coming out of the office, she was inconsolable. The work would take six months. She would need a bridge. A bridge at thirty.

"My devil-father," she cried, "and his shitty Scottish teeth. I'm rotting like he did."

"You'll have the surgery," I'd told her. "I'll go with you. They'll save the teeth."

"We don't have the money!" she'd cried.

She was right. We didn't.

And in the lobby, she buried her face in her coat and sobbed until the lapels had darkened with her tears, and when I went to her she pushed me away, screaming that she was humiliated and that she was broken. Broken. The abandonment by her devil-father, the early death of her saintly mother; the bloody suicide of her best friend; the too-early death of another—it was all too much. She was broken forever, and there was nothing I could do to fix it, she said. Nothing anyone could do. And then she turned away, collapsing onto the floor of the lobby and sobbing uncontrollably.

From several sources I borrowed the money.

She needed the bridge, but it was toward the back and barely visible. The dentist was able to save two of the teeth. The gums healed. Within six months the work was over. But the depth of her initial despair had terrified me.

And now my phone was ringing again, and then the electronic tone, and then her voice—no longer howling, no longer hollow, but trembling quietly, as if she were yielding to some greater and unopposable force.

She was talking about Orin's son, Isaac. The boy they called Sparrow. He, like his father, was a sensitive, curious boy, and now he, like his father, had been left alone.

That poor little bird, she said.

She was weeping. She was so sorry. So sorry she'd called, but she had nowhere else to turn. Nowhere else to turn, she repeated.

In increments, her voice became weaker and weaker, and her thoughts slipped out of joint and out of time. Soon, she was barely audible. And then her voice seemed to recede into the ether, into an impenetrable fog that floated over a distant ocean. And then it echoed one last time, echoed like a distress signal from a ship that I had long ago abandoned. Then the voice was gone, and the line went silent.

Lying on my low bed, the sunlight beginning to angle in through the window, I thought of her swimming.

I don't know why, but that's what I was thinking about.

We had gone to a friend's house. The friend had a pool. It was the first time I'd seen her in the water. She had a crazy kind of stroke: a hitched crawl in the arms that she combined with a lopsided frog kick. It looked a little bit silly, but there was also something kind of charming about it.

I don't know why that came into my head, but it did.

It must have been my way of distancing.

Her brother was dead; I was thinking about her swim stroke.

And her dental work.

That's what I was thinking about.

Lily swimming. Lily sobbing.

And then I called her.

I told her I that I would go with her to Indian Leap.

She said that the boy would be grateful. She said that he loved me, that he looked up to me, that it would mean a lot to him. She wanted to bring him back to New York.

Would I really help, she wanted to know?

Yes.

Would I come to the apartment?

Yes.

Did I still have the keys?

Yes.

When would I come?

Now.

Right now?

Yes.

The Apartment

On many occasions, in many different Chinese restaurants, and over many different Chinese delicacies, Pierce Sweeney had expounded the following philosophy:

"An absurdly cheap, Upper West Side, rent-controlled doorman apartment that has been in the family for over fifty years is the birthright of every Jew in New York City. It is yours and yours alone. It wasn't meant for some shiksa bitch. Don't give it away."

The apartment in question—the same apartment toward which I was now hurtling in a black livery cab—was a two-bedroom spread on Columbus Avenue with panoramic views of Central Park. It had been passed down from my grandfather to my mother. Then my mother passed it on to me. Sweeney knew the facts. He had it right. Succession was based on blood.

"But I promised to give it to her," I protested.

Sweeney would have none of it. Gifted in the art of semantics, he pounced. Morally it was mine, ethically it was mine, and ethnically it was mine.

"But the guilt," I said. "The guilt!"

To even think of taking it from Lily made me feel guiltier than the guiltiest creature. There would be complications, of course, such as the matter of the stock certificate, and certain rules and regulations regarding government buildings, and the tendency of the various management companies to lose or misplace crucial documentation. But I had to give it to her! And to listen to Sweeney rant as we greedily gobbled pan-fried dumplings by the half dozen; to rationalize with Sweeney as we slurped up sesame noodles like overgrown infants suckling at the breast; to nod my head along with Sweeney's ironclad assertion that I should take back what was rightfully mine as we binged on beef with broccoli; to conspire, yes, to conspire with Sweeney over a sumptuous three-course Chinese feast while millions of children were starving in the streets—all this made me feel like a snake.

The ninth circle of Dante's *Inferno* had been reserved for the betrayers of kin, and Lily was still, at some level, kin.

All this, and more, I had said to Sweeney; all this, and more, he refuted.

He told me to leave Dante out of it. To get down to "brass tacks." Snatching the last piece of broccoli, he made his closing remarks. I had done enough for Lily. Enough.

"She left you, you crazy son of a bitch," he added.

"But where will she live?" I asked.

"Astoria."

"Astoria?"

"That's right. Astoria."

"But how will she—"

"The N or the R…like everybody else.…"

I pretended to listen. And after pretending with Pierce Sweeney, and pretending with other friends, and pretending with my family, to deliberate on whether or not I should give the apartment to Lily—when, in fact, I knew all along and had always known that I would give it to her—I gave it to her.

Actually, I was still in the process of giving it to her. This involved endless seas of red tape and the enlisting of a lawyer who informed me that it would be best if I pretended to still be living there.

"For how long?" I asked, glancing at the framed photos that littered the mahogany desk: the lawyer sitting on his power lawnmower while his knockout Brazilian wife looked adoringly up at him; his son, solemnly reading from the Torah at his bar mitzvah; his little girl, laughing and trying to put a tiara on their golden retriever. Pictures of a life that had eluded me.

Was it really appropriate for a divorce lawyer to decorate his desk like this?

"At least, I would say, a year."

"A year what?" I asked.

"You should make it seem like you still live there," said the lawyer. "You know, pick up the mail, joke around with doormen, chat with neighbors."

And so I did. But it was an unpleasant performance to give, and the audience was depressing.

Almost everyone who lived in the building was in their sixties or older. This meant that they had already succeeded as much as they could, or failed as much as they would. This meant that they had, for the most part, stopped striving, and it was this quality that they inadvertently passed on to their children, many of whom still lived with them. Nobody was going anywhere or doing anything. Except for those who were dying.

With little else to do, they had devoted themselves to petty gossip and had formed a board of directors that bestowed upon its members all sorts of perks, such as free parking spaces and first dibs on the more desirable units.

Flimflammers themselves, the board had made it their job to look out for other flimflammers, of which I was now one, and the revolving door of bureaucratic functionaries who managed the building presented further danger.

Fueled by my noble intention, I proceeded with criminal caution.

The bed, the big stuff, I would leave. The things that I needed, I would take out a few pieces at a time—the idea being that I would come back to walk the dog often enough that no one would realize I was gone.

At odd hours, I snuck in, ransacking my own belongings and stuffing them into my gym bag or into one of the plastic shopping bags I pulled from under the sink. Then I got down on my knees, nuzzled my dog (nice doggie), scratched behind her ears (crazy doggie), whispered her name (good Millie, good doggie), gave her a biscuit to keep her quiet (no barking, no barking), turned out the lights, locked the lock (sh, sh), and high-tailed it down the hallway.

Outside, my trusty Ross three-speed bicycle was waiting, but the overstuffed plastic bags were a problem. For balance, I hung them from the handlebars in homage to the time-honored tradition of the bamboo carrying pole, a technique I had first seen illustrated on the wallpaper of an underground Dim Sum Palace in Chinatown and had later encountered in the Asian wing of the Metropolitan Museum of Art. (My unpracticed, Western eye noted no difference in the quality of the brush strokes.)

In those ink wash paintings of peasants toiling in terraced fields, there was a peaceful dignity. A sense of the sacred nature of men and women at work.

I, on the other hand, looked like a ridiculous circus performer—like the earthbound clown who clumsily bicycles around the ring before the high-wire artist is brought in to defy gravity and astound the audience with his skill and grace.

I felt particularly ridiculous when I pedaled past the swimming pool that lay just north of 125th Street and Amsterdam. At that juncture, just as I barreled across the busy avenue, I would see black boys punching beach balls and black babies wrapped in red-orange life vests or pinched into floating tubes shaped like animals, and there were black bathing beauties in bikinis, dripping with droplets of water and sweat, sparkling in the summer sun. And as I pedaled past, all stopped their talk, their play, their strutting and preening, and all eyes turned, transfixed by the sight of a modern-day Don Quixote struggling on his two-wheeled steed, his rusted Rocinante.

The sight of me! My pork-pie hat, like the helmet of Mambrino, barely balanced upon my head, the pregnant plastic bags hanging from the handlebars. The sight! A struggling, wobbling white man tilting his bony body hard into the steep incline of Harlem's Sugar Hill.

Alone in my unfurnished apartment, I consoled myself with the facts: once Lily was legally on the stock certificate we could divorce, and the back and forth would be over. But that would take at least another year. That was what the lawyer with the knockout Brazilian wife had said. And so twice a week I dutifully trudged down from 128th and Convent to check my mail, walk the dog, and wander around the place, talking to the ghosts.

Now the stakes had been raised. With Lily's brother gone and with Sparrow coming, it was all the more imperative, in my mind, that I keep up the front. The boy had already been through hell, and more hell, and he deserved a safe, secure place to live. Probably, I thought, I should come to the apartment a little more often. It would be less risky. Maybe I would help the boy with his homework. Be there when Lily wasn't.

I could come to him two times a week, and he could come to me two times a week. Or however much he wanted. Ah fuck…not with Cesar the timbale player living next door.

Lost in thought, I looked out the window at the blurring buildings.

The small bag I'd packed was jammed under my elbow, and the black livery cab that I'd hailed—there were rarely yellow cabs in Harlem—had now turned off Cathedral and was barreling down Columbus. The driver was hitting all the lights, just barely, and the apartment was coming into view. Just before we got there we hit a red.

"Fucking shit," grumbled the guy.

In restaurants and in cabs I am easy to please.

"Right here is good," I said, throwing the driver a ten.

I grabbed my bag and walked.

The face of the building seemed to darken with my moods, and sometimes the tower seemed to curve over me like a mechanical flower. But even on those days when the edifice stood like an edifice there was the matter of the doormen.

The rotating team consisted of three Latinos, a French-speaking African named Francoise, and a very unassuming man who had recently immigrated from Jaipur, India. His name was Chakor; his presence, a comfort. But the other doormen were serious threats.

Chicho was the one I saw most often. Always, he smiled. And yet there was something vaguely sinister in his service. Maybe it was that he knew I didn't really live there anymore. Maybe it was that I knew he knew. Or maybe the discomfort existed only in my worried mind. Or maybe it was because I thought he might be a closeted homosexual.

What this had to do with anything, I wasn't sure of, but the ambiguity added subtext to our short interchanges, which mostly concerned the minutiae of weather.

Then there was Placido, whose countenance was just as his name suggested. He was dark-skinned and plump; even his bones seemed soft. But his vocal pattern suggested hidden meaning: his *"Co-mo es-tas, mi a-mi-go?"* with its sing-song melody sounding like, "I know what you're doing; I know what you're doing."

Lotario was the third. Muscular, masculine, broad-shouldered, he scared the shit out of me. He was no-nonsense. His upright carriage combined with a plain sturdiness. And his entire bearing wordlessly implied that I was doing something unethical.

Lily liked him. "Lotario's got mojo," she'd once said.

To which I'd replied, "And he's built like a brick shithouse."

Even Lily had to laugh.

When I finally got to the door, Lotario was there. He knew. He knew what had happened and why I had come. Coming out from behind his desk, he grabbed my hand and my shoulder and said, *"Haré lo que usted necesita. Cualquiera.* Whatever you need, hombre; whatever you need."

I thanked him, turned the corner, and pushed the button for the elevator.

The Zebra and the Lion

The elevator came immediately. Within seconds the metal doors had opened and straight-backed, silver-haired, Señor Augusto came out, touching two fingers to the brim of his hat:

"*Buen día, Señor. Como esta, usted?*"

"*Bien gracias. Y usted, Señor Augusto?*"

"*Muy bien, gracias,*" replied Augusto as he turned the corner, the taps of his leather-soled shoes quick as castanets on the hard linoleum.

For a moment, I listened to the echo, then pushed the button.

The elevator reached the fourteenth floor.

On sea legs, I stepped out.

The doors closed behind me.

Closer to the apartment door, I could hear her voice. She was on the phone.

The door was cracked open. I let myself in.

She mouthed a "thank you" and motioned toward the couch.

I sat.

She was talking to her sister. "It's that place," she was saying, "that cursed, wretched place."

She used words like *cursed* and *wretched* easily. Though she was not from money—old or new—or from a family of any particular standing, her character was imbued with a kind of aristocratic sensibility, perhaps inherited from her poet father, perhaps from being the youngest of three. Or maybe it was because she grew up in a university town. Maybe it had evolved as a way of conferring a sense of status that she secretly felt she might not deserve. Or maybe it was because she had been an actress.

That was how we'd met.

In the small state college we'd both gone to, she was the star of the drama department, and she'd been given the lead role in *Antigone*, a Greek tragedy in which a young woman demands proper burial rites for a traitorous brother who has been killed under the hoofs of his own horse while leading a revolt. When her uncle, the king, insists that the body be left to the vultures, the woman defies him and attempts to bury her brother with her own hands. Enraged, the king seals her in a cave. Abandoned by her sister, her family, the state—and with no hope of escape—the heroine hangs herself just before her lover, the king's son, can come to her rescue.

The first time I saw Lily was at the first rehearsal of this tragedy. Having had aspirations to become a playwright, I had managed to get myself a position as a dramaturge—an utterly useless invention of the contemporary theater— while also serving as an assistant to the director. The set for this tragedy, I remember, had been designed with an extreme rake, which was supposed to tilt the actors menacingly toward the audience. The intent, the set designer had told the bewildered cast, was to make the audience *complicit in the action of the play*. Mostly, though, the steep slope made the student actors seem incredibly clumsy and awkward.

But not Lily.

She was wearing, at that first rehearsal, a brown V-neck blouse that plunged not quite sluttishly low but low enough that I couldn't look at anyone else, or, for that matter, think about anything else. Her skin was pale; her dark thick Scottish hair, which she had pulled in all directions to demonstrate her Greek grief, was messy and wild; her shoulders were pulled defiantly back; her strong, sturdy legs were spread and anchored into the ground; and her exotic, almond-shaped eyes were glaring at the director—a nice Jewish man in his late forties whom I happened to be sitting next to and who had just given Lily an acting note she disagreed with.

The argument escalated.

Lily was less than five feet tall, but on the stage she was imposing. Experienced with temperamental actresses, the director stuck to his guns and calmly repeated the note. I lowered my head. Though I was not the object of her rage, I was the assistant to the object of her rage, and so for the next twenty minutes, as they argued about blocking, objectives, obstacles, actions, and whether or not there could be subtext in a Greek tragedy, I pretended to be writing in my notebook, hoping that she wouldn't see me. But she did. She did see me. Even though I was cloaked in darkness and she was blinded by the spotlight—and even though she was busy telling the director that she couldn't understand why on this God's earth her character would meekly retreat downstage right, especially given what the actor playing the king was doing—she had seen me. She had fixated on me, and she suddenly seemed—maybe it was the extreme rake of the stage—to be coming toward me, though she was not, at that point, moving and had not moved so much as an inch. And I think that it was at that precise moment—I realize that I'm probably being a bit dramatic, but in my defense, it *was* a play rehearsal—that she decided she would weld herself to me.

What she saw that caused her to feel this, I don't know. Possibly, because I was sitting next to the director, she thought I would one day *be* a director and would therefore be able to give her roles in other plays. Possibly, in an instinctual, animal way she sensed that I might take care of her. Possibly, she sensed that I feared her. Possibly, she sensed that if I feared her I would not leave her. But mostly I think that she welded herself to me because she recognized that I was a man to whom she could weld herself.

I doubt it was intellectual. I doubt it was premeditated. I doubt it was avoidable.

In that moment, we were welded.

In that moment—as she stood in the spotlight with her arched eyebrows arching, her breasts nearly bared, her sturdy legs spread, her hands held defiantly on her hips, her hair like a storm—we were married.

It was tempestuous from the beginning. There were misunderstandings, fights, countless breakups, and inevitable reunions. Often, she fell into horrible depressions. Her father had abandoned her and had refused any attempt at contact. Her mother had died after a long illness. The winter before I'd met her, her best friend had committed suicide, had cut his wrists at the edge of a forest and had walked as far as he could from civilization, leaving a mile-long trail of blood in the untouched snow. Her sister was an alcoholic and a drug addict. They rarely spoke. All of this she told me in bits and pieces. I listened. I tried to comfort her. But despite her openness, she seemed to be keeping me at a distance. She said she was damaged goods.

Physically she was difficult too. When I touched her, it felt almost as if her body was protected by some invisible armor that lay just under the skin. Sex was a problem. It was difficult for her, she'd told me. She'd been hurt and betrayed too many times and she'd shut down. And yet there were intimations of earlier lovers, better lovers, intimations that I was doing something wrong, that I was at fault. I developed performance anxiety. It took me a long time to get hard, and when I finally did, I had to fight off coming too fast. I felt inadequate and unsatisfied. We were beginning to be welded to each other's unhappiness.

Her apartment was in a house just outside of Boston, one of those triple-deckers particular to Massachusetts that I've always found particularly depressing. The rooms were small and dark, the heat never worked, and there were big water stains on the ceiling. She lived with another acting student, a skinny blonde girl who looked like a street urchin but who happened to be the daughter of the mayor of Providence. There was also an orange tomcat, a big, fat aristocrat of a cat who let itself in and out through the ground-floor window, coming and going as it pleased.

The cat was imperturbable.

But the mayor's daughter was unstable.

The first night I stayed over, she sobbed all night long in the next room. On my second night, she had sex with her boyfriend, though to me it sounded more like rape. After three hours of blood-curdling screams that seemed totally unrelated to any semblance of pleasure, I considered calling the police, but Lily told me not to. Apparently the boyfriend had had some kind of glandular problem—I think with the pituitary—that had delayed the onset of puberty. To correct it, he'd gone on a regimen of obsessive weightlifting, hormone therapy, and steroids, which had turned him into a muscular, acne-ridden, rage-filled fucking machine. I could hear the bedsprings creaking, could hear him grunting, and could hear her calling him a selfish motherfucker while begging him not to stop.

"Jesus," I'd said, "he's been fucking her for a really long time."

We turned the radio on to drown out the sounds, but it didn't help. Intimidated by the weightlifter's performance, I didn't even attempt to have sex with Lily.

When I woke up the next morning, the mayor's daughter was sitting in the kitchen with her bathrobe falling open. She was drinking coffee from a gigantic mug that made her look like a character out of *Alice in Wonderland*. When I came in she didn't bother to close the robe. Her neck looked bruised.

The weightlifter had been rough with her, she said, leaning forward to give me a better look at the bruises on her neck and breasts. But she'd liked it.

I asked if he was still in the bedroom.

She told me he was gone. Probably for good.

I said it was for the best.

She lit a cigarette.

"You are so fucking bourgeois," she said.

And then Lily came in, saw the mayor's daughter sitting nearly naked in front of me, and went totally fucking ballistic. She screamed at her, called her a cunt, and threatened to kick her out. The imperturbable cat jumped out the window. Then Lily turned on me. It was clear, she said, that I hadn't wanted to fuck her the night before because what I had really wanted to do was to fuck the mayor's daughter. It was an ugly scene.

The next day at rehearsal, the actor playing the king cornered me. His teeth were crooked and yellow, he smelled of cigarette smoke, he had a lisp, and he was much older than all the other students—which, given his lack of talent, was probably the only reason he'd been given the role as the king.

"What's going on with you and Lily?" he asked.

"I don't know," I lied.

"She's in the dressing room. She's upset. She's worried you're going to leave her."

I didn't know what to say.

"Let me tell you a little secret," he said with a lascivious lisp—he really should have been playing Richard III. "She's in love with you."

I went into the dressing room and found Lily sitting at a long table under a row of naked bulbs, dressed in a rehearsal skirt. She'd been crying and was wiping stage makeup from her face. She could look quite hard, like one of those fifty-five-year-old society ladies you imagine meeting at a fancy party who can cut you to the quick with a few words or haughty glance. But whenever she thought she might be losing me, she softened.

She said she was sorry. She knew the mayor's daughter was totally fucked up and that I wasn't doing anything wrong. She was sorry she was so jealous. It was the play, she told me. The role, you know. It brought up so much *stuff*.

And she was worried about the girl playing her sister, who was totally anorexic. Was I attracted to the girl? No, I said. Of course I wasn't. She apologized again for her jealousy. It was just so upsetting that the actress playing her sister onstage was just as fucked up as her real-life sister.

"I guess what they say is true," she said.

"What?" I asked.

"That life imitates art," she said.

Turning back toward the mirror, she started to cry. She was distraught. I went to her. I held her. I told her I understood. I kissed her. She kissed me. She told me to wait while she locked the door. She told me to sit in the chair. She took off her rehearsal skirt. Usually it took me a long time to get hard with her, but that time—I don't know why—I was hard instantly. I could see myself enter her in the mirror, the row of naked bulbs leaving nothing to the imagination. I thought, for the first time since I'd been with her, that my cock looked really big. It was one of the few times I felt I was satisfying her. I had comforted her emotionally, and now I was fucking her like the weightlifter had fucked the mayor's daughter. Not with his violence, but with his stamina. In the face of her instability I could be stable; in the face of her anxiety, I could be calm; in the face of her fear of abandonment, I could stay. I could save her. I could be a man.

Six months later we got married.

Fifteen years after that we were separated.

Now life had imitated art again, and her brother had been trampled not under the hooves of his horse but under the metal and glass of his car, I thought as I sat in the apartment we had once lived in together, as I sat and listened to her talking to her sister.

"It's that *cursed* place," she kept saying. "It's that *wretched* place."

The howling I'd heard on my answering machine was gone. The initial shock had for the moment subsided. She was in control. She was acting, I think. Being theatrical. She was distancing herself. But she was in control.

And then her mask began to drop.

"His blood alcohol level was what?" she was saying. "Point-two-six? I don't know what that is. What does that mean? I don't know what that means."

And then she was silent. Listening. The only sound in the room was her breathing and the unintelligible voice on the other end of the line. For several minutes she just listened. Suddenly she was shaking badly, telling her sister that she was going to hang up the phone and that she would call from the road.

When she hung up, I went to her. I went to her the way I had gone to her a thousand times, in a thousand places, but her body felt foreign and her smell was no longer familiar.

"My sister says he was drinking," she was saying. "My sister says he was drunk...point-two-six...but I don't know what that means."

Her legs weakened. I sat her down at the kitchen table. In fragments, she repeated what she had been told, barely catching her breath in between.

"Late...it was late...the bars had closed...he was trying to drive home... people saw him swerving...there was a curve in the road...an embankment...and no guardrail...and it was dark...and he went off the road...and somehow he was thrown from the car...he was driving slowly, they said...but the car rolled...because of the embankment...and he was underneath...and it crushed him...crushed him... they saw the car crush him...they saw the car...my brother...my brother..."

We are sitting at the kitchen table.

"Point-two-six," Lily keeps saying. "What does that mean?"

She is begging for an explanation.

She is fixated on that number.

"What does it mean?" she asks. "How drunk? Tell me?"

"I'm not sure."

"You know," she says, "you know these things. Tell me. Was he slurring? Was he stumbling? Was he throwing up? Is it a little drunk? A lot drunk? I want to know."

"I don't think he was throwing up," I say. "He might have been slurring his words. He might have been wobbly on his feet."

"Then why," she asks, "would they serve him? Why? And Fred, his friend Fred was with him. Why wouldn't he have stopped him?"

"Because Fred was drinking too…"

"How do you know that?"

"I don't know…I'm guessing…I don't know."

"But was my brother stumbling…was he slurring his words?"

"I don't know…"

"You said he was."

"I said he might have been…"

"But if he was, why wouldn't somebody have stopped him?"

We both fall silent.

I say nothing, but I think:

He must have been stumbling and slurring. At point-two-six, he would've barely been conscious. He would've staggered out of the bar. He would've had trouble finding his car. He would've groped blindly for his keys, struggled with the door, and collapsed into the driver's seat. He would've barely been able to put the key into the ignition. And then the engine would've turned over; and the gravel crunching under the wheels, and the reflection of streetlights in the windshield, and the other headlights blurring, and the sound of car horns honking as he swerved over blurred double-yellow, and dotted-yellow, and dotted-white lines. And then the lights disappearing as he moved from the town to the winding country road, and the ghostly glow of birch trees, and the road curving, and one last set of lights, and the sound of a horn, and a moment of confusion—and then blackness. No pain. No consciousness. Any movement would be automatic. Muscle and nerve reacting without brain or spirit. The soul intact. Somewhere else.

Sitting at the kitchen table, this is what I hope: that there was no pain, no horror, no thought of what had been left behind.

I believe—I want to believe—that the body knows how to die. That it is *designed* to die. That it allows each of us to slip away in some kind of peace. A secret that only those who are gone know.

I think of the lion and the zebra.

While the zebra is free, it runs. When it is first caught in the jaws of the lion, it struggles. But at the instant that the lion's teeth tear into the zebra's belly, it surrenders.

Orin, at the time of his death, had been drinking, and alcohol confers its own kind of forgetting. Even if he'd lived, he might not have remembered that night.

Sitting at the kitchen table, I tell Lily that Orin did not suffer. Though the truth is that I don't know. And, perhaps, sobered in an instant by the car that was turning, tumbling, and crushing him, Orin was awake—awake, in great pain, and suffering horribly, wanting nothing more than to go home and to see his son.

This possibility, I force from my mind.

Instead, I sit silently with Lily's hands in my hands. Silently I pray. I don't usually pray, but sitting with her I pray. I pray that Orin didn't suffer. I pray that he is at peace. I pray that the poets are right and that all things, living and dead, are part of one great indivisible unity.

None of this, though—none of this thinking, or theorizing, or philosophizing, or praying—is of any help to Lily.

She is in terrible emotional pain. She is bereft.

And because there is no consolation I can offer, I do the only thing I can do.

I tell her that I will bring her to Indian Leap, to her brother.

I pick up the phone.

I call to rent a car.

I help her get her things together…though I feel a little like Charon…ferrying the dead to the dead.

The Drive

She managed to pack her bag; she managed to call for someone to take care of the dog; she managed to walk, one foot in front of the other, out the door; she managed to tell the doorman she would be gone for a week; she managed to sit quietly in the cold light of the car rental office while I handed over my credit card. But as soon as she was strapped inside the metal womb of the car, safe from the gaze of strangers, she began clawing at the seat like a caged animal.

I drove. I had to.

The route was familiar: take the West Side Highway (watch out for the Jersey drivers swerving to catch the exit for the George Washington Bridge); pass the Cloisters (medieval manuscripts illuminated with lapis and vermillion); cross over the Henry Hudson Bridge (whirling waters of Spuyten Duyvil below); shoot past Riverdale ("neither suburb nor city; neither fish nor fowl," according to Sweeney); then head north on the Saw Mill River Parkway (navigate steep inclines and blind curves, watch for diseased deer and flash floods).

I drove and said nothing.

I wanted to comfort her, to hold her, but the truth was that I had not held her for the last two or three years of our marriage. Or had it been longer? I couldn't remember, but at some point, an impenetrable wall had been built, and rather than trying to tear it down, we'd labored in darkness like modern savages, each secretly adding stones while arguing endlessly over who had built it.

She felt that I had. I felt she had.

My friends—Sweeney especially, of course, Sweeney—had said that she was the chief architect. "It's fucking ridiculous," he'd said. "I like Lily, but she's got you thinking that every woman needs a three-course dinner, a four-hour conversation, and a five-hour backrub before she'll *allow* you to fuck her. Well, guess what? Normal girls with healthy sex drives don't need all that. They *want* to fuck. Take a look in the mirror. You're a sort-of-good-looking, mostly straight, fairly well-built, kind-of-tall guy with a decent-sized cock, and if she *won't* fuck you, there's something wrong with *her*, not *you*. End of story."

That's what Sweeney had said. But then, Sweeney was not exactly neutral, and friends are supposed to say stuff like that.

My sense of the "problem" was probably more nuanced and definitely more conflicted than his. But even if Pierce Sweeney was right—he always was—and the wall had been mostly of her making, it was small comfort. The fact was that the death of our sexual life (and the resulting physical separation) seemed to kill some part of me. Yes, I wanted to fuck, but there was also the desire to pet, to be touched.

Maybe I'm not the best-looking guy in the world, but I'm not a monster.

I'm sexual. I like sex. I like women.

What's so wrong with that?

"Nothing," Sweeney assured me. "It's not *your* problem."

But I couldn't stop blaming myself, and I couldn't let it go. Over one of our customary dinners at Charlie Mom I pressed Sweeney for clarification.

Was there something else I was missing? Was I doing something wrong? Was the wall built partly from some shortcoming of my own that I was unable to perceive?

"No, no, and no!" said Sweeney, grabbing a dumpling and dunking it deep into the soy sauce.

But despite his support—and the comfort of the sesame noodles and sugared tea—I couldn't help questioning myself, turning on myself, blaming myself.

The essence of Lily's argument, as I understood it, was simple. It was black and white: she said I was sexual, not sensual; she said intimacy was difficult for me; she said I neglected foreplay and, as a typical male, I was overly focused on the genitals.

Apparently, I only touched her when I wanted sex, and while that may not have been true at the beginning of the relationship, it became true at the end.

The argument had an uncomfortable resonance. Maybe she had a point.

"Fuck that feminist bullshit," said Sweeney, piling pork-fried rice onto his already crowded plate. "She has no case. *No case*! It boils down to this. When you don't rub her back, she doesn't fuck you. When you *do* rub her back, she still doesn't fuck you. And I'd be willing to bet that if you cooked dinner by candlelight and covered the bed with rose petals while reciting Bryon, Keats, and Shelley, she *still* wouldn't fuck you, so fuck her. Now listen to me, you silly little freak, and listen good: she's a frigid, withholding, castrating bitch! You're in the right here!"

Sweeney's fist slammed down like a judge's gavel.

"Case closed!"

When I told my therapist what Sweeney had said, he wondered why Pierce, who wasn't even married to Lily, was angrier than I was. Luckily, I had an answer.

"Because I'm totally unaware of my own feelings and totally codependent," I said.

Stroking his red beard (it looked like some of his lunch was tangled in there, maybe a piece of bagel or something), the therapist nodded sagely and laid the whole thing out as an inverse mathematical equation whose all-too-human variables were roughly as follows:

"She says, 'If you won't rub my back, I won't fuck you.' You respond, 'If you won't fuck me, I won't rub your back.' I think you're both withholding. I think you're both hurting. Why don't you both come in and see me?"

We didn't come in. Things didn't get better. The wall stayed up.

We separated.

Hours before, in our apartment, the immediate shock of Orin's death had brought the wall down, had dissolved in an instant the fifteen years of hurt, disappointment, and distance.

During the drive, stone by stone, the wall rebuilt itself.

I drove. I had to. Lily was clawing at the seat, and she was in agony, but my job was to get her to Indian Leap. That was what I told myself. And then another voice spoke. "Don't leave her in pain," it said. "If you are here to lend comfort, lend comfort. Be a human being. Who gives a shit if you are divorcing? Once, she was your wife. Now she is clawing at her seat like an animal. So she stopped fucking you. Guess what? In a marriage, that sometimes happens. If you think she needs to be held, hold her. To not offer some kind of physical comfort would be cruel."

At the next exit, at Danbury, I pulled into a gas station and found a parking spot. She didn't know what I was doing, but she didn't stop me. I took her in my arms. I held her. During our marriage she had often told me how to touch her, which had always pissed me off. Now I tried to remember what she'd asked for. Tried to remember how she'd wanted to be touched. It didn't help. The crying was worse. She'd always liked it when I rubbed her back. I tried rubbing her back. It didn't help. I tried holding her tighter. She said she couldn't breathe.

"Too much," she said.

"I'm sorry."

"It's okay," she said. "I'm okay."

I didn't know what to do next.

"Maybe we should get gas?" I said, but when I looked down at the gage I saw that the tank was nearly three-quarters full. "I don't know…"

And then in her confusion (or was it calculation?), in her wish to reclaim me (or was it in sorrow for denying me?), in her desire to pleasure, to punish, to feel (or was it to forget?), she clumsily, like a teenager, was grabbing at me, pulling my belt off, and fumbling with my zipper. I didn't want that. I needed an excuse. I looked over my shoulder.

"Lily…"

There was another car parked nearby but nobody in it. Midday, but nobody seemed to be anywhere, save for the steady river of traffic flowing on the nearby interstate.

In the front seat of the car, she was wrestling my hips up off the seat. I fought her as she pulled the jeans partway down. Awkwardly, she reached into my boxer shorts. Her hand was on me. I wanted to stop her, thought consciously that I *was* stopping her, but my body was now acting autonomously, asserting its own primacy, and as she continued to grab at me, I found that I was taking my shoe off—just one shoe—so that I could as quickly as possible pull the jeans mostly off, so that I could get my legs open and my cock free. And as my mind ran through a quick series of the usual equivocations—I'll just let her touch me for a minute and then we'll stop; I'll just get to the edge and then tell her that I can't; I'll just touch her for a little and then tell her we shouldn't—I found that I was jerking off and watching while she pulled her skirt up and her black tights down. And then she reached for me and was working me so fast that her hand was a blur, and I felt like I was on the verge of coming, not from pleasure but from the pure mechanics of the act. And I didn't want to come.

I didn't want to come because I didn't want to be back with her. I didn't want to come because I didn't want to embarrass myself by coming in two seconds. And I didn't want to come because I knew I would be so fucking depressed afterward. Grabbing her wrist gently, I pulled her hand away, while my cock— stupid and swollen—pulsed against my thigh, as if straining to complete on its own what she had begun. Oh shit…if she touched it now, I'd come. If she touched my balls or my ass, I'd come. If she ran her hands on the inside of my thigh, I'd come. If I tried to pull my pants up and the fabric touched it, I'd probably come.

I told her we should stop. She didn't seem to hear. Twisting quickly in her seat, she pulled my hands between her legs. The tights were still at her knees, and I could feel her trying to push my fingers inside, but she was dry and couldn't.

"It's okay," I said. "Let's stop."

"No…"

Determined, she tilted her hips up and pushed down. She was breathing hard, with little catches. The windows were fogging. It was cold, but I was sweating. A half sneer crossed her lips. A contortion of her mouth that seemed like a mixture of desire and disgust. She mumbled something, but I couldn't understand what she was saying. I leaned toward her.

"The last time…" she whispered.

"The last time, what?" I asked.

"The last time we had sex…" she said.

"What?"

"What did you say…?"

"What…?"

"What did you say…?"

She was clawing at me, clutching at me. Outside, the winter sun had disappeared behind a sea of winter clouds. Inside, the windows had completely fogged, sealing us off from the rest of the world.

Her voice was hoarse: "Tell me…" she pleaded.

I remembered. The last time we'd had sex I had tried, stupidly, to make a grand gesture, or what I thought was a grand gesture. I think I was trying to save the marriage. "You taste," I'd said, "like honey. And you are still my wife…and you are still mine." It was sentimental, and I don't know if I meant it, but I'd said it. I'd said it and she hadn't responded, and the sex had been bad, and I'd felt foolish for saying anything at all. But she'd heard it and wanted to hear it again.

"What did you say…?" she asked, as she tried to force my fingers farther inside of her.

"What did you say…?" she asked again, almost begging.

Worried I was hurting her, I tried to pull away.

She reached for me again.

Something hot spilled out of me and ran down my thigh.

"Please…" she begged.

I was trying not to come, but she was using the hot that had spilled to move her hand over the length of me.

"Please…"

And I was thinking that it might be cruel to remind her, cruel to give false hope, cruel to mislead, but as I moved to stop her, her thumb found the dense gathering of nerves underneath me, and I lost all sense of what to do, or what not to do.

I told her: "I said you tasted like honey…"

Her hand moved rhythmically, relentlessly. "And what else…?"

I was on the edge now. "Oh, fuck…"

"Please…"

"I said, 'my wife…'"

"You said, 'my wife…'"

I had raised my hips off the seat.

"I said 'my wife tastes like honey.'"

"Tell me," she begged, taking two of my fingers inside of her, "Tell me again…"

"You taste like honey…"

"But tell me the whole thing…"

I couldn't hold back.

"I said, my wife…my wife…tastes like honey…sweeter than honey…"

And more hot spilled from me and hot spilled from her, and the smell of sex was in the car, and I think I felt her come. And the whole thing was sad. So sad. But it had gone too far, and I couldn't stop it.

"Oh God, oh God," she said, pushing my two fingers just under the pubic bone up inside.

She shuddered.

And she was moving her hand on me faster and faster, and still—as crazy as it was—I was thinking: "As long as I don't come…" And then I was pulling my hips away and grabbing her wrists again to stop her, still thinking to myself: "As long as I don't come" even as I came, even as the stuff flooded out of me, not in spurts but flooded like a river of thick milky stuff, spilling over my thighs and down onto the seat below.

Spent and shaking, I sank backward. She grabbed hold of one of my legs. On the skin that was still exposed, my sweat was evaporating, which sent a chill through my body, and I just wanted to find something to clean myself with, but her head was curled onto my lap, and I didn't want to move her, didn't want to disturb what seemed like a moment of peace. A gust of wind rocked the car. She held closer. I put my hand on her back. Her body, no longer animated, felt fleshy, bulky.

The narcotic effect of sex was rapidly wearing off and reality was settling back in: a rest stop, a rental car, an existential errand of great magnitude that I realized I had just fucked up. The rolling clouds had gathered above. The sun was gone.

It was still only midday but felt like night.

Snow was starting to fall, and the temperature was dropping, but I hadn't turned the ignition, and neither of us had moved.

Underneath her, my leg had gone cold and clammy. It felt like my body was rejecting her.

She would expect that. Would expect me to reject her. The rules as she understood them were simple: those who are closest disappoint you, or they leave you, or they are taken from you. That was her worldview. This would make it worse.

I listened for a while to the quiet hum of the nearby highway, lost in thought until she called my name.

"What, Lily?" I asked.

She picked her head up off my lap. "It's okay," she said.

And then she handed me my shoe and started putting herself, as best she could, back together.

"What's okay?" I asked, struggling with my pants.

"I know...I know you're just taking me...I know," she said.

And then she touched my cheek.

It had been the same when I had finally left. After a nightmarish week of talking, she had said: "I know that you have to go, and it will be okay." That's what she had done. She'd sat simply at that kitchen table—where most marriages end—and she had released me. And now she had done it again.

I wanted absolution, and she had given it to me.

I couldn't say anything.

And then I turned over the ignition so we could get some heat in the car, turned on the defroster and the wipers, and we pulled back out on the road.

The Road Taken

At Hartford, there was a fork.

To the right, Route 84 ran into the Massachusetts Turnpike, which led to Boston (where we had met) and to Cambridge, where the Greek gods of Harvard were rowing their sculls on the dirtied currents of the Charles River. Just a little farther down Massachusetts Avenue (Mass. Ave. to the locals) on the right-hand side of the street and down a flight of stairs was the cramped stage of the Cantab Lounge, where Little Joe Cook and the Thrillers used to perform nightly. And just a few blocks down from the Cantab, kids with curly hair, thick eyeglasses, and pockmarked skin were studying Newton's mechanics, and curved space time, and the aerodynamics of viscous fluids (including, one assumes, their own). Across the river from MIT was the historic Back Bay with its alphabetized cross streets (Arlington, Berkeley, Clarendon, Dartmouth, Exeter…was it Fairfax or Fairfield?). If you kept walking, you passed the Eliot Hotel (I'd stayed there once and never forgot how comfortable the bedding was) and then Symphony Hall. In my college days, a favorite poetry teacher—after spotting me in the pool and sharing a steam and shower with much talk of Whitman and Ginsburg—had taken me to a Stravinsky concert, gracefully expecting nothing but my company in return for the free ticket. He was a brilliant teacher, a lovely man. Probably still reviewing classical music for WBUR. And if you kept walking toward Roxbury, there was that hole-in-the-wall jazz club, Wally's, where you could see white boys from Berklee pretending to be black men from Harlem. And in the hundreds of dormitories that dotted each historic neighborhood, thousands of unsupervised young people were having insane amounts of unprotected sex while discussing the works of Chomsky and Zinn and MacKinnon and Fanon.

But Route 91, the route I was now taking, was a different road; it led to a different kind of place.

Route 91 took you to Western Massachusetts, to cities like Springfield—northern industrial cities suffering from rising unemployment, rising crime rates, and lowered expectations. Some of the suburbs that surrounded Springfield were affluent. Many, like Chicopee and Hadfield, were not. Indian Leap was one of the worst—a town where the rape, robbery, and assault rates were respectively two, three, and four times higher than the national average.

It was a depressing place.

The first time I'd seen it was after we'd started dating in college. I'd driven out from Boston in a heavily dented, army-green, eight-cylinder Oldsmobile that had cost me two hundred dollars. I was wearing my favorite coat—a brown leather jacket with wide 1970s lapels—and my hair, under the pork-pie hat that I always wore, was long and stringy. Except for the brown jacket, all my clothes were black. Nobody dressed like that in Indian Leap. When the neighborhood teenage toughs saw me get out of my Oldsmobile, they thought I was an undercover cop and ran off into the woods. This happened every time I went there. The adults distrusted me for other reasons.

Not understanding that I dressed poor because I *was* poor—and not understanding that anyone who really cared or knew about fashion would probably have had me arrested for my garishly bad and totally outdated taste—they took me for a city slicker and viewed me with envy and suspicion. Even among some of Orin's closer friends (like Claude Laroche and Jerry Robidoux), I was kept at arm's length, and everywhere I went I encountered nasty little strains and suggestions of anti-Semitism. Or in some cases, balls-on-the-table anti-Semitism, which usually amused rather than angered me. Either way, it was never a surprise. Anti-Semitism had a good long history in that particular neck of the American woods.

When the Puritans had first arrived, four hundred or so years before, they needed an ideological framework that would legitimize their claim on the land, and they found that framework in the Bibles they'd brought with them. Combing through the books of the Old Testament, Increase Mather, their self-proclaimed religious leader, discovered that the New World had been divinely promised to the English pilgrims. Proof of the good Reverend's exegesis lay with the Indian language, which sounded to the tin-eared English like Hebrew, a coincidence that convinced Mather and his followers that Indians were Amalekites, the lost tribe of Jews whose extermination God had sanctioned.

And so the Puritans began, Bible in hand, to take more and more land. They converted the Indians to Christianity; they set up English schools; they proclaimed the Indians subject to their English courts.

Pushed too far, the Indians pushed back.

In October 1675, a force of Nipmucks and Agawams burned thirty houses in Springfield to the ground. The Puritans retaliated by attacking the nearest Indian village. Badly outnumbered and unwilling to surrender to the muskets and swords of the heavily armed white men, their chief, Roaring Thunder, wrapped his only son in a tribal blanket and leaped to his death from the high cliffs that lay just behind Orin's house. The rest of his tribe followed. None survived. This was how the place came to be known as Indian Leap.

It seemed fitting. A shitty history for a shitty place.

Suddenly, I heard a truck honking. A moment later I felt it pass uncomfortably near to my left shoulder, and then a mass of displaced air pushed our rental car to the right.

I had drifted across two lanes.

Remembering a trick I'd learned to stay awake, I tried, every five seconds or so, to shift my focus.

Ahead were some trees, some hills, but mostly just the kind of crap that crops up on the side of interstate highways.

Welcome to America: land of chain stores, strip malls, gas stations, and rest stops. A continuous blur of shit that leads to a town named after the mass suicide of indigenous peoples.

Indian Leap...

I hadn't enjoyed going there even in good times.

Now I was going back.

Indian Leap

The triple-decker building stood at the end of the road. The beams and braces were groaning under the combined forces of gravity and time, the wood shakes on the roof were infested with mold and rot, the paint was peeling off the clapboard, and the back porches—each apartment had its own—were piled high with the detritus of rural suburbia: rusted bicycles and tricycles; rusted chainsaws; rusted lawn chairs with ripped slats; deflated inflatable wading pools; broken baseball bats; hibachi grills caked with kerosene-blackened gunk; and God-knows-what-else buried under frozen-stiff tarps. And as the wind whipped and whistled through the warped siding, it seemed that the building was breathing its last breaths.

The grounds were no better.

Deep ruts had been dug into the frozen, black mud of the driveway; the backyard was torn up and, badly scarred; the silvery-white bark of the nearby birches, wounded with rot, fungus, and other fatal signs. And beyond those dying trees, on the other side of the icy river, lay groves of willow and groves of black alder, weeping.

Even in daylight there was an unrelenting darkness about the place.

When we first got there, I took Lily up to the apartment. Her sister, Lavinia—drugged-up and a little drunk—said that Sparrow was down by the river. Lily stayed in the apartment. I went to get the boy.

On the way, I noticed the driveway was empty. Orin's pickup truck—the instrument of his death—was at the police impound, but his motorbike was still standing out back by the shed. Amid the decay, it was the one object in perfect working condition. Orin had taught Sparrow how to properly maintain all of its moving parts, and together they'd bored out the pistons to get a little more power from the engine. It ran quiet and strong. I knew the boy would want to keep it and would want my help, but I didn't know anything about mechanics. Maybe I could learn, but the truth was that motorcycles scared the shit out of me. And the idea of letting the boy ride in a city like New York was inconceivable. If anything happened, Lily would jump out the window. I'd have to figure out a way to talk him out of taking the machine.

In no rush, I made my way to the end of the road and took a small path to the edge of the cliff. On the horizon, I saw still more birch trees, their ghost-white trunks and etched lines of black dissolving into the gray of the winter sky, and I heard the sound of water running over rocks and bits of ice breaking off from the bigger sheets on the river. All else, save for a little wind in the bare trees, was quiet.

At the edge of the cliff, I grabbed hold of a tree branch. In the distance below, I saw him. He was on one knee on the south bank of the Chicopee River, and he had a geologist's small pickax in his right hand. From my vantage point, it was impossible to tell what exactly he was doing, but it looked like he was breaking apart and studying something—maybe a rock, or a piece of shale—studying it as if it had some secret magical power, or as if it concealed some hidden answer.

Watching this solitary, sad stalk of a boy, alone on the riverbank, I thought of wheat, which had originally been perennial and green like grass before it adapted to harsher climates by passing through a grain stage to prevent it from perishing. So too, I thought, with Sparrow, who must be learning to shut down—even partly, to die—in order to survive.

At first, his mother had raised him. I had seen only one picture of her, and she was extremely beautiful. But even in that single picture it was impossible not to notice the slightly disoriented look in her eyes, the tension around the grim line of her mouth, and her nervous, electric energy. After her relationship with Orin ended, she denied him any access to the boy. They weren't married, and Orin, thinking he had little legal recourse, complied and left town. It turned out that she wasn't well and under the pressure of raising a boy alone her mental illness became increasingly pronounced. Fearing that some clandestine branch of the government—the FBI or the CIA—might take Sparrow from her, she stopped sending him to school. To protect him from the police, both state and local, she put multiple locks on the doors and windows. But these measures were, in her mind, inadequate. Her paranoia escalated. It would be safer if she could become invisible. The curtains were drawn and the blinds pulled down. Coats of black paint were applied to the walls and to the windows. In the absence of light, her hearing became acute. Eventually a voice emerged. The voice told her not to go outside. Even for food. The voice told her that the federal government had poisoned their water. She stopped bathing herself. She stopped bathing Sparrow. Stopped feeding him. He became emaciated and developed scurvy. Her family tried calling. Assuming it was the FBI, she ripped the phone from the wall.

Orin found out what was happening. With her family's blessing, he came for Sparrow. He came for his little boy and took him back to Indian Leap. For five years Orin cared for him, clothed him, fed him, and loved him. But by then, Sparrow was older and painfully aware of his mother's mental illness.

He turned his attention to things he could make sense of.

At first, he studied what was around him. He studied plants. He studied flowers and trees. Then he decided to study the history of Earth. He learned the geologic ages in their proper order; he learned when each new species appeared; he learned when mammals first crawled from the primordial muck. He knew rocks, minerals and metals—sedimentary, metamorphic, and igneous. He knew mudstone and shale. He could plunge his hands into the waters of the Chicopee and tell you the composition of the silt.

Watching him—he was still kneeling in the cold mud with the pickax in his hand—I remembered a time when I had been closer to the earth. At the age of five, digging in the woods at Pound Ridge, I'd unearthed an Iroquois arrowhead. It was a talisman. I became obsessed with the American Indians. I learned about the different tribes and memorized the names of their great chiefs. I learned how they hunted, fished, and how they dressed. Using a pattern I found in a library book, and with my mother's help, I made a pair of moccasins. I insisted on wearing them everywhere, even in winter. After school, I wandered through the woods that lay behind my house, picking berries, making arrows out of sticks, and imagining that I was hunting the deer that I sometimes spotted in the meadow or near the edges of Sugar Pond.

And now, in the distance, about one hundred yards below me, Sparrow was raising the small pickax to dig deeper into the riverbank. The movement struck me. His connection to the earth, to the archaic, and to the mythical was something that still existed in my own nature, but I'd become an urban animal. No longer did I dig in the dirt. No longer did I run in the woods. I'd lost touch with the earth, had become almost squeamish about the very thing I, as a child, had longed to be near.

Resolving to stop being such a prissy city boy, I climbed over a rotting log I'd been trying to figure my way around and began making my way down the trail that led to the riverbank.

When I got to him, he didn't seem surprised to see me. Poking in the mud with his pickax, he spoke first.

"I heard you and Lily split up, but I figured you'd come," he said.

I wanted to go to him, but it didn't seem like he wanted to be touched, so I let him be. I wished he were eight, like when I first met him, so I could just scoop him up.

He could barely look at me. Coming a little closer, I squatted down and asked him what he was digging for.

"I wouldn't kneel in that water with those pants if I were you..."

"They cost nineteen dollars at Filene's Basement, so I'm not too worried about them."

"Oh..."

I put my hands down in the dirt. "What are those?" I asked.

"These are sedimentary rocks, and these are igneous—probably Precambrian, or maybe Paleozoic," answered Sparrow. "I can't remember which. These are crystalline. These rocks probably were brought during the last ice age by glacial meltwater."

I nodded, and the boy began a brief geological survey of the area, starting with the finer points of sandy loam. "Well, in Springfield it's actually loamy sand, not sandy loam," he said, quickly correcting himself. "Up there it's all stratified sand and gravel. Of course, there are also deposits of stratified drift and recent alluvium. Not to mention some calcareous spar, some limestone, and some reddish rock."

Continuing, he talked about the difference between shale and sandstone and having satisfactorily described the geology, went on to talk about the fish that swam, or might be swimming, right at our feet. Mostly he caught pickerel and perch, but he'd heard that there were also shad and salmon and striped bass where the Chicopee met the Connecticut. Mostly, though, it was just pickerel and perch.

Looking around in the silence, he exhaled. The droplets of moisture were white in the winter cold. The sun was dropping behind the bare branches of the birch, and the wind picking up. But he wasn't ready to go inside yet. He had more to say.

Industry, pollution, and dams, he went on, had made it pretty tough for the fish. Then there was the Putts Bridge Dam. The Dwight Dam. Just less fish in general. He and Guga, his Portuguese friend, barely caught anything anymore. Things just weren't like they used to be.

I said I knew how he felt and then told him how impressed I was. I just couldn't believe how much he knew about so many different things.

He told me it wasn't that much, really, but that he thought it was important to understand nature.

"Maybe I don't know what I'm talking about," he said, "but it seems like people have forgotten some pretty basic stuff."

"Like what?"

"Like how to be parents…I guess…for one thing…but I probably shouldn't say that right now…"

"I think you can say anything you want."

I asked him if he wanted to see Lily.

"I don't know why, but maybe not yet."

"Okay…when you want."

"I can't see anybody right now…I don't think…"

Behind us, the last arc of the sun disappeared behind a grove of birch trees and an abandoned shack. The days are short in February, and the day was done.

Neither of us spoke. Everything was gray and dismal. At our feet, the water was running faster over the rocks. Standing together, we listened. And then, without warning—as if he had decided that knowledge didn't protect you against anything and probably wasn't worth much—Sparrow threw the pickax into the icy mud. Handle up, it stuck. Then he turned away, crossed his arms, slipped his bare hands into the sleeves, and, as much as he could, burrowed himself into his winter jacket, which was just a bit too big for him. Inside the coat, his shoulders were shaking.

"Sparrow?"

From underneath the jacket came a constricted cry, a sharp stab of pain that quickly swallowed itself in the silence of its own grief.

And then the boy contracted in a sudden spasm as if he had been stabbed in the heart. He staggered blindly in the frozen mud in a small half circle until he was involuntarily facing me. Snot and sputum and tears ran down his face. But before he could turn away, I went to him, and there, at what felt like the end of the world, I took him in my arms, and I held him.

Sonnets From the End of the World

On the top floor of the triple-decker building, Lily was making phone calls and Lavinia was working out funeral plans. Hoping to distract the boy, I took him around the corner for a pizza.

The owner was an Italian woman. Her name was Agnes. Agnes had lost her husband a few months after burying her mother. Then she'd lost her only son. She dressed only in black: dresses, stockings, shawls, and shoes. She lived alone, slept alone and worked alone. The restaurant was traditional. The tablecloths were red and white, the pizza was thin crust, and the sauce was fresh. On the walls were flags, trophies, paintings, and photographs: her husband in full military uniform; her son in full military uniform; her mother as a young girl, smiling and waving to the photographer; the Leaning Tower of Pisa; the Roman Coliseum; Sophia Loren; Rocky Marciano; and the *Mona Lisa*. The place was a kind of temple in which all the sacramental objects pointed in some way toward the corrosive effects of time.

When we walked in, Agnes came out from behind the counter. Indian Leap was a small town, and she'd already heard. She took Sparrow's hands in hers, then she touched the boy's face. For a long time she did not let him go. Eventually, she led us past the crumbling remains of the Coliseum to a small table in the back. Her husband and son watched us as we ate. When we had finished, Agnes came and sat with us. When we left, I could hear her praying in Latin.

Back at the apartment, Lily was still calling people. Claude Laroche had stopped by and had said he would come back first thing in the morning. Lavinia had started drinking. At some point it was decided that I would sleep in Orin's study. Lily and Lavinia took the extra bedroom. Intermittently, there were visits from the tenants below. Nobody knew what to say. More people came. Mostly neighbors. I didn't get all the names. At eight thirty, Jerry Robidoux and Aldo Romano, Orin's closest friends, showed up. Robidoux rode dirt bikes harder than I'd ever seen anybody ride. He was so reckless on the track that Orin had refused to ride with him. Romano was Robidoux's polar opposite. Handsome and contained, he was a man of few words. At times he seemed to have an almost Zen-like quality. Or maybe he was just a little weird. I'd always suspected that Lily was secretly in love with him, but even if she wasn't, there was something about being around the guy that always made me feel that I was on the verge of being usurped—though exactly of what, I wasn't sure. Maybe my manhood. After a half hour of mostly awkward silence, Robidoux and Lavinia said they wanted more beer. Romano offered to drive. Sparrow took refuge in his small bedroom. I retreated to the study.

A little while later, Lily came in.

She was upset, and in her hands was a small book.

The book was titled *Sonnets From the End of the World,* and the author was a man named Hamish O'Mordha. He was Lily's father. I'd never met him.

O'Mordha, who had changed his name from Muir to its older Scottish form, was a poet and a professor. He taught at a college in Charlesburgh, Pennsylvania, where he also lived. He wrote sonnets. He slept with his students. Eventually, he chose one.

I had seen pictures of the girl. She was plain, pasty-white, slightly overweight, and wore thick-lensed glasses.

Her main charm was her youth; his, his status as a professor and published poet.

Though he was thirty-three years older, they married.

Within three years, she'd given birth to three children: all girls.

"Very Chekhovian," he would say.

She did the cooking and the cleaning. She corrected and graded his students' term papers. Freed from the responsibilities of family, housekeeping, and teaching, he turned to writing villanelles, or "villain-elles," as he joked, having proclaimed himself to be the Rasputin of Charlesburgh or sometimes, the Socrates of Charlesburgh, but with a pen for poetry instead of philosophy and with an eye for little girls instead of little boys.

Set up in his new life, Hamish O'Mordha abandoned the old—abandoned his son, his two daughters, his grandson, and everyone else connected with them. Now, twenty years later, he was coming to Orin's funeral, and Lily, realizing that there was nothing she could do to stop him, had decided to steel herself as best she could against the inevitability of his arrival.

In her hands was a book of his poems. She wanted me to read them.

"I want to know," she asked, "if they are any good."

I told her that I wasn't qualified to pass judgment. What had I produced?

"But I trust you," she said.

I told her that it would just be my opinion and that my opinion didn't mean much.

She persisted.

I realized I was entering a minefield.

Did she want me to hate the poetry so that she had absolute and final proof that her devil-father's life was totally without meaning and that unlike, say, a Picasso or a Caravaggio, his life would never be redeemed, not even in his art? *Or* did she want that little volume of poetry to be a magnificent artistic achievement, an achievement so great that she could justify the pain he'd inflicted on her, on her mother, and on her beautiful brother, Orin, whose death she was now convinced he'd indirectly caused.

Or was she seeking smaller comfort? Did she simply want me to find, buried somewhere in her father's verse, or secreted somewhere in his metaphor, some sign that he had not forgotten her? Had not forsaken her? After all, she was from his loins, had been born of his blood, was made of his marrow. Was all of his father-stuff poison? Or did his soul, his spirit still contain, despite the facts of his life and the actions he had taken, a small but indestructible kernel of truth and beauty.

And then there was the matter of Sparrow, who despite the lateness of the hour was still awake and who would be listening to every word spoken about his mysterious, long-absent grandfather. If the poems were bad, I didn't want the boy to hear me disparaging his flesh and blood.

But while I was busy debating all this in my busy, busy brain, Lily had taken action, forcing the book into my hands. And she wouldn't take it back.

There was no getting around it. I would have to read it, and I would have to give an honest appraisal. White lies, diplomatic evasions? Not for her. The duality of the soul? Also not for her. She had no time for it. You were charitable or greedy, faithful or idolatrous, a liberal or an asshole. You agreed with her, or you didn't. Period. What she wanted, at any cost, was the truth. That much I knew. As to which answer she wanted...that I *didn't* know. In fact, she herself didn't know. At least not consciously. But what she *did* know was that she *had* to know, and knowing *that* much, she had determined that she would bring the sonnets to an authority and that she would receive from that authority a final verdict on her father's sonnets and, by extension, a final verdict on the value of her father's life. I had been chosen as that authority. I had been chosen to deliver that verdict. There was no avoiding it.

I sat.

I read.

The first four sonnets were love poems. I recognized the woman's name. These were written for Lily's mother and presented a special problem. If I said that these four were no good, would I be criticizing, in some sense, the subject? Would I be inadvertently judging her mother's worth?

I reread. The sonnets were Italian and the words were those of the Romantics: words like *darkling, thrush, dismal, murky, primrose, bleared, smeared,* and *weeded*. A reference to "the low, Levant sun" seemed familiar, and the phrase "fell of dark" seemed like it might be borrowed, but overall, the language was evocative.

The colors were gold, crimson, vermillion. The smells were of ploughed earth. The lovers met in wheat fields, marshes, bogs. He met her at ebb tide, on riverbanks at midnight, and in fog-shrouded forests of birch and elm. They wet their bodies in cool streams; they lay down in wide, grassy meadows. Her body was his sanctuary. He wanted to taste her dark, dewy obscurity.

That, too, seemed familiar. Beautiful but borrowed.

I pushed on to the final stanzas of the section.

She lived in anguish; he was her pale master. He was her madman, and her slave. He was despotic, and he knew it. Yes, he had destroyed her. And he knew that too. At the end of these four sonnets he had written the word *Requiescat*.

Looking over my shoulder, Lily interrupted my reading. I hadn't realized she was still there.

"I forget. What does that mean?" she asked.

"It means 'rest in peace.'"

"That fucker. The nerve. He destroys her and then he has the balls to write that?"

She checked herself. "Will you keep reading?" she asked.

I said I would.

The second four sonnets were written for his children: three for Orin and one for Lily.

Orin was dark and doomed. He had been conceived in heartbreak and delivered in pain. He had come into this world cloaked in shadow and shame. And Lily. Lily was a black Lily; Lily was the darkling child. For her, he had no words of wisdom. No valediction. This middle section struck me as particularly needless and cruel. At the end Hamish had written: *Nōlī timēre. Ego sum etiam vestri abbas.*

"And what does that mean?" asked Lily, again pointing to the Latin.

"I'm not sure," I said. "I forget what *etiam* means, but I think it's something like…"

"Like what?"

"Well…*Nōlī timēre* is 'don't be afraid,' and I think the second part is 'I am still your father,' or something like that."

"Is he kidding? He has got to be fucking kidding. That's what it says? Oh God…"

"I think…"

"What's wrong?" asked Sparrow, who'd just come into the room, rubbing sleep from his eyes.

"My father," said Lily, "your grandfather…"

"What about him?" asked Sparrow.

"I gave your uncle a book of his poems to read."

"Those are his poems? In that book?"

"Yes. Why don't you go back to bed, and I'll be in to check on you in a little bit. Okay?"

But the boy didn't want to go, so Lily told him that he could sit right next to us on the couch. And then she went and got him a blanket and wrapped it around him. It felt to me like we were three little vessels floating on a dark sea, lashing ourselves together for safety.

I read on.

The last four sonnets were meditations on Hamish O'Mordha's approaching death. The second wife, and the second set of children that I had seen in the photograph, were not, as far as I could tell, mentioned. In these last four, Hamish O'Mordha was alone, facing the void.

He'd lived in falsehood, vice, and idolatry. Now he was spent. Had palsy and gout. Was fit for the graveyard and nothing else. He would return to having no face, no name. Like the phoenix, he would be consumed in fire, but he would not, like that mythical bird, rise from the ashes, nor would anyone weep for him. He had not lived in the world of the spirit and therefore would not live in eternity. His life was concrete, temporal, done. And he knew it. At the end of the last four sonnets, he had written: *Nusquam res.*

I stopped reading and looked up.

The boy and Lily had been staring at me. Half an hour had passed, and they had not moved.

"What do you think?" asked Lily.

Not knowing what she wanted to hear, I tried to play the middle.

"It's good," I said.

The boy seemed happy with the answer; Lily was reading between the lines.

"Good?"

"Very good."

"But?"

"You know...they *are* sonnets and so the language is naturally going to be a little...anachronistic."

"What's does that mean?" the boy asked.

"That the words he uses are old words," I answered. "Words used by great poets like Shelley and Keats...and some words he's using, like *darksome* and *pitchblack* remind me of Hopkins...although I don't know Hopkins that well... but this line here," I continued, as I picked through the pages, "this line about 'the darkling plain' is taken from a poem by Matthew Arnold, which is also about broken faith...and this...this is good..."

"*But?*" asked Lily.

"But," I said, carefully trying to gage her response while I spoke, which she knew I was doing and which infuriated her even more, "it is derivative...a *little* derivative."

"What does that mean exactly?" asked Sparrow.

"It means that—"

"He's copying," said Lily. "It means that he's copying other people's work."

"But it is still *very* good writing," I said, sensing the boy's upset, "and he is writing in a *very* difficult form. And I couldn't do it. I wouldn't even try."

Sparrow nodded and said he was tired. With the blanket wrapped tightly around him, he disappeared into his bedroom. It seemed like the wind had been knocked out of him. His grandfather had "copied." That meant his grandfather was a failure. I regretted saying anything.

Lily was ecstatic. Hungry for the kill.

"Is it shit?" she asked. "Is it total shit?"

With the boy out of the room, I thought I could speak a little more honestly.

"No, it's not shit. But it's academic, it's pretentious, it's been done before, and it's been done better."

She started to cry.

When I went to her, she pushed me away.

A little while later, I went to check on the boy.

His bedroom was decorated with dinosaur posters and maps of the universe. Over his bed was a chart that illustrated the correlated history of Earth. The chart was made up of columns. The first column dealt with plate tectonics and geology. The second column listed eras, periods, and epochs. It began four-thousand-million years ago, with the Precambrian, when the continents were a single mass, and it continued all the way to the Holocene, the present. And there were other columns that marked the emergence of the earliest plants, invertebrates, fish, amphibians, reptiles, birds, and mammals. Man was in the upper right-hand corner of the poster, his history dwarfed by the epochs that had come before him.

Australopithecus had begun walking upright about three-and-a-half million years ago. But even after he began walking upright, Australopithecus was still not man.

Man, Homo sapiens, *man-who-knows,* had not started remembering his dead until one-hundred-thousand years ago.

Underneath the chart, the boy was still awake, staring at a picture of his father.

Der Zauberberg

The night wore on.

Big John, a big crazy angel of a man—mentally retarded but sweet like a child—came for a bit and left in tears. He'd wanted to see the boy but didn't realize how late it was. He said he'd come back in the morning.

In the kitchen, Jerry Robidoux was talking with Aldo Romano about a local restaurant called Hung Lee.

"Every friggin' time I drive by that place," Robidoux was saying, as he rubbed at his reddened eyes, "what I always want to know is, does the guy who owns the place, this Mr. Lee, know that 'hung' means 'big dick?' I mean, he's been there forever, so wouldn't ya' maybe-think somebody might-a' told him? Like maybe his kid would-a come home from school one day and said: 'Hey Dad, guess what? I think we should change our sign.' Or a concerned customer. I mean, c'mon, call me fucking nuts here, but I think it's kinda hard to believe nobody ever took this guy aside and said, 'Hey, pal, just so you know, in English, as it is spoken here in the United States of America, your sign means 'big dick.' So he's gotta know. Right?" said Robidoux getting up to grab another beer.

"But, see, I think he thinks he can get away with it because he thinks we'll think because he's a Chink, he don't know. And if he does know what it means, my next question is: does he have a big dick? And if he has a big dick, does he have a big dick for a Chink, or does he just have a big dick, period? Either way, it takes balls, right? Big balls! I mean, c'mon, Aldo. It'd be like me opening a motorcycle shop and calling it 'Big Dick Jerry's.'"

Aldo Romano wasn't amused.

Robidoux didn't notice.

On my way to the bathroom, I glanced toward the kitchen.

Robidoux was now madly running both hands through his brush-cut blond hair as though he were a legendary actor on the English stage assaying the role of Dr. Faustus and grappling mightily with some metaphysical mystery—in this particular case, that mystery being the precise length and girth of the inscrutable Mr. Lee's penis. He probably would have gone on at much greater length if Romano hadn't told him that it wasn't the time or place for that kind of talk.

Robidoux obediently quieted down, but in the bedroom by the porch, Lavinia had started ranting about how fucking shitty it was to work for her new arrogant-asshole-of-a-manager at the Tiki Lounge because in addition to switching the computer system and accepting coupons on weekends and not letting you put on a fifteen-percent gratuity, Mr. Shitbag had also made the whole staff wear tighter T-shirts and shorter shorts, which meant you got groped even more, so now it definitely felt like she worked in a friggin' whorehouse, which is what it was, and she was already gonna quit anyway, "oh, yah," but now that this little jerk-off had taken over, who'd only got the job because he was somebody's friend's son—"you know how the world works, Lily: it's all who ya' know"—she was so outta there just as soon as she paid off her car, and she wanted to know if Lily knew how you got started as a dental technician, because a friend of hers, this married guy who she'd gotten pretty close with—"don't be judgmental, Lily. I'm not gonna sleep with the guy unless he leaves his wife, okay?"—said he'd heard from an acquaintance of his that they were hiring at an office over in Hadley.

Maybe I was just imagining it, but even after I had retreated back to the study, I thought I could hear Lavinia's teeth grinding. I considered trying to quiet her down for Sparrow's sake, but I knew it would only make things worse. She didn't like being told what to do, especially by some snobby-asshole, New York intellectual, which was how she'd always viewed me.

Lavinia had graduated from Hampshire College with honors. Like many of her classmates, she wore hippy dresses, didn't eat meat or dairy, and refused to wear makeup. She'd joined NOW, NARAL, and an offshoot of the SDS. After graduating she'd gone to live in Europe "to figure things out." She became fluent in French and picked up some Italian. Lily said she'd never been happier.

But when she came back home, she had a hard time adjusting. First, her mother died. Then her father checked out. In a letter sent from Charlsburgh, Pennsylvania, where he had just taken a teaching job, he told his daughters that he'd finally realized what a "toxic" human being he was. He intended to purify his soul in a book of sonnets, the same sonnets I'd just read, to heal himself, if he could, "through his muse." In the meantime, it would be better for all involved if he withdrew.

After that, Lavinia changed. She moved out of Northampton and into the south end of Springfield, where the rent was cheap. A friend got her a job at the Tiki Lounge. The money was good, but she gained weight from all the fried Polynesian food. It was the eighties. The hippie dresses disappeared. She started wearing makeup. She dyed her hair blonde, then jet-black, then bright red. The eighties ended; the nineties began. Depressed, alone, and nearing forty, she began to loathe the way she looked. The girls she worked with convinced her to try cosmetic surgery. Just some little stuff. First came the Botox and collagen injections. Then she had black liner tattooed under her eyes. Then she had the eyebrows removed and drew black, highly arched lines in their place. Alcohol aged her. Cocaine gave her a strung-out, animal look.

It upset Lily to see her.

She couldn't understand how her hippie sister had transformed herself into a Springfield townie, but she had, and her metamorphosis was striking. She now thought liberals were pretentious. So were those hippies over in Northampton. Europeans were "superior-acting assholes." French was "for faggots." Lily wondered where her sister had gone.

It seemed to me like they came from different families.

One night, a few months before Lily and I had married, we'd all gone out drinking in Boston at a bar on Boylston Street. At some point, she and Lily had had a fight. Lavinia wanted to go back to Springfield. I took her to the bus station. It was late. Almost four in the morning. We were very drunk. She hugged me good-bye. Then she tried to kiss me while she fumbled at my belt buckle. When I refused her, she slapped me across the face hard enough to draw blood. I was scared of her. Especially when she was high. And now, sitting in Orin's study, I was still scared of her.

Lily was too.

Despite her grief, she was patiently listening to Lavinia's rant and telling her that becoming a dental technician sounded like a great idea and that she would try to help in any way she could.

I stood and began pacing, feeling as if I had been newly incarcerated. The study had cheap carpet and yellowed, peeling wallpaper. Not that I was used to better accommodations. My apartment in New York was a complete shithole. But this place had its own particular kind of Western-Mass-gone-to-hell feel that unsettled me.

I looked down.

On the ground at my feet was a twenty-pound metal plate with a string attached to a cylindrical piece of wood. That was for the forearms. Next to it were two dumbbells and a barbell. By the door, some running clothes were hanging on a hook along with a plastic yellow poncho.

The smell of Orin's clothes—slightly sour and salty—reminded me of my father, who had also been a runner. My father was sentimental, a trait I had inherited. Thinking of him, I had an impulse to go into Sparrow's room and tuck him into bed, although he was probably long past the age when boys want that.

Maybe I would go in after Lily and Lavinia left—if he was still awake.

I paced some more and poked around some more. Through the poorly insulated windows I could hear Lynyrd Skynyrd, Led Zeppelin, and Aerosmith blaring from the passing cars, which made me feel like I'd been transported back to the 1970s, and the weights and workout equipment, which reminded me of the rooms of countless friends' older brothers, only heightened the effect.

I'd always thought that each city, each town in these supposedly united states is stuck in its own particular decade. Indianapolis, for example, is stuck in the fifties. Albany, when I was last there, was still struggling to get out of the eighties.

Outside, another car rolled past, blaring the flute solo from Jethro Tull's "Aqualung"—if a flute solo could be blared. I was now living in 1973.

Most of the traffic was coming from Quebec Street. Quebec was the town's underbelly. On a previous visit, I'd seen hustlers and hookers hanging out on porches, leaning in doorways, sitting silently in cars. Dark shapes sitting and waiting. An urban scene being played out on a smaller stage.

Some nights there were shootings.

I began browsing through Orin's bookshelves.

There was some stuff by Hesse, a stack of *Popular Mechanics*, and several car maintenance manuals. Shoved in next to the car manuals was a book on running by Jim Fixx, the fitness expert who'd died of a heart attack. On the top shelf, in the middle, was a copy of *The Magic Mountain* by Thomas Mann. Lily said the book had been her brother's favorite—a touchstone, she said. It had also been a favorite of mine, but we'd never talked about it.

Flipping through, I looked for signs of Orin in the margins—scribbled notes, a coffee stain—some sign that he had lingered on a particular page, paragraph, or passage.

Things were quieting.

Robidoux had stopped talking, Lavinia's rant seemed to have exhausted itself, and the traffic from Quebec Street had slowed to a trickle.

In the reprieve of the silence, I read.

The plot was straightforward. A young engineering student of ocean steamships named Hans Castorp visits his ailing cousin, Joachim, in a tuberculosis sanatorium high in the Swiss Alps. During the visit, a moist spot is found on the young man's lung, a diagnosis that keeps him on the Magic Mountain for the next seven years.

Separated from his study of ocean steamships and from the everyday world below, Castorp slowly settles in to a very different kind of life, taking long walks through fields of flowers, hiking on mountain paths, eating seven-course meals, seeing a Freudian therapist, having an affair with an older Russian woman, and indulging in a series of long and fruitful philosophical conversations.

Deep into the star-lit nights, swaddled in blankets to ward off the alpine chill, Hans Castorp reads books on the natural sciences, physiology, psychology, philosophy, anatomy, astronomy, and botany.

Orin, I imagined, must have hungered for that kind of life, hungered for a place where he could rest, fall in love, indulge in his passion for reading, thinking, and learning.

Buried under house payments, car payments, and loans, and responsible for a young boy, there was little time to indulge in anything outside of drinking. But the local bars that lined Main Street couldn't provide respite. The women were depressed; the men were distrustful. It was a New England thing. If you weren't born in Indian Leap, and Orin wasn't, you were an outsider.

He told Lily he felt trapped and alone.

I turned to the chapter called "Snow" in which Castorp, skiing through a terrifying winter storm, gets lost. Seeking shelter, he stops at a small shed. The shed is locked. Leaning against a wall for protection from the winds, he fortifies himself with a sip of port. The temperature drops. Near death, he begins to hallucinate. The Mediterranean appears. He sees children, sea, and sun. Boys on horseback pass him, and a girl dances beside a sparkling bay. It is Eden. Then the vision turns. Walking on the warm sands, he comes to a foreboding temple. He enters. At the bottom of a winding staircase, two half-naked old women with drooping witches' breasts, their nipples as long as fingers, are dismembering a child with their bare hands in savage silence.

Exhausted, I put the book aside and turned out the light.

Something seemed to be moving in the room. Half-asleep, I remembered reading about the omens and portents that the Puritans had reported seeing in Massachusetts: the perfect form of an Indian bow appearing in the air; a female child born with two heads; a great piece of ordinance shaking the earth; a running of the horses when there were no horses to be seen. And then, half-dreaming, I heard drums passing, going westward, and then a single gunshot rang out.

I was awake.

I went to the window.

Outside on the street below, lit by the flickering pink streetlight, I saw a man. He was nearly seventy, and his combed-over gray hair was flapping in the wind. In the dim light, the hair looked like a piece of skin, lifting up to reveal the exposed skull. The man looked familiar, but I couldn't place him. The gunshot, if there had been a gunshot, must have come from Quebec.

I left the study and went into the kitchen.

Robidoux and Romano were gone.

I came back to the study and went to the window.

The street was empty.

The man had disappeared.

Somewhere in the apartment, Lavinia had started talking again. But she wasn't talking about her new manager at the Tiki Lounge, or about becoming a dental assistant in Hadley.

She was talking about the night before. She was talking about Orin's death.

Still at the window, not moving—my reflection dimly superimposed on the dark woods that lay just beyond the dead end—I listened.

Lavinia

"They came," she was saying. "Two cops came. One cop had a moustache. He said he was Sergeant Maloney. The other cop was a big guy with blond hair and bad skin. You know…pockmarked. Like you could see he had acne as a kid. Officer O'Rourke, I think…I don't remember. They both stood in the doorway with their hats off, and they were looking at the ground, and I knew something was wrong.

"Maloney asked if I was Orin's sister. I said I was. He asked me if Orin had any 'next of kin.' I said he had a son, Sparrow. He asked if I knew where the boy was. I said he was probably at Claude Laroche's because he always stayed there on Saturday nights. I told them where Laroche lived. They said they knew the place. Then Sergeant Maloney told me something had happened. That there had been a bad accident, a crash, and that Orin hadn't made it. He said he wanted to take me to get the boy.

"I said I didn't believe them.

"The big cop explained that they had run the plate. He said Orin's wallet was missing, but that they'd pulled up his picture from the plate number.

"He said he was sorry.

"But I still didn't believe them, because, you know, what if the car was stolen and whoever was driving was the one who died, and Orin was just passed out at some girl's house or something? But Maloney said they already checked, and it hadn't come up stolen.

"So I explained to them how people were always borrowing his car…taking advantage of him.

"And Maloney stood there, still looking down, and he kept saying that he was very sorry, but the picture on the license matched up with the body, and that

69

they were sure it was him.

"The big cop, he didn't say anything. He just kept staring at the carpet. And the Maloney guy, the sergeant, he finally looked up, and he looked right at me, and he told me that Orin had been hurt pretty badly, and it might be difficult... difficult for me...

"I started crying. I said I didn't care how difficult it was. I said I had to see him.

"They asked about the boy. They asked if I wanted to tell him first.

"I said the boy was only twelve. And I told them that Laroche was old and that his mother was in her nineties. They said they knew Laroche but didn't know his mother was still alive. I said I didn't want to wake them all up in the middle of the night. I thought it would be better to go in the morning.

"They asked if there was other family. I said I had a sister. They asked where? I told them you were in New York. I told them I would call you after I saw Orin.

"Maloney said Orin was in the morgue in West Springfield. He asked me who I'd be comfortable going with. I thought it was a strange word to use. Comfortable. They must tell you to say that in the cop-training book. Who would you be 'comfortable' going with? They asked if I wanted a chaplain, or a priest.

"I said I wanted to go alone.

"So they put me in their patrol car. In the back. It's like a cage back there. We drove to the other side of the river. After the bridge, we headed north. We passed that monastery up on the hill on Riverdale Road. I wondered if the monks were already awake. I wondered if they were praying. Then the police radio came on. The big guy with the bad skin, he picked up the mic, and he had a conversation with someone, and then there was another call, but I couldn't hear what they were saying. And then it was quiet again, and we came to a big building off the main road.

"The cops helped me out of the backseat. They walked me up the steps. They rang a bell, and they took me inside to a waiting room. A woman came in. She said her name was Ellen. She sat me down on a couch and got me some water, and she told me how sorry she was. She explained that I could look at a photograph if I wanted. She said that they'd made an identification and that I only had to see the body if I wanted to.

"I figured the cops must have called her and told her to try to keep me from seeing him. That was probably what they were talking about on the radio. I said I wanted to see him, and I didn't understand why everyone was trying to stop me. And she said she just wanted to make sure, and she said she understood it was important for me to see him and that she would take me, and she asked me if I could wait for a few minutes. So I waited.

"Next to the couch, they had this metal rack with all these different pamphlets. One of the pamphlets was about grief. I took it. I tried to read it. It said grief was a process. It listed all the things you might be feeling. It said grief was a personal emotion. It said the initial shock wouldn't last for long. The woman, Ellen, came back in. She said she was ready for me. The cops offered to come. I told them I was okay and they could just wait, but when I stood up I was shaking and I could barely walk, so the big cop took my arm.

"The woman, Ellen, she led us down a long hallway.

"It had a stripe painted down the middle so you knew where to go. I said it was just like a hospital, and she said it used to be.

"'I guess they gave up on the living,' I said.

"Then we went through two sets of metal doors and down a flight of stairs, and we were in another hallway underground.

"I heard a humming sound.

"I asked her what it was.

"She tried to answer matter-of-factly, you know, saying it calmly and not hiding anything, like I bet they're trained to do. That's what she was doing. That's what the cops were doing. What they're trained to do.

"She told me the humming was the sound of the refrigerators.

"The humming got louder and it got colder, and I smelled a smell I'd never smelled before, and it felt like my brain was shutting down. That's what it felt like, Lily, like my brain was just slowly shutting down.

"We walked past two stacks of pine boxes. There were big ones and there were also some small ones. I didn't ask what those were for.

"At the end of the hall we came to a big room, but I couldn't see what was in it because they'd curtained it off with this blue plastic sheet they'd hung like a shower curtain.

"Ellen said she was sorry but that it was the middle of the night and they hadn't expected me, so they hadn't been able to get everything ready.

"She got me a chair and squeezed my hand, and she told me she'd be back in a few minutes.

"I waited.

"It smelled like bleach…like buckets of bleach.

"Then one of the cops got a call. On his radio. And they both moved away from me. And while they were on the radio, this old black man—a janitor with a mop and a bucket—came out. He smelled like gin. I could smell it on him. And I don't think he noticed me, because when he came out, he moved the curtain and I saw.

"I saw bodies.

"Three bodies.

"There was one that was covered, but I could see the feet, and it looked like the skin was gone, like the flesh had melted away, because I could only see bone and nails. And I could see the tag. The tag they put on your toe. Like you're a piece of meat. And there was another body. A woman's body that looked like it had been burned.

"The cops saw that the curtain had been moved, so they yelled at the janitor guy. And then Maloney, the one with the moustache, whispered under his breath to the big guy: 'I thought we fucking called ahead. I thought they knew we were coming.' The big cop saw that the janitor hadn't moved, so he yelled at him to put the curtain back like it was. But he was old, Lily. He was old, and he couldn't move fast.

"And Ellen, she must have heard the cops yelling, because she came rushing back in, and when she saw the curtain had been moved, she got upset with the janitor guy too, but I could tell she was trying to control herself. And the janitor guy, he was shaking and he was upset, saying, 'Sorry miss, sorry miss.'

"So Ellen, she put her hand on me, and she explained she didn't know the janitor was working that late. They were all circled around me, the cops too, because I think it looked like I was gonna pass out.

"I asked about the woman. I don't know why, but I wanted to know if she'd been burned. And Ellen said no, the woman wasn't burned. She explained that the woman died facedown and that the blood had pooled in the front of her body.

"Then she said that she knew it must be traumatic to be in a morgue and to see that, and she asked me if I still wanted to see Orin, or did I want to come back in the morning with a family member?

"Then I got angry. I said I didn't know why they were all trying to stop me from seeing my brother. The big cop, he said he was sorry, and the sergeant said he was sorry, and Ellen said she was sorry, and Ellen said she would go and bring Orin to me right away.

"When I saw him I knew why they didn't want me to see him. He was on a metal gurney. He was covered with a sheet. They had the sheet so you could only see one side of his face.

"Nobody asked me, but I said it was him.

"I just stood there. I wanted to touch him, and I wanted to talk to him, but I couldn't. He was so hurt I couldn't even look at him. He was so hurt, Lily. And this woman, Ellen. Somehow she just knew. She knew it was too much, and she knew I couldn't be with him any longer. She knew and she put her hand on my hand. And she looked at me.

"I just nodded. I just nodded my head up and down because I couldn't talk.

"And she took him away."

Claude Laroche

The next morning came slowly, the gray light gradually illuminating the now familiar landscape of burnt-out, triple-decker houses, sagging porches, and fenced-in front yards. Next to the houses were gravel driveways crowded with pickup trucks, trailers, boats, and bikes. At the end of the driveways there were storage sheds, rusted swing sets, and tangled power lines. And still farther back, under the canopy of branches, were the haunted corridors of the Indian trails that ran alongside the river.

Leaving the window, I buttoned the shirt I'd slept in and went to the kitchen. Lily was with her sister, making coffee and still figuring out plans for the funeral. It was as if they'd never gone to bed.

A lot needed to be done. Bank accounts had to be closed, the insurance company had to be called, social security had to be contacted, and an obituary had to be written. There was also the matter of the death certificate. Lily wanted someone—she couldn't do it herself—to go to the police impound to see if Orin had left anything in his truck. I offered to pick up the death certificate and to go to the impound.

When I went downstairs to go, the boy followed. It had snowed a little in the middle of the night, and I was wiping off the windshield when a small figure, waddling like a seal on a slippery rock, came toward us.

"Hey, Sparrow!" Guga called out.

Sparrow mumbled back.

I hadn't seen the kid since Pierce Sweeney and I had taken both boys to Rye Playland. During a ride on the whirligig (the kid barely made the height requirement) Guga had thrown up all over both of us, after which Pierce had referred to him alternately as "that little fucker" or, when his mood lightened,

74

"that little Portuguese prick." In the end, won over by the chubby kid's eccentricity, Pierce adopted him as a personal mascot. It was hard not to like Guga. But now, as he came closer, I noticed that he'd lost some of his baby fat, and it seemed as though a little meanness had crept into the corners of his mouth. At age eleven, he was already hardening. Indian Leap did that to people. Maybe his family had noticed. They'd decided to take the boy back to Portugal, and Guga had come to tell Sparrow.

"When?" asked the boy.

"In a couple of weeks," said Guga. "The fishing is better over there. You know...the whole country—well, most of it—is right there on the ocean."

"You'll catch some pretty amazing stuff there, I bet."

"Yeah, my dad told me you could even catch marlin."

"Wow. That's a big fish. You have to be a real sports fisherman for that."

"But," continued Guga, "they have regular stuff too. You know...hake and cod."

"Well, we have lots of cod here. Maybe you'll even catch one that gets away from me."

"Maybe," said Guga.

"Do you know what your new address is so I can write you?"

"Nope. We're staying with relatives until we get our own place, but I don't know the address."

Sparrow looked up at me.

"Is it okay if I go over to Guga's for a little while?"

I didn't know what to say. It was the first time I'd ever had a child ask for permission.

"Don't you guys have school?"

Guga looked disgusted. "It's winter break," he said.

"Okay, then you can go," I said.

The boy hugged me.

I watched them disappear, but before I could head out for downtown, an old Buick—the driver invisible behind tinted windows—slowly pulled in front of Orin's triple-decker. Then the driver's door was pushed open, and the rubber tip of a metal cane tapped tentatively at the ice-slicked pavement. A moment later, an old man's head, splotched with pink and sparsely covered with gray curls, poked from the shell of the car. The eyebrows were arched in a vague expression of what looked like surprise; the nose (reminiscent of Nixon's) suggested some kind of internal corruption. One hand gripped tightly at the cane, maneuvering it toward a secure patch of pavement; the other, pinched like a crab's claw, grabbed at the doorframe. Then there was a sharp intake of breath and Claude Laroche was standing.

During the Korean War, Laroche had been stationed on the eastern flank of the Pusan perimeter. One morning, just after daylight had broken, he heard a gong sounding through the narrow valley his platoon had been patrolling. That was the last thing he remembered. During the mortar barrage that followed, he was badly wounded, nearly losing his right leg. He had used the cane ever since.

There was something almost feminine about Laroche. A moustache covered a cleft in his lip, but it didn't cover the slight sibilance.

Laroche played the horses. That was how he made his living. With his winnings he bought local real estate; and the more property he bought, the more rent money he took in; and the more rent money he took in, the more he gambled at the track; and the more he gambled at the track, the more he won.

By Indian Leap standards, he'd become as rich as Croesus.

It was said that he had piles of cash hidden all over the house. It was said he still had his service rifle and that he was a skinflint. He took care of an elderly mother, but outside of that, he sure didn't seem to spend much.

Eight years earlier, he'd told Orin that he should buy a triple-decker, multiunit apartment building. "You can live in one unit and rent out the others. That way the tenants will be paying your mortgage. It'll be security for you and for your son," he'd said. Orin didn't have the down payment; Laroche told him he'd lend it to him. Orin said he didn't want to take on any more debt; Laroche said he'd give him the money. He didn't care if Orin paid him back or not.

"Stuff's cheap here, and it'll go up," he'd said.

Lily didn't like the arrangement. She felt that the loan, or gift, or whatever it was, had bound her brother to a man who was beneath him and that the building had tied him to a place where he didn't belong. And maybe she was right. Orin himself often told her that the property was an albatross. But he also believed that the building was the only way he could provide for the boy, and that it would, in the long run, secure a better life for them. When the mortgage was paid off, he would pay Laroche off. Then they would leave Indian Leap.

The day that Orin had closed on the building, he and Laroche had gone out for a celebratory dinner at Leone's and then to the Regal Beagle for drinks. Orin had had too much. Laroche drove him home and helped him to the couch. Sometime later in the night, something disturbed Orin's sleep: the vague awareness that his shoes and socks were being removed. When he finally managed to open his eyes, he found Laroche massaging his feet. In a panic, he called Lily and told her what had happened.

Lily pounced.

"Do not," I had heard her saying into the phone, "do not let that loathsome man near your boy."

But his home was now half Laroche's. He began to doubt himself. Maybe he hadn't remembered right. Or perhaps he'd misunderstood. He had, after all, been drunk. Within a week, he'd pushed the incident with Laroche from his mind.

One night, not long after 'the foot incident,' as Lily called it, we'd been invited into Laroche's home for dinner. Lily had begged off. I'd ended up going with Orin and the boy. After a meal of brisket and boiled potatoes, they went into the kitchen to help with the cleanup. Laroche poured himself a scotch and told me about his time in Korea.

A colonel, who was head of the psychological operations unit in his division, had taken a liking to him. Concerned that there'd been a communist infiltration, this colonel—'a real tough son-of-a-bitch'—had asked if he would help interrogate a South Korean soldier who he was sure was spying for the North. Laroche, who'd already lost six men in his platoon, said he'd be honored to. They interrogated the man in the mess tent.

"This colonel," Laroche told me, "takes out a tumbler, and he pours himself a jigger of good old Kentucky bourbon. And he has me heat up some oil in a frying pan, see. Meantime, the sergeant goes over to the prisoner and puts a knife blade to his ear, holds it with just enough pressure so that the man feels the blood beginning to drip down his jaw. And then, the colonel, see, he dips two fingers into his bourbon, and he flings a few drops into the frying pan so that that prisoner can see just how hot it is. And he looks that boy right in the eye and says: 'Now listen, son, if you don't tell me what I want to hear, I'm gonna have this sergeant cut your ear right off yer head, and I'm gonna fry it up in this pan, and I'm gonna eat it right in front of you. And if you still won't talk, I will do the same thing with the other ear. Understand?'"

"Jesus," I said. "He sure was a tough son of a bitch."

"Real tough son of a bitch," echoed Laroche.

"You didn't ever tell Sparrow that story, did you?" I asked.

"No," said Laroche. "Of course not. But I did show him pictures."

"What pictures?" I asked.

The sound of dishes halted. I was certain that the boy was listening.

Oblivious to my alarm, Laroche pushed himself from his armchair, limped over to one of the closets, reached up, and took down an old shoebox. Inside were black-and-white pictures of men in combat fatigues. There were pictures of men under fire: climbing barren hills, crawling along narrow ridges, and hiding behind berms. There were pictures of haunted barracks and makeshift shelters and pictures of spent shells and crumbled cities of stone. Among them were pictures of the dead.

"I showed him these," said Laroche, "so he can see what war is."

Lost in the photographs, Laroche began talking about the closeness that can happen between men in the midst of battle.

He lingered over the image of a young American soldier who had just been shot dead. The boy's arms were spread out like Christ on the cross, and his eyes were still open. The genitals were clearly visible. Laroche couldn't let the picture go.

Later, after I told Lily about my conversation with him, she'd begged Orin to break off relations with the man. Orin must have told him what she'd said, because every time we visited after that, Laroche kept his distance.

For the past five years, we had barely spoken to him.

But with Orin gone, we would have to talk things over. And that's what Claude Laroche had come to do.

"I hear," he said, planting the red rubber tip of the cane onto a dry patch of sidewalk, "you're thinking of taking Sparrow back to New York City."

Speaking slowly, Laroche had broken the word *City* into two distinct syllables, pronouncing it as though New York was located in some foreign country.

"We are," I said, "thinking about it. We have a pretty big apartment on the Upper West Side…"

"Don't know where that is."

"Well…it's on the West Side of Manhattan and a little bit north."

"Safe?"

"Very."

"Uh-huh," said Laroche, tapping absent-mindedly at the sidewalk with his cane, as if he were discussing the matter with a rather charitable civility on an exclusive golf course at which I was an uninvited, barely tolerated guest.

"In Manhattan," I added.

"Manhattan," repeated Laroche. "Manhattan's pretty safe these days?"

"Oh yes."

"Expensive?"

"Yes."

"And you have enough money for that?"

"We'll get by."

"Well, of course, the government's gonna give you about two hundred dollars a month. That ought to help. You know, social security gives you that on account of Orin's death."

"Didn't know that."

"They do."

"Wasn't counting on that."

(Why was I slipping into Laroche's drawl and dropping pronouns?)

"Now of course, you already got the forty thousand that was Orin's share of this place coming to you…"

"To the boy," I said. "It's not mine to use. We'll put it away for college."

"Well, you've got to live. What do you do down there? Put it in the stock market, make a little money off it, then give him the principal? That how you do it down there?"

"Do what?"

"Make money."

"I don't make that much."

"But you said it was expensive."

"I did."

Laroche said nothing for a minute and then continued.

"So I think we'll just go and see Henry Dargis," he said.

"Who?"

"A lawyer friend. And we'll have him hold on to Orin's share. Make sure it stays safe. And we'll have the government money go through his office just to make sure it stays in the right hands."

"You want the boy's money to stay in your lawyer's hands?"

"I didn't say that."

"I don't think that's a good idea. We'll let Lily take it. She can put it in something safe, like a savings account—"

"And you're her husband, so I'm sure you'll have some say, and my guess is that you'll want to play around with it in the stock market down there, the way I know you people like to."

"I don't see any reason to sit down with your lawyer," I said.

"You're not gonna walk out of here with that boy."

"That's up to Lily."

"No…it isn't."

"Oh yes it is. And if she wants to take him with us, which is what I want, then we will."

"Then it's gonna be over my dead body. Because you're not gonna walk out of here with his government money, and Orin's hard-earned money, which I helped him invest, and his social security. I know your kind. I know who you are and what you are and what you do."

"Well Claude, guess what? I know *your* kind too."

Laroche stopped. His whole body, as if jellied, was shaking, and the pink splotches on his skull had gone bright red.

He raised his cane but stumbled back against the side of the car. Sweat dripped from his chin like a baby's drool. He spoke in a rasp.

"I'm like that boy's grandfather. I took him to school when Orin couldn't, and I picked him up in the afternoons. I took him fishing, I bought him presents on his birthday, and on Christmas, and I put my own money into this building so that he could have a safe place to live. This boy is my life, you dirty money-grubbing—"

"What, Claude?"

"You dirty…money-grubbing… Jew…playing with my boy's money…with my money I saved for him…"

Watching the crippled man struggle toward the driver's seat, I felt myself turn as ugly as I ever had. And I wanted to stop myself, but I couldn't. It was as if I was speaking from a dark pit that had opened somewhere near the bottom of my stomach.

"You dirty old faggot," I heard myself saying, as I watched Laroche struggle.

"I served this country in a war!" he shouted back. "I sacrificed everything I had for this country. And I sacrificed everything for Orin and for his boy. Go down with me to Henry Dargis and you'll see. Every penny I have is going to that boy. Every penny. Right there in my will. And you call me by that name. I love that boy, and if anyone tried to harm him I would kill him. And I know what it is to kill. And I would kill again for that boy. And you call me by that name? You don't know who I am. You think you know, but you don't. You don't."

I was paralyzed. Laroche was crumpling toward the sidewalk, and there was nothing I could do to help him.

And then Big John, like an archangel, came walking up from the woods and wordlessly took Laroche in his arms. Gently, he helped him into the driver's seat. Then he went to the passenger side and sat with him.

Sick to the pit of my stomach, I went back into the house.

From the window in Orin's study, I watched as Laroche drove away.

Cyclops

Lily had been watching. Returning upstairs, I was greeted as a conquering hero, though I sensed there would be some cosmic payback for yelling at the old man.

I drank a cup of coffee to calm myself. Lily called the police station and the police impound. She asked if someone else could pick up Orin's things.

Cupping the phone to cover the mouthpiece, she asked if she could say that I was her husband.

I nodded, yes.

The police station was on Main Street. The property clerk was on the second floor, down a blue hallway. On the counter was a desk bell, the old-fashioned kind that you sometimes see in hotels. I rang it and waited. A clerk appeared from behind the wall of wooden cubbyholes and checked my name against a list. She had a solemnity that seemed appropriate to her office. Wordlessly, she disappeared back behind the wall. I had the odd feeling of being a parent, picking up his kid's belongings at a camp or a school, and the cubbyholes and walls, which had been painted chalkboard-green, accentuated that feeling.

There are certain shades of blues and greens that you only see in police stations, hospitals, and elementary schools. I remembered Lavinia saying that the Springfield morgue had originally been a hospital. Had the police station once been an elementary school? Had the world given up? A few minutes later the property clerk returned.

The clothing was in a plastic bag. The shirt had been neatly folded, but it was covered in dried blood. Picking the bag up, I noticed the pants were also neatly folded. And the undershirt and underwear. The shoes were in a separate bag. They had been tied.

I looked back up at the woman.

"Did you fold these?" I asked.

"They fold them at the morgue and send them to us like that," she answered.

I thanked her and asked for directions to the impound. Five minutes later, I was lost. Orin's clothes, now in the backseat, were unnerving me, and one of my contact lenses, the right one, had clouded. I couldn't make out the street signs, or read the map that sat open, like an old accordion, on the seat next to me.

Out of my left eye, I spotted the armory—a fortress of red brick, topped with towers and turrets. It had been the site of Daniel Shay's rebellion. Not far from the armory, I passed St. John's Congregational Church, where John Brown, the abolitionist, had once worshipped. There'd been some good old revolutionary, radical fervor on these grounds. The town had history, but it had faded badly.

In the main square, there were government buildings made of brick, and City Hall with its great Greek columns, a grand old clock tower, and a statue of Miles Morgan, defender of Springfield during King Philip's War. But just past that main square everything turned to shit—to a drag of strip bars, fast-food chains, liquor stores and boarded-up buildings.

Downtown had been abandoned.

I drove aimlessly, as if in a trance. My vision was getting blurrier.

An hour later, I finally found it.

At the front gate, chained to a tow truck, there was a pit bull with eight engorged teats—a low-rent Cerberus, guarding the underworld tangle of steel, chrome, rubber, metal, and glass. A fat man appeared wearing aviator sunglasses, motioned me inside a small shed, had me sign a clipboard, and pointed me toward the back of the lot. The dog barked and bared her teeth. The fat man, watching TV in his shed, paid no attention.

Scanning for Orin's blue pickup, I passed cars sitting up on blocks, cars on top of cars, cars with the doors torn off, with hoods open, with windows smashed. Flattened cars, crumpled cars, twisted cars, and stripped cars—wheels, rims, hubcaps, hood ornaments, and mirrors torn off by vultures. I'd written Orin's plate number on a piece of scrap paper. I didn't need it. At the back of the lot, near a chain-link fence topped with barbed wire, I saw the truck.

This Car Climbed Mt. Hood was plastered on the bumper.

When I'd lived in Boston with Lily, I had seen that truck pull into the parking lot behind our building a thousand times. And then Sparrow would practically jump out of the passenger's side, a little bag of bones, the sweetest boy in the world, and he would attach himself to me like a baby chimpanzee, begging me to play wiffleball.

"Don't let me win. This time, I want to really win on my own!"

"I didn't let you win last time. You won fair and square. I just didn't realize you could hit the curveball in the clutch."

"So we can play?"

"We have to play. I need to redeem myself."

And then, after I had promised I would play and had sworn up and down that I wouldn't let him win, the dog, an old cocker spaniel, would come limping out with its tongue hanging and its ears nearly dragging along the pavement. And then the driver's door would open, slowly, and Orin, usually limping like a warrior from some motocross or running injury would emerge from the driver's seat, handsome, with thick, dark, wavy hair. He would walk slowly toward his sister, Lily—the only person left in the world who he felt could truly understand him.

Orin did that once a month. Drove the hour and a half from Indian Leap to Boston.

But now, the driver's side door was gone, Boston was gone, my marriage was over, the old cocker spaniel was dead, and the time when Lily could salve her brother's hurt soul while I took the little boy and swung him up toward the heavens in celebration of an astonishing homerun or great come-from-behind-victory was over.

I climbed in and sat in the driver's seat. The windshield was spider-cracked, and when I moved my head, even just a little, the world outside broke apart as if I were viewing it through a kaleidoscope. But I could still see, between the two low red brick buildings that stood just behind the chain-link-fence, a pink neon sign that said *Girls*—preternaturally bright against the dull gray sky. Underneath the neon sign, a man, slightly hunched and split in two by the windshield, was standing, trying to look casual.

I wondered if Orin had ever gone into the club.

Sitting in the front seat, I pried open the glove compartment. Inside were maps of Vermont, New Hampshire, Maine, and Canada, an insurance card, a manual for the car, and a picture of Sparrow. It was a school photo. Four pictures, printed on the same sheet. The boy was wearing a black shirt and a white tie; his hair had been carefully combed and plastered across his forehead. He looked very pale and very skinny.

Turning the photo over, I looked at the date. It was the first year that Orin had raised him. Fourth grade. I returned to the small pile of maps—maps of all the places that Orin had taken the boy. And he'd taken him just about everywhere that a boy that age should be taken. He'd taken him to mountains, woods, lakes, and rivers. He'd taken him to motorcycle races and to county fairs. He'd taken him on fishing trips and on hikes. He'd shown him how to work on cars, how to tune a motorcycle, how cast a line, and how to camp out in the woods.

Depressed or not, he had made the boy, as best he could, the center of his life.

Orin had a disease. He was an alcoholic, and the boy had to endure that. But he had been a father, and a good one.

Things happen: fat guys work at junkyards, lonely married guys go to strip clubs, and depressed guys drink. Sometimes, even when they drive slowly, they die.

Later that day, I watched as Lily wept over the shirt. When she finally put it down, I took her back into Springfield to close bank accounts and pay bills. Afterward, we went to the funeral parlor that Lavinia had picked.

The proprietors were hideous and ghoulish. Their spines were curved from bending over their work—from draining fluids, the last of the life-stuff, from corpses. One of the men, the shorter one, kept quiet. It was clear he'd been told not to open his mouth. The slightly less ghoulish one did all the talking.

We looked at coffins. The prices were outrageous. We settled on what Lily knew Orin would have wanted: plain pine. A church was chosen. A priest was picked. We went to see him. He had thick black eyebrows, thick lips and though he was an older man, very thick, dark hair. It was as if celibacy had accentuated rather than diminished his sexuality. He barely knew who Orin was. Lily felt everything was horribly wrong: the church, the priest...everything. And she was right.

Everything was wrong.

The Funeral

It was a bitter, brittle cold—black ice on the bridges and back roads and sidewalks, icy stalactites, like rows of shark's teeth, hanging from the power lines. The snow fell against the gray sky, mingling with the purplish smoke that rose from the chemical plant.

Lily was worried that nobody would come. She thought her family would stay away, and she had little faith in Orin's friends.

But they came.

The cousins from Vermont on Sparrow's mother's side, blond and pale and pinched; an aunt from Virginia on Orin's side, a maker of Scottish crafts; Big John, the broken angel, in his black leather jacket and red flannel shirt; Aldo Romano in a pinstripe suit, a Windsor knot in his yellow tie; Jerry Robidoux, red-eyed, rumpled-jacketed, his shirttail flying, his belly hanging over his belt; Fred—the man I had seen standing out on Quebec Street the night after Orin's death—gray hair combed over his bald spot, shoulders slumping, the stink of booze on him; Laroche limping, not looking in my direction, his hand on his mother's wheelchair; Laroche's mother, shriveled under blankets, coat, scarf, and hat; men from the Westover base in full military dress; Guga, black hair carefully combed; kids from Sparrow's school and their parents—each pulling up into that gravel driveway car by car until the lot was full and then walking the thirty yards through the bitter cold to the chapel.

First they milled around in the back, in the recreation room.

There was subdued chatter, hugs, and hellos. In the hush, people discreetly pointed out other people. That's his sister. She's his cousin. That's the uncle. She worked with him. In the background, a few church volunteers stood guard over the plastic platters of food, plastic silverware, Styrofoam cups, and a dented coffee pot.

Lily went in to speak with the priest.

Then the door opened and there was a bitter blast of cold shot through with the acrid smell of resin from the chemical plant, and there he was: Hamish O'Mordha himself, wearing a black greatcoat, his white hair brushed straight up, his face stained scarlet from drink, and his eyes an electric blue.

Behind him the door closed. A church worker took his coat. The suit underneath was worn but elegant. A small crowd gathered around him. Despite the years and the miles, the devil was still magnetic. He still had the life force.

Hamish O'Mordha had not moved from the doorway, had not moved at all, but I found myself drawn toward him. Coming closer, I heard the voice: a gravel whisper that rattled out from his chest. The thoughts were broken, or left unfinished. He seemed not to care if anyone listened, or understood. But it was impossible not to listen—impossible not to wait for the next crumb, no matter how small. I couldn't hear much, but I heard him say something about *wine* and *milk* and *bones*. Then the aunt from Virginia, the craftsmaker, apparently his sister, went to him, and he repeated those same words: wine, milk, bones. I wanted to know what they meant, but before I could get any closer, the sound of the organ flooded the room.

In the front row, Lily, Lavinia, and the boy were waiting for me. I grabbed hold of the boy's hand and Lily's.

The priest entered and placed the gospels on the altar.

He had a thick Boston accent and a pronounced lisp that the microphone amplified to the point of parody: "In the name of the Fah-tha, and of the Thun, and of the Holy Thpirit…"

He read perfunctorily, barely looking up from his text. The Kyrie was sung. Gloria. The Lord's Prayer. "Our Fah-tha, who art in heaven, hallowed be thy name."

I mouthed along as best I could.

The priest called Lily to the altar. It was her turn to speak.

I tried to concentrate on what she was saying while glancing at my notes. It had been decided that I would speak for Orin. This was because Orin's friends couldn't or wouldn't, Lavinia couldn't, the boy was too young, and Lily thought it would be terrible if only she spoke. Besides, the priest was a hack, and I, at least, had known Orin.

Then things got blurry. My right contact lens was drying up again. So was my throat. I could barely breathe. I gave up on my notes and listened.

Lily was brave and eloquent and magnificent.

Then the priest called me to the altar. I could barely walk. I began by talking about how *The Magic Mountain* had been a "touchstone for Orin." But everything I said sounded hollow, stupid, and pretentious. I tried to return to my notes, but my right eye had worsened. My throat tightened. I went back to talking about *The Magic Mountain*.

I told the mourners that I saw Orin in the rarified air of the Swiss Alps, wrapped in a blanket on a lounge chair, staring up at the constellations and contemplating the universe. The faces in the front pews—the only ones I could see with my blurred vision—were blank. Somewhere near the back, I thought I heard Robidoux snicker. I was aware of my own irrelevance. Gripping the lectern to hide my shaking hands, I went on.

I said that Orin's boy, Sparrow, was a Hans Castorp in the making, a continuation of what was best and most beautiful in Orin. I don't think anybody knew what I was talking about. I looked down at the last page of my notes.

I found the quotation I'd wanted to close with.

For the sake of goodness and love, man shall grant death no dominion over his thoughts.

I began to read, but when I got to "no dominion," my voice cracked and I couldn't finish. For the first time now, I wept. Not for Orin but for my own inadequacy as a man.

I had failed. I had failed the boy.

Mercifully, the priest stepped forward and motioned for me to sit.

Finally, it ended. The Bach cantata Lily had picked filled the little church, and it ended. Lily rose from the bench and went to the altar to offer a last prayer. The boy went off with Guga. I walked to the back of the church and sat alone in the last pew.

A voice, somewhere on my left, came from the dark.

"So you're the husband?"

"Yes…"

There was a long pause.

"I'm sure she gave you the story. I'm the devil. I abandoned her. I don't get to give my side. I know the rules…no sense in defending."

"I'm sure she's glad you came."

"She hasn't said a word to me. Her mother hated me. You can't imagine how much. Oh God…she hated me. Passed it on to her daughter like some kind of virulent fucking, incurable virus but—here I am. Undeniable. The devil is here. The devil's come to carry his son's casket."

"I'm sorry," I said.

"I'm sorry too. I'm sorry too," he said, sliding along the pew, coming closer.

"Do you know what they've done?" he was saying. "Do you know what they've done to my son?"

"Who?"

"Over there," he said, pointing an accusatory finger toward the undertakers.

"Those two desecrated my boy's good clean body. Desecrated it…you see. I know all about that. How they prepare the body…Wrote about it…in a poem."

"I read some of your stuff."

"Didn't think much of it…eh?"

"Actually, I thought a lot of it."

Hamish nodded, pleased, then lowered his voice and came closer, putting a warm hand on my shoulder. Amazing the constitution of a real drunk. Blood pumping no matter how much rotgut they put in the tank.

"So those ghouls over there," he said, "play dress-up. Paint your face. Cut you open. Take out the innards. Have to do that. If you don't, you get a greenish discoloration. The Etruscans had a god of death painted the same color. Aquamarine. Goes to black eventually, of course, and then the skin comes off in sheets. Intestines leak out through the rectum. The world will not end in fire… but water. So says Eliot. But we don't let nature have its way. I would have soaked his bones in milk and wine…that's what I would have done."

I looked at him closely. Even with his son dead, he seemed, on some level, to be performing.

"You think I'm a clown, don't you?"

"No..." I said.

Neither of us spoke for a while after that.

Lily was still praying at the altar. She and her father had not yet spoken, or even looked at each other. I told him I thought he should go to her.

"Can't...she calls me devil."

"You abandoned her."

"Because she wouldn't have me."

For a minute, he sat in silence. Then he went.

Slowly, with a slightly herky-jerky gait, Hamish O'Mordha made his way down the aisle, through the now empty nave, and went toward the pulpit, where Lily, his daughter, was standing.

He was below her, at the altar, looking up.

He said something to her, which I couldn't hear.

She said something to him.

He answered.

Then her face turned to stone, and she whispered something else I couldn't hear.

His shoulders sagged a little. His head dropped toward the floor. He was swaying side to side, like a boxer who had just taken a devastating punch.

There was very little light in the church, but I could see lines of hatred etched in the white mask of Lily's face.

I could see only the dark outline of the father's form.

After a moment, he raised his head proudly.

I could see again the shock of white hair.

He looked at his daughter, and spoke.

"I am not your father," he said.

And then he turned on his heels, steadied himself, walked down the aisle, passed the mourners who were waiting to go to the graveyard, grabbed his greatcoat, and walked out the door.

Henry Dargis, Esq.

Henry Dargis's office was located next door to a small two-story structure that housed Indian Leap's lone museum, a one-room exhibition space devoted solely to the sinking of the *Titanic*. In addition to displaying such artifacts as the wireless message that warned the ship of the fatal iceberg, it was also home to The Rivet Counters, a group of enthusiasts devoted to constructing detailed models of the ship from the poop deck down to the propellers.

Whether this odd museum kept Dargis on retainer, I don't know, but I thought it appropriate that someone who made his living off the misfortune of others should be operating in such close proximity to the remnants of an American tragedy.

Although he was not slick enough to be a shark, Henry Dargis—maker of wills, settler of estates, arbiter of acrimonious divorces—was a bottom-feeder, and he looked the part. Short and squat, with a piggish, pinkish face and thinning, frizzy gray-blond hair, he sported a spectacular comb-over, the likes of which I had not seen since 1973 during a childhood visit to one of my father's favorite Greek restaurants in Astoria, Queens. But despite his singular unattractiveness, or perhaps because of it, Dargis was continually checking his appearance in the gilt-framed mirror that hung in his otherwise modest office. So captivated was he by his reflection that he paid only passing attention to the rant his client was unspooling.

"I'll want a bond," said Claude Laroche. "I'll want a bond of surety, because that boy has thirty thousand dollars worth of equity in his father's building, and I have thirty thousand. So that's sixty thousand all together, all told. And when I die it's all his—right Henry, that's what we put in the will? And I'm sorry, but I don't want it squandered in the stock market, and I don't want it invested in some harebrained scheme, and I don't want it spent in fancy restaurants or on fancy clothing.

"In fact, I'll tell ya straight out, Henry, that I just don't want their hands on it at all. I don't want their hands on that property, or on any of the proceeds issued from any said sale of said property. Not one red cent of it. It's not theirs now and never was to begin with. And furthermore, that boy is entitled—because of his father's death and because he is a minor—to social security. Now, social security is gonna amount to over seven hundred dollars a month, and I want to see to it that that government check—every penny, nickel, and dime of it—goes to the boy and only to the boy and that she isn't spending it on God-knows-what-they-spend-it-on-down-there—getting her nails done and such."

"Oh my God," said Lily and sighed in total disgust.

Here, Henry Dargis, his voice unexpectedly sonorous and deep, interrupted.

"Claude," he said, checking his hair in the office mirror and pushing his glasses up on his nose, "let's be fair. Women get their nails done in Springfield too. So put the brakes on and calm down. Everybody wants what's best for the boy, these two included."

"I know that Henry," said Laroche. "I was just using a figure of speech to make a point. It's not just about the money. It's also about where they live. And I'm sorry, Henry, but I'm not a big fan of New York City. That boy likes hiking in the woods and riding his bike and fishing in the river. He loves nature, he loves going to the horses with me just to watch them run, and I just don't think city life is much of a life for a boy like that.

"Now. Lavinia says she's willing to move into Orin's apartment right away. She can take care of him, keep the place in order, and collect the rents. That way, he stays in school and stays near his friends. I can drive over and see him anytime. He can stay with me whenever he likes."

Laroche kept talking. Lavinia was grinding her teeth. Her jaw looked like it had been carved in granite. Whenever the subject of money came up, I could see the hunger in her addict's eyes. Probably, she was coked up. Or would be later. Either way, she'd clearly been told to keep quiet.

Laroche was her mouthpiece, and he was putting on quite a show.

His accent, for example—which had started just over the Mason-Dixon Line—had gradually worked its way down through the Carolinas and Georgia. By the time he'd gotten to the part about Sparrow fishing and watching the horses, he damn near sounded like he'd been born in Barbour County, Alabama, jus' a piece down the road from Mista' George Wallace.

The good ol' boy accent had a purpose. He was a country mouse, and the boy was a country mouse. We, on the other hand, were city mice, and the particular city we chose to inhabit was, in Laroche's view, a stew of drug dealers, crack-addicted teenage mothers, conniving pawnbrokers, and brutal mobsters—in short, the kind of characters whose absence from the ever-gentrifying island I had long lamented.

Eventually, Laroche exhausted himself, and it was time for us to make our case.

With some difficulty, Henry Dargis—that vaingloriously ugly troll—tore himself from the mirror.

"So," he began, turning toward me, "I understand that you're separated from your wife, that you're currently unemployed, and that you live on one of the biggest drug blocks in Harlem."

Laroche, looking like the cat that swallowed the canary, grinned slyly at me. Lily went cold. Lavinia's enormous jaw, which now seemed to be wired shut, twitched violently. She was already spending the social security on blow.

But I wasn't ready to let the boy go.

"Lily and I are not separated," I said. "I'm not unemployed, it's not a drug block, and I don't live there."

"Then why are you on the lease?"

I took the lease so that I could learn about Santería from a Latina high priestess didn't seem like it was a good answer, so I improvised.

"I took the lease in order to sublease, which is perfectly legal. Along with the superintendant of the building, I'm in the process of furnishing the apartment and subdividing it into two units so that I can sublet it, at a profit, to two Columbia University students. When the students leave in the summer, I plan to use the space to tutor at-risk high school students, which is why I chose that location."

Had I gone overboard with the "tutoring at-risk kids" stuff? Dargis seemed unfazed.

"Then why aren't those students' names on the sublease?" he asked.

"Because the super and I are still remodeling and because it is illegal to sublet until after the first six months."

"So there are no students living there yet."

"No."

"But you said the students went to Columbia?"

"Yes. The university is nearby, and that's the plan. That's who I assume would need cheap rent and wouldn't need much space. You know how college kids live."

"So you still live at seven eighty-nine Columbus?"

"Check my credit card bills, bank statements, and electric—everything gets sent there. Call the management office. Speak with the doormen. They all know me. They all know I live there."

"Lavinia," Laroche said, "told me you two had separated."

I knew Lavinia wouldn't speak. And I knew Dargis could see that she was an addict and wouldn't necessarily trust her. So I pushed it a little.

"We've had some problems, like all marriages do, and Lavinia might've misunderstood. And it is true we considered taking some time apart. But we haven't separated, and we're not going to divorce."

Lily grabbed my hand under the table.

I told myself I was doing this for the boy. I told myself that Lily and I could separate later, once the boy was safely with us, that I could still be in his life and help provide him with a home and a good education and a good start.

On my lone visit to the Titanic Museum, several years before, I had discovered that the wireless operators onboard the doomed ship were paid primarily to relay messages to the wealthy passengers in first class. Consequently, when a nearby ship attempted to alert the *Titanic* to the fatal field of ice floating just ahead, the wireless operator, overrun at that moment by what may have been the world's first text messages, replied: "Shut up, shut up. I am busy."

This made me consider the possibility that denial might be our most natural state, enabling us to survive in one moment and killing us in the next.

PART TWO

PART TWO

Der Untergang

I had read somewhere that Oswald Spengler's *The Decline of the West* might be better translated as something like *The Downward Movement of the Land of the Setting Sun*, a title that struck me as being even more poetic and foreboding than the one that ran up the spine of my worn copy. Written during World War I as fifteen million people were perishing, this philosophy of history described in voluminous detail the religious, political, and artistic cycles that occur as a civilization falls. I had never been able to make my way through the whole damn thing. But after I returned from Indian Leap and moved back in with Lily, I found myself once again thumbing through its pages. Perhaps I was projecting, but as the millennium approached, it seemed that Spengler's downward movement was everywhere.

The second George Bush, though not yet president, was slouching toward Washington; the Twin Towers, though still standing, had already been attacked; banks, drugstores, and Starbucks—markers of greed, sickness, and fatigue— were spreading their tentacles, rendering the city rootless and sterile, "dead to the cosmic," as Spengler would have put it.

Lily was grieving. I felt trapped. It was nerve-racking.

Once a week I took refuge with Pierce Sweeney, going out for our customary Chinese dinners and late-night drives. His mood was darker than usual, and he had fixated, with fervor, on the assassination of John F. Kennedy, hoping, I guessed, to lose himself in the details of a tragedy other than his own. Even before he had lost his wife he had gravitated toward the darker side of life, insisting that I immerse myself in his peculiar interests and obsessions by creating a rather odd curriculum of coursework for me to master.

The following catalog is partial but representative.

Organized Crime in New York City: This was a general survey of the five major mob families with a special emphasis on the Sparks Steakhouse murder of Paul Castellano.

Racism and Economic Inequality in America: Special topics included the busing crisis in Boston and *Brown v. Board of Education*. There was also guided fieldwork in Bed-Stuy, Brownsville, and Bushwick.

Urban Planning and Political Corruption: Pierce, under threat of revealing my one homosexual experience to our entire high school graduating class via certified mail (in 1979 I had allowed a really nice gay guy to give me a hand job in Bryant Park) demanded that I read all 1,169 pages of *The Power Broker* in one month.

The Manson Family and the Murder of Sharon Tate: Course materials included Vincent Bugliosi's *Helter Skelter*, the Beatles' *White Album*, and the early films of Roman Polanski.

For his current obsession with the Kennedy assassination, he wanted me to read *The Death of a President*, the definitive study by William Manchester, and he had called the morning of our dinner at Charlie Mom to inform me that the book was mandatory. Before answering, I considered the facts. Sweeney had a core belief in the entity known as Sweeney, a belief that was set in stark relief to my utter lack of belief in the entity known as myself. Resistance was futile. I was fucked.

Pacing the living room, phone in hand, I explained that I was currently reading Oswald Spengler and Thomas Mann and that I would try to get to it at some future date.

He wanted to know why a Jew would immerse himself in the literature of a country that had attempted to wipe his people from the face of the earth. When I protested that neither man had participated in the Holocaust, he told me to stop splitting hairs. Then he called me a pretentious cocksucker.

I could feel myself crumbling.

In Sweeney, black bile and gall predominated, making him one of Galen's "melancholics." And yet he could, when roused, argue with the greatest of the legendary trial lawyers. Had he chosen a career in law, he would have been slick, fearsome, and rich.

He was—to borrow a new age term—*fully realized*.

When he wanted to eat, he ate, gorging on cold sesame noodles, broccoli with garlic sauce, pork fried rice, and General Tso's chicken. Afterward: ice cream, donuts, cookies. He knew that his diet would lead to weight gain, high cholesterol, and heart failure. But he knew what he wanted and got what he wanted. And what he wanted now was for me to read *The Death of a President*.

At nine p.m., we'd been seated at our regular table at Charlie Mom. We'd ordered two appetizers and three main dishes. Pierce had asked for a Coke. Then he put his elbows on the table and lit into me.

"Listen to me you silly little freak and listen good! This is a minute-by-minute account of the Kennedy assassination, from Thursday, November twenty-first when he wakes up until midnight on the twenty-fifth when Jackie places a bouquet by the eternal flame and everything in between."

"Everything?" I asked, pouring myself a little sugared tea.

"Everything. What's in his suitcase, how he puts his back brace on, who dresses him, what's in his wallet, what he has for breakfast. Get this: Zapruder comes to work without his camera and his fucking secretary tells him to go back and get it, and then he worries he's too short to get a good picture. Jackie's late for breakfast because she can't decide what gloves to wear. It's all the shit you know you want to know about—LBJ, Connally, the Secret Service."

"What was in his wallet?" I asked.

The dumplings and sesame noodles had arrived.

"Good question. Brilliant fucking question. Just the type of shit I wanted to know."

"So what was in the wallet?"

"Nothing. Just a driver's license. He's the fucking president! He doesn't need any money. Fascinating stuff. Fascinating. Very interesting psychological stuff about Oswald—and I don't mean Oswald Spengler, you pseudo-intellectual son of a bitch. I'm talking Lee Harvey! LHO!"

Noting the arrival of the fried rice, I attempted to serve myself, but my chopsticks were useless in the face of the occidental fork Pierce was wielding.

"Everything and more than everything," he continued, digging into the dish like a madman. "As Manchester gets closer to the moment, the detail just explodes like a mushroom cloud. He tells you what every person even remotely connected with this president is thinking and doing. Minute by fucking minute! It's twelve twenty-one Central Standard Time, nobody knows yet. Barry Goldwater is flying to Muncie; Jackie's sister is hanging out at Buckingham Palace."

"What was she doing at Buckingham Palace?" I asked.

"What would you be doing if you were there, asswipe?"

"I don't know. Trying to make the guards laugh, I guess."

"*Exactly*, that's *exactly* what she's doing there."

"What about Teodoro?" I asked.

"Teddy's running the Senate, half of the cabinet is headed for Japan, and Pierre Salinger is on that plane."

I hadn't heard that name in some time, and for some reason it reminded me of my childhood and the bread my mother used to make.

"Pierre fucking Salinger..." I repeated.

"Provi Paredes, the first lady's maid is shopping for Christmas presents."

"Provi Paredes, the first lady's maid. Two internal rhymes and some nice alliteration. Impressive."

"That's right, my friend. Whitman, Dickinson, and all those other poets you read ain't the only ones playing around with language, if you catch my drift."

"I'm not sure that I do."

"Meanwhile, Eunice is having lunch with Sargent Shriver."

His energy was infectious. He was getting to me. "Was Sargent really his first name?" I asked.

"Yes it was."

"Okay. Where was the staff?"

"Another good question. McNamara summons the joint chiefs, the Cabinet turns around over the Pacific, the phone system shuts down, they suspect sabotage. LBJ is sworn in, but Caroline's at a play date; she still doesn't know.

Life. Nobody knows it's about to stop."

He picked at what was left of the pork-fried rice.

"You know…it was cloudy that day…and Jackie wanted a bubbletop on the car."

I noticed he had somehow managed to finish the General Tso's chicken and the broccoli with garlic sauce.

"They thought there might be a thunderstorm that day…If the weather had stayed bad, *if* the sky had darkened, the car would have had a bubbletop on and Oswald would never have had a clean shot. If the sky had only darkened…if, if, if. After it happens, total chaos. Zapruder is screaming even as he films. Some people just go catatonic. The whole chain of command breaks down. The mayor of Dallas whispers the same thing over and over again."

"What?" I asked.

"It didn't happen. It didn't happen."

Pierce fell silent.

"Are you finished?" I asked.

"Talking? Why? Am I annoying you?"

"No, are you finished with the broccoli?" I really hadn't had much to eat.

"I'm finished," said Pierce. "I'm finished."

We sat quietly.

It had been five years since his wife had died. The anniversary was coming up.

I didn't know if he was ruminating on Kennedy or her. Or maybe both.

I sat and thought about Orin. I remembered Lavinia telling Lily each detail of his death. And I thought about Manchester's book and about our obsessive need to know.

When we resurfaced from our private thoughts, the place had emptied.

The waiter came with the check.

We split it, leaving the kind of outrageous tip that only people who feel really badly about themselves leave and walked out down the long mirrored hallway.

He grabbed a toothpick. I took a mint.

We stood outside. Sometimes in Manhattan, you can see a few stars. If you look hard enough. I pointed out the North Star and the hanging quarter moon.

Pierce, miming a tennis forehand, paid no attention.

His voice drifted through the air, soft and wistful.

"Nellie Connally won't even talk to Jackie at Parkland Hospital, that fucking bitch."

Turning from the sky, I saw that he was holding the keys in his outstretched hand. The cowlicks in his blond hair were rustling in the night air, each with a direction and intention of its own.

We got into his car.

I drove. Pierce lounged in the passenger's seat operating a police scanner, seamlessly switching to the appropriate frequency as we moved through the various precincts. Working the scanner was no simple matter. It required a certain kind of autism and a Buddhist-like facility for extended periods of repose. He was also responsible for the map.

That night we'd decided to check out Brighton Beach.

"So you're back with Lily, eh?"

"Yup."

"I don't like it..." he said.

"It's for the boy."

"Then I'll allow it," he said.

"Thank you."

"So he's coming to live with you?"

"Yes. I hope."

"Where is he now...in the brother's apartment with the crazy coke-snorting sister?"

The police scanner crackled.

"Yeah. Hopefully he'll want to come live with us in the spring."

"And if he doesn't?"

"If he doesn't, we'll get a lawyer and fight for him."

"That's expensive."

"I know."

"How are you gonna pay for that? Is there some Jew money somewhere in the family?"

"No. No Jew money."

"So what are you gonna do?" he asked.

I didn't answer.

After we'd spent a few hours out in the nether regions of Brooklyn checking out Gravesend and Brighton, I drove back to the Upper West Side and pulled in front of Delilah's Bar and Grille, where I used to bartend.

It sat just off Broadway, on the south side of 79th Street, under a faded white awning and down nine steps. Delilah, the owner, had big, blue, wide-set eyes, one wandering, and big breasts that spilled out of her bra, the prominent nipples pointing in divergent directions as she wiggled through the crowds of inebriated adorers. She was all over the place. Thirty years earlier, she'd been a bunny at the Playboy Club. Now, in her own restaurant, she was queen and den mother to a group of regulars that the bar manager called "the library of losers."

Delilah was still a sex object, but she was a sex object from a different time— from the Plato's Retreat–Studio 54 era, when women were still women in all their glorious imperfection and the sex was dirty and druggy and good.

"Are you thinking about going back there?" Pierce asked.

I knew he was having visions of drunken, middle-aged women and nubile, needy waitresses, with me as pimp and procurer.

"I don't want to. I really don't."

And then the night porter opened the door, and I had a quick glimpse of my former and future life.

Delilah's

The place had the feel of a cave and brought to mind Plato's allegory: each denizen seemingly chained to his, or her, chair—in this case by alcohol—and the light of the sun reduced to a mere shadow on the leprous walls from which great flakes of paint fell like the sloughed-off skin of some long extinct beast.

Across from the warped wooden bar, running along the wall, was a long, low banquette upholstered with a faded flowery pattern and bookended by two plants—both dying. The music was thunderously loud, the ceiling low, and the hanging clouds of smoke formed an autonomous weather system that operated without regard for the natural law of the outside world.

In the back, just past the cramped kitchen, there was a little café. In the little café, there were more plants—also dying.

As were the people who came there. They too were dying—purposefully, willfully. They drank as though they were being pursued by some malignant fate.

When I finally left Delilah's, taking a low-paying job at a community college, I had sworn that I would never go back.

But things were changing.

Across the street, the door was still open and the night porter was hauling the black plastic bags up the nine steps and wrestling them into submission on the sidewalk. Behind him I could see the pestilent, rolling fog of cigar smoke, cigarette smoke, and the smoke of burnt offerings from the small kitchen, and I could just make out the strange yellow light of the votive candles and curved lamps reflecting off of the peeling walls as if squeezed from a tube of paint, pooling irregularly.

And I saw in that irregular, yellowed light, closest to the door, a Rubenesque woman wearing a wide-brimmed hat, wielding, like a conductor's baton, a black cigarette holder. And I saw the bald-headed Loan Shark, the last of his dying breed, nearly eighty but still bulky and ox-strong, a white towel hanging from his boxer's shoulders, and I saw the tall, elegant Greek reclining and smoking his veined, fat, phallus of a cigar, and I saw the Priest, defrocked and drunken, dancing some strange jig, a dance of death. And I saw the Bishop and the Painter huddled together. And then the night porter, finished with his nightly task, closed the door, and they disappeared, but their images were so strong, and the delineation of their particular character so sharp, that, in my mind, I saw them still—the Rubenesque woman, the Loan Shark, the elegant Greek, the defrocked Priest—drinking deep from their goblets and glasses in the flickering, oily, yellow light. And I saw two middle-aged, Eastern European men—one from Berlin, the other from Prague—clad from head to toe in leather, inseparably huddled in the middle of the bar. And I saw an African man leaning against the jukebox, and I saw the law enforcement guys, and I saw the black man with the Stetson hat grinning like a Cheshire cat and another black man called the Prez, and more black men—old black crows perched on the knotted branch of the bar, and I saw a gaggle of girlish women, garishly made up, grabbing at the last of their youth, flirting as best they could.

I hadn't been there in over a year, but I could see them, and I could hear them: their particular voices, their particular vocabularies, their pet phrases, their physical ticks, their favored topics, and their sexual proclivities hinted at in jokes or nakedly revealed in drunkenness.

I knew the signatures of their being.

And though the door was shut, I could hear the music, maddeningly loud: low-down blues, Dixieland, swing, big band, bebop, soul, Latin, Afro-Cubano—the throb and thrum of the bass pushing the walls outward like the chambered walls of a weakening heart. I could see the head bartender—his skull a death skull, his cheeks hollow and haunted, his body all sinew, his genitals visible under the silk of his single-pleated pants like the exaggerated genitals of a primitive idol—creating elixirs from a bowl of exotic fruit while pulling white, perfectly folded packets of cocaine (pure mixed with pharmaceutical) from the silver register. Still sitting in the silent womb of the car, I could see him moving like a tango dancer toward the stereo, turning the volume clockwise with one long finger, and I could hear the music, Afro-Cuban, blasting, and I heard the old Loan Shark calling out the names of the musicians:

"Willie Bobo!" he cries. "Willie Bobo on timbales; Mongo Santamaria on conga; Cal Tjader on vibraphone! Am I right? Am I right, Vincent?"

Vincent—the head barman, the de facto boss of Delilah's—answers.

"My main fucking man," he says. "You got it."

And the old black man in the Stetson hat—I can see him as if he is right in front of me—flashes his black Cheshire cat smile.

"Shit, motherfucker, you got it! You got it, baby! This motherfucker knows his music. Shee-it!"

And the bald man, the old Loan Shark—touching thumb to middle finger in a gesture from the Gita—twirls his hand in small circles above his head: a black mass, a shadow blessing.

"I grew up with these guys in Spanish Harlem. Tito Puente lived across the street. All day, I heard him practicing. He still gives me tickets whenever he plays."

From his pocket, he pulls a thick roll of dull green.

"This doesn't matter," he says. "It's about respect," he says. "You fuck me, I fuck you," he says.

"You right, motherfucker!" says the Cheshire Cat. "Shee-it. I hate a phony. I like good people. All good people. Be who you are, motherfucker!"

"He's right," says the Loan Shark. "I never disrespect anybody until they disrespect me. Take my wife. I tried to have her killed three times this week, but every time I give the guy money to do it, she pays him more to kill me! Ha! Ah-hah! Ah-hah!"

And from the Contessa, the Rubenesque woman with the wide-brimmed hat and long cigarette holder, comes a shriek of pain that passes for laughter.

"Sweetheart," she screeches, "you don't know the half of it! I'm writing a book on the subject."

The two men in leather rise from indolent repose.

"What is this book you are writing?" asks the Berliner.

"Yes, Contessa, what is it?" asks the Czech, adjusting his dark glasses.

Her chin lifts. The cigarette holder is angled at forty-five degrees. Her red scarf, purchased in Paris, accents the theatricality of her movement. As she twists her body toward the men, her ass sways. It is tidal in the force of its motion. This is the ass that a Puerto Rican painter named Pablo Carreras has become obsessed with. He has rendered it in charcoal, acrylic, and oil.

The Berliner lowers his leather cap. He is a coquette: pale-blue, watery eyes, soft gray stubble, and a skinny body built for a bathhouse.

"Tell us, Contessa," he demands. "Don't keep us in such suspense. What is it?"

"It is about my marriages," she says. "*All* of them. And it is called…" Here she pauses, exhaling three perfect rings of smoke for effect. "It is called *Seven Oysters, No Pearls.*"

The bar stops. Completely stops. There is disbelief. Astonishment.

"Seven times? You've been married seven times?" asks the Berliner.

"Yes."

"Seven?"

"Yes."

"Unbelievable," says the Secret Service guy. "I got to hand it to ya, Contessa."

Jukebox George raises his eyebrows in agreement.

"Who was the first?" the Berliner wants to know.

The Contessa—sly, triumphant—turns to her questioners, and all eyes turn toward her. Her mouth is a red slash, her hair slicked and jet black, her eyebrows pencil thin, her skin powdered. She has girth. She is an object. This is why Carreras paints her. This is why men look at her. And now the stage is hers.

"It all started," she begins, "with the beautiful, dark-skinned African prince."

An interruption.

"He was *African* African?"

"Yes, sweetheart. African African. He spoke French, his tribal language, some Italian, and beautifully accented English. He drove a black Cadillac, an enormous old car that we called Toots Latour. His skin was darker than night.

He was big-boned and had muscles for days. His chest was God's chest, and his voice was deeper than a river…and he turned out to be gay. So that was number one—"

"Wait, Contessa! Stop," shouts the Berliner.

"What is it, sweetheart?"

"Would you mind," he asks, slyly pulling his cap over his eyes, "giving me his number?"

A shriek of laughter. The law enforcement guys throw their hands in the air. The Czech is beside himself.

"What about me?" he cries to the bar.

"I love you," says the Berliner, "but I have a weakness for black men."

From the stereo, a military drum roll from the forearms of Art Blakey and the Jazz Messengers kicks off the next tune, "Gee Baby, Ain't I Good to You."

Everyone is relaxed now. The Greek reclines farther back in his seat, draws deeply from his cigar, and brushes the falling ash from his Savile Row shirt.

"Philistines," he says, chuckling. "You're all Philistines."

And with that he orders a pink gin, drink of the Imperial British.

"Gosh," says the defrocked Priest, pirouetting toward the bar to refill his vodka (half tonic, half soda). "I used to know something. Now I don't know anything."

"Nobody doubts the latter part of your formulation," adds the Greek.

"And what about the second husband, Contessa?" asks the Secret Service guy. "What did he do, darling?"

"Oyster number two was a violist."

"Ah, yes, Contessa, you said he had 'issues,'" says the Berliner.

"Honey! He had a subscription," she adds.

"He was confused?" asks the Czech.

"Aren't they all, darling?" answers the Contessa.

"You are amazing, my darling," says the defrocked Priest, kissing her hand.

"Why are you kissing her hand?" asks Prez.

"My father was a hand kisser," he answers, still bent, still kissing.

"And probably a dicksucker," adds Prez.

Another old crow perched nearby clarifies.

"Definitely a dicksucker."

From some indeterminate place, a voice: "What are you thinking about?"

I had become so engrossed in my memory of Delilah's that I had forgotten that I was sitting in a car and that Pierce was with me.

"Oral sex, black men, defrocked clergy, barely closeted alcoholics," I answered, somewhat regaining my temporal equilibrium.

"I like it," said Pierce.

"What's not to like?" I asked, gazing at the door, still slightly disoriented.

"So are you going to work there again?" he asked hopefully.

"Do I have a choice?" I asked.

"What do you mean?"

"I think I have to," I said. "The boy is coming."

Vincent

Early the next morning, I walked over to 79th, went down the nine steps, and knocked on the wooden door. Through the small window I could see Vincent coming toward me.

He was just over six-foot-one and dressed in his customary black clothing, custom-made from Hong Kong tailors. As he opened the door, I could hear the bluesy swells of a Hammond B-3 organ pouring out of the speakers. He looked at me and then down at his watch.

"Five of eight."

"Yes, sir."

"My man, Johnny on the spot. You're back."

"I'm back."

"What happened to the teaching job?"

"Not enough money."

"What did those cheap cocksuckers pay?"

"You don't want to know."

"What about the wifey-pooh?"

"I'm back with her."

"I thought you guys were splitting up."

"We were, but we got back together because we're trying to get custody of our nephew."

"Her side or your side."

"Hers. Her brother's kid."

"Where's the brother?"

"Died in a car accident."

"What about the mother?"

"Crazy."

"I get it. My mom was nuts."

"His mom is on the streets."

"Oh Jesus."

"Yeah."

"Oh that poor fucking kid. And now you're gonna take him in?"

"Yeah."

"She got you back with the guilt-sy-pooh."

"I love the kid."

"You must be pissed the fuck off, my man."

"Nah..."

"I'd be angry. How old is the kid?"

"Twelve."

"Good kid?"

"Great kid."

"Sensitive?"

"How did you know?"

"When shit like that happens, my man, you either close off and become a real prick, or you get real sensitive, because you know what it is to really hurt. So this kid is a sweetheart?"

"Yeah."

"What's his name?"

"Sparrow."

"What kind of a name is that?"

"A nickname."

"Where is he now?"

"Up in Springfield, Massachusetts, with his aunt. My wife's sister."

"Oh what a fucking toilet. They got a lot of donkey-do-rights up there?"

"They do."

"Why can't he stay with the sister?"

"She's a drug addict."

"Okay. So you gotta go and do a little recon and get him out of there. You take care of him, my man. You give him a break. You take care of him like he's your own."

"I'm going to."

"Now remind me—what the fuck was wrong with you and your wife?"

"She didn't want to have sex."

"And what about now?"

"She still doesn't want to have sex."

"She getting a little part-time dick somewhere else?"

"No."

"So let me get this straight: you're back with her for the kid, but she ain't fucking you?"

"Right."

"Don't worry, my man, there's plenty of pussy here, and we'll get you making some serious shekels again. C'mon in and we'll get set up. I'm almost done squeezing the lime."

I knew the routine.

After the limes came lemons and oranges. Then a couple of quarts of egg whites.

"We're gonna get good and fat back here," said Vincent.

Every Friday morning we'd go to Fairway with a red hand truck, returning with cases of lemons, limes, oranges, and whatever else was fresh. Then we'd descend into the bar's barely lit basement to squeeze it all by hand, and when we had filled the quart containers with fresh juices and mixes, our hands would be stinging from the acid in the citrus, and the garbage pails would be running over with pulp and rind and egg shell and yolk. Then we'd go back upstairs. Vincent would put some music on the stereo, and he'd show me how to make one of his drinks while he held forth on pre-Columbian pottery, or the proper way to make clams with raspberry champagne sauce, or how good it felt to fire a .50 caliber handgun.

"I showed you how I do the Bloody Mary, right?" he asked.

"Yeah, but I'm probably a little rusty."

"Don't sweat it, my man. We'll go over it right now, and then you can prep it while I finish squeezing the juices."

"All right," I said.

"You like the music?" he asked, popping behind the bar.

It was "The Sermon" by Jimmy Smith, one of my favorites. A straight ahead blues in the key of F that goes on for about twenty minutes. Jimmy kicks it off with a long solo on the Hammond B-3 organ. And right before the guitar comes in, he repeats an F note. It's simple. It's the root. But the way he repeats it, kicks everything up a notch. And as each instrument comes in, it just keeps building and building. Like a great sermon.

"I love it."

"That's Art Blakey on drums," he said.

"And Kenny Burrell on guitar," I said.

"How do they do it? How do those niggers swing so fucking hard?"

"I don't know."

"I don't either, my man. And it sounds so easy when they do it."

But before he could start his own sermon on the Bloody Mary, the phone on the wall rang.

Vincent answered: "No…we don't take reservations for brunch…I am one of the owners…I just told you…we don't take reservations for brunch…The other owner isn't here…Her number? Her number is two-one-two, fuck-fuck-you."

He slammed the phone back down into the cradle. "Fucking Jewish bitch!"

"Probably one of my relatives," I said.

"Jesus. I forgot how motherfucking sensitive you are."

He could be a scary guy, but I knew him well enough to give it back to him.

"You just called Jimmy Smith a nigger," I said.

"I'm sorry, my man. I shouldn't have. I love Jimmy Smith. But when I was in the service one of those motherfuckers stabbed me, and I got soured on their whole tribe."

"And you're an anti-Semite," I continued.

"Hey, Rabbi," he said. "Relax. I'm part chosen myself."

"I didn't know that."

"Fuck yeah. My mother's mother was one-hundred-percent Heeb," he said, as he took a mixing glass and placed it just to the right of the bar mat. Then he took another glass and shoved it into the ice.

"You build a drink from the bottom up. Remember? Three-quarters ice in the glass. Always three-quarters. Fresh lime, Worcestershire, jit-stain of Tabasco, horseradish, celery seed, ground pepper, tomato. Booze goes in last. That way, if the donkey suddenly decides he wants Stoli, you don't have to throw the whole fucking drink out."

"The donkey?"

"The donkey-do-right. The motherfuckin' Hee-Haw," he said, baring his front teeth and braying obsequiously and stupidly. He took out a seven-inch boning knife and cut a perfect oval of skin from a lime. Skin down, he squeezed it over the drink.

"I finish it off with lime oil. The lime oil puts the fifth star on it. Now taste it."

"No ice?"

"It's a cocktail. You've already shaken it. It's already cold. Why would you want to put ice in it, you prick? Taste it."

I took one sip and then another.

"It's really good," I said.

"I know. Because it's subtle. Balanced. Now you do it."

I put ice in the mixing glass. Disgusted, he took out two cubes.

"You *are* rusty. Three-quarters."

I put in the ingredients in the order he'd showed me, but I moved the glass once, and he didn't like it.

"My man, you picked up some bad habits while you were gone. Always work around the glass, remember."

I started to shake the drink. He stopped me again.

"I hate to shrink your dick up, but you got to lock it in. Then put your thumb on the back and your mother-fuck-you finger on the front. Like this."

I tried it.

"No. Get behind me and put your hands on top of mine so you can feel what I'm doing."

I'd had enough. "Jesus fucking Christ, Vincent. I think I know how to shake a fucking drink."

"My man," he said, "I know I'm sticking it up your ass a little but dig this: most bartenders suck hind-tit. Most of them are donkeys. But you ain't like most bartenders, and I don't *want* you to be like them. So what I *want* you to do is calm the fuck down, get behind me, and learn something."

I don't know why I loved him so much. He could be ugly and racist. But he was also sweet and paternal, and it felt good to be close to a man, and to be mentored.

Resisting him was futile. Reluctantly, I got behind him.

"Good. Put your hands on my hands. Feel that?"

His movements were as rhythmic and sure as the music on the stereo.

"That's what it should feel like. Now you do it."

I took the shaker back.

"Keep your elbows out more and relax your shoulders. Get out of your head."

My body tensed up. I was getting it wrong.

"Oh, motherfucker!" he said, laughing. "Now you're gonna have Jewish fucking guilt about not being able to shake a drink right."

"I'm not having Jewish guilt."

"You gotta stop worrying so much, my man, or you're gonna end up with chronic diarrhea."

"I already have it."

"I ain't surprised."

He took the shaker back.

"Don't worry. You got good hands. You'll find your spot," he said, dislodging the mixing glass from the metal with the heel of his hand. Then he grabbed the strainer, poured red liquid into a chilled glass, and garnished the drink with a lime twist.

"Now taste what you made. Most bartenders don't taste what they make, so they have no idea what they're making. How is it?"

"I think it's good."

"Then it is good. I don't make the drink for them, I make it for myself. No matter what I do, I always try to bring my art to it. You know what I'm talking about. You're an artist. You were teaching theater, right?"

"Directing. At a community college."

"You ever direct professionally?"

"No. Just taught."

"That's okay. You're still an artist."

"I don't think so."

"My man, you know music, you appreciate it. Who's this playing right now?"

Art Blakey had just kicked off another chorus, Jimmy Smith was stabbing at the keys of the Hammond B-3, and the blare of a trumpet filled the empty bar.

"That's Lee Morgan," I said.

"See. You know who motherfucking Lee Morgan is. You're not like the insensitive Wonder Bread motherfuckers who come in here. You're an artist. So bring some art to this while you're back here."

"I'll try."

"Fuck 'try.' Do. And stop worrying so fucking much."

"How can you tell I'm worrying so much?"

"It's all those lines in your fucking forehead. You gotta stop sweating shit so much. Stop worrying about that shit with your wife. I know how it is. I was married."

"I didn't know that."

"Oh yeah, my man. Ten years I was married. I'll show you a picture sometime. She was one sexy bitch, and very provocative—the kind of kid you follow down the street. Everybody wanted to fuck her. When I first met her, she was going out with King Faisal. I'm not making it up, my man. She was that fucking gorgeous. Then I fell in love with her, and we got married. When I came home after a shift, she'd get on the table and strip for me while I beat off. I used to run home to see her. We're slaves to our dicks. You know that. Wherever it points, we've got to follow. Marlon Brando said it: confidence is a very hard penis. That's hard, we're on. We're not gonna fail. Oh Jesus, what a prick he was. For acting, nobody can come near him. That motherfucker. Have you seen *Last Tango in Paris*?"

"Yes."

"That casket scene? There's nothing like that. Great actors quit acting after him. There's nobody like him."

"So what happened with your wife?" I asked. "Why'd you get divorced?"

"She had a drinking problem. And when she got sober, she became a Jesus junky and left me. Women. You can never figure them out. All right, my man. You make the Bloody Marys, just like I showed you, and taste every one so you get good and fucked up. I'm gonna go downstairs and squeeze some lemon and lime."

And then he was gone.

106th Street and Amsterdam

In Indian Leap, things weren't going well.

Lavinia had allowed a man named Stan to come live with them. When we called, the boy told us that they were doing cocaine together.

"Do they bring over other people?" I asked. "People you don't know?"

"Not really that often."

"How much more school do you have?"

"A week, I think."

"Okay. Look. The papers are ready. We can come get you now, or whenever you want."

"Can I finish school, here?" he asked.

The next day Lily and I went out to buy a bed and ended up at a discount warehouse in Queens that sat under the BQE. The guy who ran it had slicked-back hair, bad breath, and no sense of personal space, but he was funny in a sleazy-sales-guy kind of way.

"Single bed?" he asked. "That's some fucking budget you two are on."

We told him it was for our nephew, who was coming to live with us.

"You taking him in?"

"Yes," said Lily.

"How old?"

"Twelve," she said.

"Okay, I got something nice for you, and I'll give you a good price."

After we bought the bed, he insisted on tying it to the roof of the car we'd borrowed. His technique was incredible. Lily and I were mesmerized.

"What do you call that?" I asked.

"That's a buntline hitch," he said. "Fucking impossible to untie. You'll have to cut it loose on the other end, but I can guarantee it won't come undone."

He checked the bed on all four sides, then stepped back and lit a cigarette. His eyes watered. I thought it was from the wind and the smoke. But he looked away.

"That's not fucking going anywhere. That's a good bed," he said. "He'll sleep good on that."

The guy was right. It took me thirty minutes to cut the thing loose. When we finally dragged it upstairs, there was a letter waiting under the door. It was from the agency that was managing the building. They'd found out that we'd messed around with the documents, and they'd decided to kick us out.

After a frantic month of apartment hunting, we found a place up at 106th just east of Amsterdam Avenue.

The neighborhood wasn't great.

There was a mural of an angel painted next to our vestibule, but the white wings had been smudged with soot, the halo had been covered in graffiti, and the Dominican drug dealers and their steady stream of buyers madly swarmed under the angel's blurred gaze.

The main dealer was immovable—a mass of flesh named Mario. I sometimes said hello to him, and he sometimes deigned to respond, nodding discreetly like a Buddha while scanning the busy streets. I didn't know his foot soldiers. They came and went, interchangeable cogs at the lowest level of distribution. At night they sat on our doorstep. They didn't acknowledge us and wouldn't move for us. Awkwardly, we clambered around as they lounged, laughed, and insulted us in Spanish. Upstairs, in our apartment, I impotently railed against them while Lily tried to calm me. I had always loved the underbelly of the city—its sleaze, its criminal element—but now that the boy was coming to live with us, I was beginning to feel parental anxiety and rage. Nobody was gonna fuck with my kid.

Together Lily and I set about fixing up his room, a cramped polygon that sat just off the narrow hallway, awkwardly wedged between the bathroom and the front door. Rummaging in secondhand stores, Lily found a desk and chair that fit the strange contours, and I built a bookshelf as best I could into the narrow nook next to the shallow closet. By the time we'd finished, it looked like it was straight out of *The Cabinet of Dr. Caligari*, and I worried that Sparrow would go mad from claustrophobia.

When he finally came to us in the spring, the block was bathed in sunshine, the graffiti had been scrubbed off the angel, and the vitality of street life—rapid-fire shouts of Spanish, blasts of salsa, little girls jumping rope on the sidewalk—outweighed the suffering. Upstairs in his new room, he placed books on archeology, geology, Native Americans, and natural history onto the jerry-rigged shelf I'd built. On the bottom, in easy reach of the bed, he carefully positioned a small book I'd bought for him on Hindu myth.

Together we read the introduction, which told how Brahma, the prime mover, had placed his seed in Savitri and how for a hundred celestial years she had held in her god-womb the precious embryo that gave birth to the Vedas and to the thirty-six celestial Raginis that capture the heart.

"They're just better than we are, I think," said the boy. "It's incredible. An incredible religion. It's more beautiful, I think. More sophisticated, definitely. I mean, maybe I'm just crazy or something, but I think this stuff is beyond our religions. Definitely beyond what I learned at Catholic school. Way beyond."

Alone, he read the rest, losing himself in a tapestry of nearly infinite worlds.

Like a cloistered monk, he sought out the deities; like a budding Faust, he struggled with demons.

Nearly every night, I'd sit at the foot of his bed and we'd talk.

"I'm worried," he said.

"What about?" I asked.

"I'm worried I'll go crazy. My mom was crazy."

"You won't go crazy."

"Or maybe I'll end up like Lavinia: a drug addict."

"You won't be a drug addict."

"How do you know?"

"I know," I told him.

He worried about school.

I told him we would do his homework together.

He wanted to go everywhere with me. Even to the Laundromat. Especially to the Laundromat when he found out the owner was from India. I told him he could if he brought his homework. He brought it, but every time I looked over I could see he was lost. He couldn't focus.

"Maybe you should go back upstairs so you can concentrate," I said.

He didn't want to go back upstairs. He wanted to be with me.

"Okay," I said. "But here's what I want you to do."

"What?" he asked.

"I want you to sit down over there in the back, and I want you to do five minutes of homework. That's all. Five minutes. And once you do five uninterrupted minutes, you can do whatever you want for the rest of the day and go wherever I go. Okay?"

"Okay," he said, trotting like a skinny puppy to the chair in the back.

I timed him. After three minutes he got distracted. I pointed to the clock and held my hand up. "Just five. That's all."

He went back to work.

Twenty minutes later he looked up and called out to me.

"Hey, I did more than five."

"I know," I said. "I tricked you."

He thought it was a good trick.

During the day I took him to school. In the afternoons I tutored him. At night I was back at the bar, back at Delilah's.

It was September. The place was crowded and the money was good.

The Upper West Side was getting richer. We started getting more guys who worked on Wall Street. They'd push against the bar for drinks, unaware of the regulars' regular spots. Prez, in particular, bristled at what he viewed as "the newly entitled" every time his legroom was threatened.

"I gotta tell you," he told a young Wall Street guy who'd gotten a little too close to his seat, "I have had white people lurking behind me all day and I don't like it."

"Where were you," asked the Berliner, "the Ramble?"

"The doctor. For my checkup," said Prez.

"How'd it go?" asked the Greek.

"Well…he put on that rubber glove to check me out…"

"Yes…"

"And when he put his finger up there on my prostate, I got a hard-on."

"Yes…"

"An erection."

"Yes…I understand."

"And a little bit of stuff came out…just from him playin' around up there."

"Hmm…" intoned the Greek, leaning back in his chair.

"Well honey," said the Contessa, "I wouldn't worry about it. In my experience, most older men need their prostates stimulated to get aroused."

"Not just older men," said the Berliner, looking at the Czech.

"I don't need it," said the Czech. "I just happen to like it."

"Well, I don't like needing it," said Prez.

"You're not alone," said the Greek.

"I'm not?"

"No. You're not Prez. In point of fact, it so happens that I went for a physical last Tuesday and had a similar procedure. Though in my particular case, the doctor came out with a tub of Vaseline," said the Greek.

"A whole tub of Vaseline?" asked Prez.

"Yes. That's right. A tub. And my physician, a rather gifted young man, managed, without causing me any discomfort, to get four fingers inside. Almost his entire hand, as I recall."

"Did he find anything?" asked Prez.

"A watch," said the Greek.

"A watch?" asked Prez.

"Yes…" said the Greek.

"Was it yours?" asked Prez.

"I think it may have been, but I'm not sure," said the Greek.

The Wall Street guy looked disgusted. I served him quickly and turned the stereo up.

The music was Vincent's. That's all you heard at Delilah's. Vincent's music.

It was Cuarteto Patria de Santiago, or the Ink Spots. Or it was Helen Humes, who wasn't as well-known as Ella, but who was a musician's musician. Or it was Hank Williams singing "On the Bayou," or Karen Kushner playing Chopin's "Mazurka in B minor," or Sabicas playing "Malagueña." But whatever is was, it got into your guts.

As the night wore on, the conversation turned from prostates to politics.

The hawks were fighting the doves over the first Gulf War.

"Why are we there? Why?" asked the Critic, a Jewish man in his mid fifties.

"Don't be insulting; don't be naïve," countered the Greek. "You know why we're there. Hussein is an animal. Less than animal."

"That may be true, but we've got to stop being the world's policeman. It's not working and it makes us less safe," said the Critic.

"Yes, he's right, he's right," said the old Soprano, who'd once sung at the Met and who'd since ballooned to well over two hundred pounds.

"Oh, c'mon, sweetheart," said the Cop, sipping his bourbon. "Nothing you read is the truth. You know that. It's all disinformation."

"I don't know that," said the Soprano. "It depends, I would imagine, on what you read."

"It's *all* disinformation. *All of it*," said the Cop.

"Well, it seems to me," continued the Soprano, "that the disinformation is coming from this government."

"That's absolutely right," said the Critic, twirling his plastic stirrer. "We've got to stop sticking our noses where we don't belong."

"Don't be foolish," replied the Greek. "If it weren't for our involvement in World War Two you'd be a lampshade, or a bar of soap, and we'd all be speaking German."

"Charming, charming," said the Critic. "That's really charming."

"It's disgusting, is what it is," said the Soprano.

"And by the way," said the Critic, "your lovely little history lesson conveniently leaves out the atrocities our military has committed in places like Central America, Indonesia, and Southeast Asia."

"Bravo, bravo," cried the Soprano.

"One day," intoned the Greek, turning imperiously on his tall throne, "one day you Bolsheviks will realize that the military is the backbone of this great country."

"Thank you," said the Cop.

"Thank you," said the Secret Service guy.

"Thank you," said the FBI guy, rounding out the law enforcement triumvirate.

"That's funny," said the Critic, "I thought *democracy* was the backbone of this great country. And I thought that the *Constitution* was the backbone of this country. I thought the *Bill of Rights* was the backbone of this country! I thought that the *First Amendment* was the backbone of this country! I thought *Freedom of the Press*—"

"Yes! Yes! Yes! Yes! Yes!" shouted the Soprano, her fist raised in the air.

"Please, you two!" said the Cop. "You two haven't been outside of New York City, so you have no idea—"

"I've been to Europe. I spent a year in Chile—"

"Darling, I'm sorry, but you haven't been in a war; you haven't seen the enemy up close."

"Democracy…" intoned the Greek—testing the word, turning it, examining it—"will only take you so far. Look at the Peloponnesian War in which the liberal democracy of Athens was defeated by the conservative oligarchy of Sparta. And I suspect that we may ultimately want to move in that direction."

"Greco," said the Cop, "now even *I* think you're being completely silly."

"He also happens to be anti-Semitic and completely out of his mind," added the Critic.

"Why anti-Semitic?" asked the Greek.

"The oh-so-lovely 'bar of soap' and 'lampshade' comments," answered the Critic.

"I wasn't being anti-Semitic; I was simply stating the facts."

"But you are completely out of your mind."

"Perhaps," said the Greek, turning like a drunken monarch toward the Critic. "Perhaps I am completely out of my mind."

"No. Not perhaps. You are out of your mind. And by the way, we already *are* Sparta. We already *are* moving in that direction. We already *are* an oligarchy."

"He's right, he's absolutely right," said the Soprano, clapping her hands.

The Greek, smoothing his Savile Row suit, rose indignantly: "Maybe you want to live under Sharia Law," he said. "But I do not wish to do so."

"He's being provocative. He's being malicious," said the Soprano.

"He's also telling the truth," said the Cop.

"No. He's saying evil things. Evil things!" she countered.

"He's just being absurd," I said, attempting to calm her.

"No!" she shouted, pointing an accusatory finger. "I know evil. I've seen it up close. And what he is saying is evil!"

"If you think *I'm* evil…" said the Greek, placing his hat just so over the great gray curls that grew from his great pink head.

"I didn't say you were evil," said the Soprano. "I said what you are saying is evil."

"I fail," said the Greek looking down his elegant nose at her, "to catch the distinction, but if you are looking for evil I suggest you gaze into the eyes of the fourteen-year-old girl who's just had had her nose and ears cut off for refusing to sleep with the forty-year-old husband whom she has been given to in an arranged marriage. Or perhaps you could go to Tahrir Square, where they recently stoned a woman to death for suspected adultery. Or you might visit one of the mass graves where the bodies of murdered Kurds and Shiites lie along with the bodies of their slaughtered children. Or you might visit one of Hussein's rape rooms. And the list goes on. I'd love to continue the discussion, but unfortunately you Bolsheviks refuse to budge, and the blood of innocent Iraqis doesn't seem to have shifted you a bit from your entirely untenable position. Nor apparently, does the barbaric treatment of women in the Islamic world."

"Thanks for the Red-baiting and the ad hominem attacks," said the Critic. "It's all just so charming."

The Soprano raised her great bulk from her seat and moved threateningly toward the Greek.

"What makes you think you have the right—"

"Let it go," said the Cop, trying to move between them.

"Yeah, let it go," said the Secret Service guy.

"Let it go," I said, knowing it won't do any good. "Please let it go."

"I won't let it go. I won't be silenced. Nobody is saying Saddam is a good guy. Nobody is advocating the mutilation of young girls. You are disgusting. A disgusting man. You're a fear monger. You are and *they* are," said the Soprano, pointing to the triumvirate of law enforcement guys. "You are *all* fear mongers."

"I'm just a realist, my dear," said the Greek.

"And on that note," he added, stubbing out his cigar, snapping shut his brief case, standing, straightening his long frame, brushing stray ash from his suit, "good night."

And so it went.

High School

Like all good liberals, we believed in public schools. But after an endless tour of prisonlike institutions guarded by metal detectors and fences topped with barbed wire, after we'd visited echoing halls of madness and overstuffed classrooms with peeling paint and graffiti on the walls and bathrooms that smelled of smoke with girls' numbers scrawled on the walls next to crude depictions of genitalia—well, maybe that was nothing new, but metal detectors in schools? And cops? Girls dressed like whores and the boys dressed like pimps? Lunch was shit, libraries were subpar or nonexistent, and there were no books or textbooks. The schools were overcrowded, dimly lit hellholes; they were everything you read in the papers but worse. But the last straw—the last straw—was a school where the gym, or what they called the gym, had a ceiling that was about six-feet high. And I knew it was six-feet high because when I went to visit it I couldn't stand up straight without hitting my head. Well, maybe it was six-and-a-half feet. But it wasn't more than that. What were they going to do in there? Play jacks? Marbles? Musical chairs?

No. The boy would be lost, overwhelmed, eaten up by the system, and he would fall further and further back. Lily and I decided on private school. The problem was money—we had none. But maybe that would help. Maybe we could get financial aid or a scholarship.

I worked with him on his essay. I told him to include his personal history and everything he was passionate about: geology, anthropology, astronomy, the American Indians. He already wrote well—it must have been in his blood—and didn't need much help. The essay got him a scholarship at a hoity-toity private school on the Upper West Side.

The school was in a modern building shaped like a television set. It had open classrooms, liberal teachers, small class sizes, and outrageously precocious students. I worried he wouldn't fit in, but at least, I thought, he would be safe. At least he would get an education and an opportunity to get into a decent college.

Lily was much less reserved. She thought it was a wonderful place. There were openly gay teachers and openly gay kids. The kids wanted to be poets or writers; they wanted to be first-chair clarinetists or avant-garde percussionists; they wanted to be social activists or psychotherapists. One student—a boy who dressed as a girl to protest what he viewed as "the deeply entrenched, patriarchal power structure"—was considering gender reassignment.

Sparrow thought the kid was a weirdo.

Lily was horrified. She accused him of "not being comfortable with his own sexuality."

"What teenager is?" I asked. "Jesus. He's only thirteen."

I could see that the "permissive atmosphere" and "free thinking" were scaring the shit out of him.

"I think it's good," Lily said. "He needs to loosen up."

"Maybe," I said.

But I also pointed out that what they were teaching wasn't necessarily free thinking. Actually, it was Upper West Side, liberal Jewish free thinking, a very specific kind of free thinking that was not, and is not, free thinking.

"I always forget how anti-Semitic you are," said Lily.

"You don't have to be Jewish to be anti-Semitic, but..."

"I know. It helps. You've told me that joke ten thousand times."

"Look," I continued, "we like what they're teaching. We agree with it. But maybe it's too ideologically narrow for a young boy who's from a very different background."

"I think it's wonderful and good for him," said Lily.

"Well, you're probably right," I said.

But even though it was a good school, it wasn't the perfect situation.

Sparrow was sensitive. He was artistic and poetic. But not in the way these kids were.

His first year, his freshmen year, they read *The Catcher in the Rye*. Somehow one of the kids got it in his head that Sparrow looked like Holden Caufield. Or how he imagined Holden looked. The other kids agreed. One was a talented caricaturist. Soon, drawings of Sparrow wearing a red hunting cap turned backward began appearing on the walls. And it was true that he was in some ways like Holden. He was an outsider; he was caustic; he was funny. But he couldn't identify with a character he viewed as spoiled and privileged.

Yes, like Holden, he went to a private school, but he was on scholarship. He wasn't the manager of the fencing team, didn't own a camel-hair coat or fur-lined gloves, and he didn't live in some East Side fancy-schmancy apartment. Nope. He identified with other kinds of literature.

Lily thought the drawings were a compliment. The boy didn't agree.

"I mean for Chrissake," he told her, "when he visits his teacher at the beginning of the book, he's surprised they don't have a freaking maid!"

"I don't remember all of it," said Lily, "but he's funny like you, and he has that outsider perspective that you have."

"Outsider perspective?"

"Yes. And he's observant and honest and original," said Lily. "Like you."

"But he doesn't like old people. I like old people. Sometimes, I think I *only* like old people."

"He thinks everybody is a phony," Lily offered.

"Big deal. Everybody is a phony. I'm not Holden Caufield. I mean, what the hell is he worried about? For Chrissake! The guy has a brother in Hollywood who drives a Jaguar and he goes to a fancy school in Pennsylvania, and the only reason I go to a private school is because I'm on a damn scholarship and because they probably felt sorry for me on account of my essay!"

"That is not why," said Lily. "That is not why you got in! You got in because you're brilliant and a beautiful boy!"

"And his parents are millionaires," he continued, ignoring Lily, "and they're alive and he's got a sister who loves him. I don't have that! But just because he's scrawny and because he's bitter and talks a little like me suddenly I'm Holden freaking Caufield? I don't think it's very nice. I'm sorry, but I don't. And by the way, he doesn't know shit about the Egyptians."

At a parent-teacher conference, his English teacher, a soft-spoken man wearing a flannel shirt, expressed concern: "He's a wonderful boy, this boy, and a very original thinker, but I'm a little worried about him not making friends."

"So are we," said Lily.

"He was really hurt by the Holden Caulfield stuff," I said. "He felt ostracized."

"It was unkind and insensitive of those students, and I've talked to them about it, but I think I understand how it happened," the teacher replied. "He just reads so deeply and identifies so closely with the characters."

Lily nodded in agreement.

"Sometimes, I worry he reads too deeply," the teacher continued.

"Well, I think it's wonderful," said Lily.

"Of course it's wonderful," said the teacher. "Very, very special, and I didn't mean to suggest otherwise."

I had to admit that his teachers were exceptionally supportive. But his social interactions remained problematic.

Lily wanted him to have a girlfriend.

He didn't like the girls at his school.

He'd divided them into categories.

"It's just like a caste system," he said. "First, you've got the Brahmins."

"Brahmins?" asked Lily.

"You know. They're the privileged ones. They go to New York City Ballet and they take ballet dance lessons and acting lessons, and they go to all the museums. They wear really nice clothing, and they're super rich, and they don't really notice me, but if they bumped into me in the hallway, they'd be really nice. Girls like Rebecca Rubin."

"You should ask her out," said Lily.

"I can't. She's not in my caste."

"That's ridiculous," said Lily.

"I don't think she likes me."

"What about Tanya Jankowitz?"

"She's a Kshatriya."

"What's a Kshatriya?" asked Lily.

"I can't believe you memorized these," I said.

"Her father's a lobbyist. She's in the ruling class. I can't date her."

Lily laughed.

It occurred to me, having met Tanya only once, that in addition to being part of the ruling class, she was also in that group of precocious-private-school-Jewish-girls who have sex and lots of it. Advanced and adventurous, they smoke pot, make out with each other at parties, sleep with the metal shop teacher, and do God-knows-what-else. And the boy seemed to know it.

"I think Tanya Jankowitz is a little too much for me," he admitted.

"I think I know what you mean," I said.

She was too much. So was the third group of girls—the girls who hung out in the Laundromat across the street and openly talked about who was fucking whom and who was pregnant, and who gave whom that nasty cold sore…and so on.

Watching Sparrow avoid them, I saw a reflection of my younger self, swimming away as fast as I could from the girls who'd attacked me in the pool in the Bronx.

Then there was the fourth group. These were the girls in the nearby projects—Black and Latina girls who were very studious and carefully guarded by their hypervigilant parents.

"I guess they're the untouchables," he said.

"Are you saying they're beneath you?" asked Lily.

"No. I'm just saying I can't touch them."

I thought he was being charmingly self-deprecating.

Sparrow liked these girls. But he didn't feel like they liked him very much.

He needed a girl, he said, who wasn't from privilege and who wasn't from the projects. He needed a girl who didn't do drugs, who respected her family, and who wasn't "all concerned about money and clothes" like the kids who went to his private school. He needed a girl who didn't fit in "you know, like I don't fit in" and, preferably, a girl who looked like "those girls you see in National Geographic who are really beautiful in a really beautiful way. Like the girls you see in Africa, or in India, or in the Middle East."

He needed somebody who was from someplace else and in tenth grade she came.

Her name was Asma Ali and she had been born in the city of Hyderabad, the capital of the southern Indian state of Andhra Pradesh.

She was a slight girl with burnished skin and iridescent eyes.

He ate lunch with her everyday. He walked her to her subway train after school.

He didn't tell her much about his family, but she told him all about hers.

Asma had two brothers. Azhar was the elder; Syed the younger. Their father, Ahmed, had been a cricket player "almost to the state level." His youngest son he'd named after Syed Mohammmad Hadi, who was known as Rainbow Hadi because he excelled not only in cricket, but also in six other sports: field hockey, tennis, table tennis, polo, soccer, and chess.

Eventually, Asma invited Sparrow to dinner at her family's apartment in Jackson Heights. She asked him if he would bring his parents.

Lily was busy. I went.

Perched together on their small couch, we balanced our plates of biryani on our knees as best we could while Asma's mother attended to us as if we were visiting royalty. The two brothers—both with thick black mops of hair—were very polite, as was the father, who kept telling us that he was "very liberal."

After dinner Asma's grandfather—an old, white-haired man, with a long, silvery beard and rheumy eyes—turned to Sparrow.

"When I was your age," he said, "I left my village, and I went to Kabul. The fruit markets in Kabul had the sweetest grapes I ever tasted. And there were Tajiks and Pashtuns, and Uzbeks...and women...beautiful women. One, I remember. She was wearing a red silk chadri, her face was veiled, and she had two yellow birds in a cage that she balanced on her head. When I saw her, I thought I was dreaming."

After Kabul he'd gone into Pakistan, and from Pakistan, he had crossed into India, settling in Delhi, near the Red Fort, which was made of red sandstone and marble.

"It had many baths and gardens," he said. "And there were pools for people to bathe in. On the walls of the mosque were birds, butterflies, and flowers made of precious stones."

Then he told the boy how the British had come and destroyed much of the fort, how the baths had dried up, and how the gardens had withered.

"Now there is a highway that runs through the middle," he explained. "There are streetlights. There are traffic jams. The air is dirty. The fort is crumbling. It is in ruins."

"As happens to all civilizations and cities," added Ahmed Ali, nodding sadly.

"But," said the old man looking into the boy's eyes, "if you look at the mosque of the Red Fort at sunset, the red sandstone takes on a color you will see nowhere else in the world. Isn't this true?" he said turning to Ahmed.

"You are right," said Ahmed. "And sometimes, at sunset, birds circle the minarets and golden domes, and you feel as if you are looking five hundred years into the past. Everything else melts away, and you feel you are seeing God."

I think it was at that moment that the boy fell in love with Asma Ali, her family, and the entire subcontinent.

But as liberal as Ahmed Ali was, he was not liberal enough to let his daughter date an American, nor was the mother, who took me aside and explained politely that she wanted Asma to maintain her ties to their culture "as much as she could."

They could be friends, the parents told me, but nothing more.

I said I understood.

After we left, the boy wanted to stop at one of the markets that lined 74th Street, so we wandered through aisles packed with rows of pickles, pastes, powders, and high stacks of basmati rice, their burlap bags adorned with brightly colored scenes of women cooking or of men farming with oxen. Some of the bags were decorated with zebras or deer, all in arresting combinations of color and design.

"Look how cool the red looks next to the orange," said the boy. "Those are the colors I think of when I think of India."

Farther down the aisle I noticed a bag that said *Haitians and Asians Love Our Parboiled Yellow Basmati Rice,* which we both thought was kind of funny.

On the way out, we stopped in front of the curved glass counter and contemplated the miniature mountains of basmati rice: the golden-yellow hue of the saffron, the bright red of the red pepper, the dull red clay of the chili, and the earthen cypress green of the okra.

"The food is beautiful…isn't it?" he asked.

"Yes," I said.

"Why is Indian stuff so beautiful and American stuff so ugly?"

"I don't know."

"I mean, up in Western Mass everyone is sitting their fat asses in front of TV sets and eating crappy food and driving around in pickup trucks. And the kids at my school are so rich it's disgusting; they just don't seem to care about anyone but themselves. I don't know. I wish we could go back in time. Or to another country. I mean, it just seems like everything here is crap. What do you think?"

"I think we're fickle comedians…myself included," I admitted

"Fickle comedians?"

"Yes," I said.

"Wow…that's a really great way to put it."

"I didn't come up with it, but I think it applies. We don't live close to nature, we don't live close to our families, we don't share a common culture…"

"So what should we do?" he asked.

"I don't know. But given all the negatives, we did just have a pretty amazing night. So there are still, I think, beautiful experiences to be had. I know that's a corny way to say it. But I don't know a better way."

"Yeah…you're right…but I don't know if I want to live here."

"I don't blame you."

"I think I might want to travel," he said.

"You should. You should go wherever you want, and you should gobble it all up. It's good to get away from the craziness here," I said.

"From the fickle comedians?"

"Yes. From them."

On the train ride home I told him what Asma's parents had told me, that they didn't want their daughter dating an American.

I said I was so sorry.

He said he understood, but he was obviously crushed.

After that, he saw Asma less and started spending more time with the Rossman twins instead.

Leopold and Loeb

Kurt Rossman, the father, was a doctor who specialized in removing varicose veins from the ever-thickening legs of upper-crust women of a certain age. And though he seemed to be equally proud and ashamed of his prowess as a plastic surgeon, he was, in his very particular branch of medicine, known as one of the best.

Strangely, he did not look like I'd imagined he would.

Most men in cosmetic surgery, I assumed, were well-groomed, clear-skinned, preternaturally fit, fifty-five-year-old Viagra-popping studs—modern megalomaniacal Pygmalions who molded the middle-aged into simulacrums of idealized youth. But with his unkempt tangle of long hair, thinning a bit at the crown, wire-rimmed glasses, unshaven chin, and extensive wardrobe of worn flannel shirts, Kurt Rossman could have easily passed as a Humboldt County pot farmer.

The sons, the twins, were two gaunt white ghosts—blonde and brilliant. One was studying classical Greek just for fun; the other was a chess champion who regularly fleeced the hustlers in Washington Square Park. They were misfits, but they were ranked one and two in their class.

I referred to them as Leopold and Loeb.

The mother was alive but had a very aggressive blood cancer. Rossman had moved her to the basement apartment in his building and had moved his new girlfriend into an apartment on one of the upper floors.

The first time I met Rossman was on a weekend in the fall. We took the boys to lunch and then to the Metropolitan Museum of Art.

"Do I sound like a right-wing nut job?" he asked, after we'd been talking for just over an hour.

I thought he did, in fact, sound like a right-wing nut job.

"No," I answered.

We'd been talking about guns, and in particular, Rossman's personal arsenal, while wandering through the American Wing. Rossman was standing under Fitz Henry Lane's *Stage Fort Across Gloucester Harbor*, a desolate painting of a former military fortification. Sparrow, standing nearby, was transfixed by Thomas Cole's *View From Mount Holyoke*, which he knew firsthand from his childhood.

"So what else do you have?" I asked.

"Everything," said Leopold, wandering over to us.

"Everything," Loeb echoed from across the gallery. "He even has an AK-47. It's pretty cool."

"Isn't that an assault rifle? I thought those were illegal," I said.

"Semiautomatic," said Leopold. Or was it Loeb?

"If it's not fully automatic, it's not illegal," explained the father.

"Why do you have it?" I asked.

"Ruby Ridge? Waco? The list goes on," said Rossman. "Hard to believe it, but that's our federal government for you—a man retreats into nature, goes back to living as God intended us to, pays for a nice spot of land, and buys himself a cabin. Then, just because he doesn't answer some bogus court summons— which he probably never got—they kill his dog, shoot his best friend, kill his son, and kill his wife. Then they shoot him through the arm and chest when he's trying to bury his own son."

"Did that happen?" asked the boy who'd wandered back over to listen to Rossman's impromptu lecture.

"It did," I admitted, "but I think it was a little more complicated than that."

"It wasn't more complicated than that," said Rossman. "It was worse than that in Ruby Ridge. But it wasn't more complicated."

I didn't want to debate, I didn't want to upset the boy by fighting with his friend's father, and I definitely didn't want to get into a discussion about gun owners and gun owner's rights, especially since we had left the Luminists behind and were now passing through the hall that housed the portrait of Washington crossing the Potomac with his well-armed militia. But I couldn't help myself from drawing a distinction.

"Koresh," I countered, "wasn't Weaver. Koresh, as I recall, was sleeping with underage children."

"Not according to Texas law," said Rossman.

Great, I thought, a wonderful argument to defend a pedophile.

"What's Texas law?" asked the boy.

"We probably don't want to find that out," I said under my breath.

And then Rossman, surrounded by Revolutionary heroes, launched into a jeremiad against the state of the state.

Wall Street and the "people" who ran it—with help from the hacks in Washington—had hijacked their money. The government had regulated what guns they could own, what grass they could grow, and what God they could worship. Meanwhile, the feds were printing money. Way too much money.

"We should have never gone off the gold standard," he cried before segueing into a brief summing up of the Mississippi Scheme, which was a prime example, he said, of what happens when businesses issue too much paper. From the Mississippi Scheme he moved on to the IMF, and from the IMF he hopscotched over to the Federalist Papers, before making a jarring leap to the subject of evolution, or more specifically the newest developments in the "abstract, neomammalian brain," which he was observing in his own twin sons.

"Look at my kids," he said, pulling me under a massive canvas of the Andes by Frederic Church. "They are uninterested, concerned only with their well-being and completely unaware of the cause of their well-being. Look at how they're growing up. They push a button and the elevator comes. They flip open a phone and they talk to whoever they want. They turn a key and the car goes. But they have no idea how any of this happens. They just assume it. They expect it. Look, people have been saying this for years. Goethe said it: to live at ease is plebian. Ortega said it: mass man lacks seriousness. He's a spoiled child, given to amusement and tantrum. There are no limits on desire. Everything is allowed. Everything is allowed!"

I thought that Rossman was right, but I also thought it was the height of hypocrisy, given that his dying wife was living downstairs while he fucked his new girlfriend in the penthouse.

"What do you think?" he asked.

"I'm not a fan of Koresh, I'm not a fan of guns, and I think you're a little bit paranoid about the federal government."

"Just because you're paranoid doesn't mean you're wrong," he countered.

I laughed and we went to find Sparrow, who was standing in front of Thomas Hovenden's *The Last Moments of John Brown*. The painting showed the handsome and heroic Brown tenderly kissing a little black baby before being led to the scaffold.

"Pretty amazing, huh?" said the boy.

"Look what we do to our real heroes," said Rossman. "We hang them."

The day ended with Rossman lecturing about libertarian principles as we walked back across Central Park. When we parted at 86th I decided I'd had enough and headed south.

For once, it was almost a relief to go to work.

Annabel

"There was an archbishop in Lvov who wanted to be a patriarch," said the Bishop, swirling his old-fashioned with a swizzle stick. "I'm going back about twenty years now...and he was put into prison by the communists, and when he was finally released, he was sent to the Vatican. But because you can't have two patriarchs in the same country, they made him a cardinal, which was the ultimate insult to the Orthodox because a cardinal is lower than a patriarch. And eventually he died in the Vatican. I met him once. In Los Angeles of all places."

"And what's your point?" asked Prez.

"Point? I don't know," answered the Bishop. "I guess that we don't get what we want. That we die disappointed. That's a little dark, though, isn't it?"

"Not too dark," I said.

"I knew I could count on you," said the Bishop. "Why are you so good to me?"

"I have a thing for conflicted clergymen," I answered.

"Well, there are certainly enough of those in here," said the Bishop, pointing to himself and to the defrocked Priest, who was at that moment regaling a bewildered young couple with the story of how he'd been forced to "give up the cloth."

"I love you," said the Bishop, as I poured him a little extra bourbon.

"I love you too."

A few minutes later I was flagged down by the cornered couple; they'd had enough and wanted to pay their check so they could make an exit.

"You choke up! You choke up on the bat, and you put the bat on the fucking ball!" someone was saying, as I rang up the drinks on the register.

"He's right!" said the Loan Shark, twirling his fingers in the air.

"That was a long time ago…forty, fifty years ago," said someone else from somewhere, in the dark.

"A long time ago," echoed another voice.

It was getting late.

"He died young," someone else was saying. "Very young. A nice man."

"Who?" a voice asked.

"Ron Ziegler. Smart man. Very smart. In many ways he was a good guy."

"You've got to be fucking kidding me," said the other guy.

"What?"

"C'mon. Name two good things about Ron Ziegler."

"He was a good guy…he was…I'm sorry if that upsets your worldview."

"What I'm trying to say," the Bishop was saying at the other end of the bar, "is that they co-opt the leadership…you understand the point I'm making?"

"No," said Prez. "I don't."

And then, as it got later, I could no longer distinguish the voices, which dissolved into the language of deep-sea mammals, the mostly male voices blending together into a long, low moan, like whales signaling in the great, dark deep. And then the defrocked Priest, leaning back, vodka in hand, laughed hysterically, and the whole bar, like *The Raft of the Medusa*, sailed off into the night with the dead and dying clinging to the edges.

Later, after they left, I put on some Cuban music. The waitress and the Chinese night porter were the only ones left. The waitress counted her tips.

Her name was Annabel.

"God, this music is incredible," she said. "That singer has such a fucking beautiful, weird, sad voice. Who is it?"

"Septeto Boloña. Their lead singer was a dwarf."

"A dwarf?" she asked.

"Yeah. Maybe that's why he sounds so sad."

"Because he's a dwarf?"

"I don't know," I said. "It can't be easy to be a dwarf."

"God, it's just so beautiful it makes me want to cry."

"Lily hates it."

"Who?"

"Lily, my wife."

"Oh yeah. Your wife. I thought you guys split a while ago."

"We did, but we're back together."

"Why?"

"We're raising our nephew."

"What happened?"

"Her brother died in a car accident, and we took in his boy."

"Oh God. When?"

"About a year ago."

"How old is he?"

"Fourteen."

"So you guys are back together?"

"For now...you're still with the guy who's a comic?"

"Sort of...oh God, this is killing me."

"What?"

"The music, this music."

And then she started to dance.

Annabel's hair was red, almost orange, cut straight across, the bangs covering her forehead. Her freckled skin was pinkish and pale, her lips were thin and crinkled, and her eyes, when she pushed the bangs aside, looked like two asterisks. She was small-boned and pigeon-toed. She smelled slightly, I thought, of yeast. She was a little red-haired girl from Alabama who wanted to be a dancer. A ballerina. Neither of her parents had been in the arts. Neither had encouraged her. Nor were there dancers in the family. But her mother, she told me, had "a great body." "Great tits," she said, "but, you know, she doesn't, like, shave her pussy or anything."

It hadn't occurred to me to ask about her mother's genital grooming, but that was the kind of stuff she freely volunteered.

"So your mother was a dancer?" I asked.

"No," said Annabel. "That came from me. I just knew from the beginning that I wanted to dance."

When she was twelve—"just before I got my period and tits," as she put it—she got her big chance. Balanchine had come to Alabama looking for dancers for New York City Ballet, and along with twenty other girls around her age, she was brought in to audition for the master. She was not, even in that small pool of dancers, she told me, the best. Not even close, she said. But she'd "heard the music"—that was the phrase she always repeated—in a way that no other twelve-year-old could.

Balanchine picked her.

For the next fifteen years, she danced in the corps.

When her dancing career ended, she still wanted to be in the arts. She wanted to be an actress or a comedienne. So she got a job cocktail-waitressing at Delilah's, and every Monday she hosted an open mic night in the café. At around seven, the comics would start to straggle in; by nine, the place was packed.

She was the den mother, the master of ceremonies, the surrogate girlfriend, friend and supporter, and they came, these flocks of hurt, anxious birds, to the little garden café in the back, with its tiny stage and tiny tables. They overflowed into the narrow hallway, spilled out past the kitchen, and bottlenecked at the service bar, where they tried to hustle free drinks before they had to elbow their way back toward the tiny stage, where she, their Annabel, lovingly introduced them—swearing like a sailor and cracking jokes that were alternately infantile, scatological, overt, and taboo before ceding the stage to the talent she was trying to nurture.

All the comics wanted to fuck her, but there was one who was more successful and more brilliant than all the rest. He was an alcoholic, and he was in his late fifties. He was a stuttering, muttering, ranting and raving lunatic, and he was very fucking funny. He was twenty years older, and he'd been her boyfriend ever since she'd left the ballet. Balanchine was her first mentor; he was her second. He was her Svengali. He had the one thing she worshipped above all other qualities: he had talent. She fed off it, needed it, craved it, she told me. Talent was her weakness; it was his trump card.

But she wasn't happy in her relationship, and because I wasn't happy in mine, we found ourselves talking late into the night.

Sometimes we talked about the regulars.

The Greek, she thought, was just so fucking sad, the Contessa needed to get laid, Prez was actually pretty funny, and the Priest was so fucking pathetic, but kind of fascinating. She liked the Bishop, loved him, actually, and she wondered how the fuck the Cheshire Cat, at the age of seventy-five, could still do coke. The Critic was "kind of smart" and "okay," but the old Soprano was bitter and angry, and she hoped she wouldn't end up like her.

And the Painter. The Painter was brilliant. But he was in love with her, so she had to keep him at a distance. And the law enforcement guys were really creepy. Was it true, she wanted to know, that I'd found the FBI guy passed out in the bathroom in his own shit with his gun out of his holster?

It was true.

"What about the Secret Service guy?" she asked.

"Great guy," I said.

"And what about the Cop?" she asked.

"Also a great guy. Really, really smart."

"When he looks at you, he looks right through you. I think he's kind of scary."

"He is scary. But I love the guy."

"Quick sidebar," she said.

"Go ahead," I said, counting singles.

She wanted to know if I thought Deborah, the Jewish middle-aged manager, was having an affair with Jimmy, the Chinese chef.

"Definitely."

"Really?"

"Mm-hm," I said, now counting fives.

"And does the Loan Shark, really kill people?"

"I think he shatters the occasional kneecap and maybe breaks a leg now and then."

"And what about the Bishop? Is the Bishop gay?"

"Openly," I answered.

"Cool," she said. "I love him. But don't you think it's really weird that we have a defrocked, closeted priest and an openly gay bishop as regulars?"

"Never look a gift horse in the mouth."

Sometimes, we talked about plays. She wanted to be in a Chekov play, or a Shakespeare. A real play. Not a comedy skit. But she was sure nobody would hire her. Regional theater actors or graduate school actors would take those parts, people with money, credits, and credibility. She was struggling. If not for her rent-controlled apartment, she couldn't survive. All she wanted, she told me, was to keep doing things that were aesthetically beautiful, but it was hard when you were a woman "of her age." We talked a lot about the plays she wanted to do. I told her I had been an assistant director in college and had thought about directing but hadn't been able to find any work. We talked about Arthur Miller. We talked about Eugene O'Neill. She thought that everything I said about everything was brilliant.

The way to a man's heart is not through his stomach; it's through his ego.

"You just couldn't get the work because you weren't in the pipeline," she told me.

"What's the pipeline?" I asked.

"You know," she said, "Yale, Julliard, NYU..."

"I don't know if that's the reason," I said.

"Oh, c'mon," she said. "That is absolutely the fucking reason. The way you talk about plays is brilliant. You are so fucking talented."

One night, I asked her if she wanted a ride home.

"You have a car?"

I didn't but I'd borrowed one from Pierce so I could take the boy to Bear Mountain the next day.

She wanted to go for a drive.

"Where?" I asked.

"Anywhere," she said.

We drove down 79th and out onto the West Side Highway. It was cold and clear, and we could see the bridge and the Palisades and the lights from New Jersey reflecting on the water.

She told me more about her boyfriend, the comic. He was really more of a father figure, she said. The sex wasn't great.

"Why is that?" I asked.

"Because he's an alcoholic," she said, "and you know...alcoholics can't... you know...can't get it up...because..."

"I get it," I said, "but you stay with him because..."

"Because I've been with him so long. I think. And because he's good to me. And because he's so fucking smart and talented and funny, and because guys closer to my age are such totally gross douche bags."

Her body twisted toward me as she talked, and though she'd been a dancer, there was something almost spastic in her movements as she strained against the seatbelt. It was as if being *en pointe* on-stage with an orchestra playing transformed her into a princess, but otherwise, on the street, or sitting as she was now in the front seat of a car, she was decidedly earthbound, almost clumsy.

"I'm sure you could find another boyfriend," I said.

"Not when you're almost forty," she said. Her exact age, she never revealed. "Trust me. You have no idea how bad the options are."

And then she was gesturing wildly, telling me about the comedy show she was working on, as I swung the car around at the bridge and headed back downtown, the lights of Edgewater on my right, the hills of Washington Heights on my left, the empty road ahead.

Apparently the show was about the relationships between men and women and how they never worked out. She had been working on it, refining it, and performing it on and off for about two years. It had finally gotten her some attention. They'd even gotten paid for some gigs, and it had led to a little television writing.

"Why don't you date your comedy partner?" I asked.

"Because I hate him."

"Why?" I asked.

She sputtered: "Because he's such a...a...ugh...yucky...gross...gross guy... and he's got..."

"What?"

"Well, I don't want to be mean, but he's just got these really fat thighs and these really wide hips," she said, spreading her hands to demonstrate. "And he's got a really fat ass and I just—I know I'm being mean—but I just hate that on a guy."

"I kind of like it on a guy."

"That's funny."

"Thanks."

"But seriously," she continued, getting back to her partner, "I just don't like pear-shaped guys."

"That's why you don't like him? Because he's pear-shaped?"

"No, no," she said. "It's more than that. I mean, *a*, he's always trying to fuck me and I don't want to fuck him. And *b*, every time he comes over to my apartment, he goes straight into my bathroom and takes an enormous dump."

"How do you know that's what he's doing?" I asked as we glided down the empty highway—the streetlights, all green, the lights of Weehawken reflecting in the river on our right, and the new high-rises of what had once been Hell's Kitchen looming on our left.

"Because I hear it and because I smell it and because he takes a half an hour in there. And he does it every time he comes over. Every time! I mean, it's like he's saving it up and waiting until he comes over. I think it's really hostile."

"Hostile?"

"Yes. Hostile. I think he's doing it because I won't be his girlfriend and I won't fuck him."

"Well, I don't think he's helping his cause."

"No. He's not. I mean, seriously. Would you do that? Even if it was a girl you weren't fucking but just working with? Would you go over to her apartment and take a giant dump?"

"No. In fact," I said, "I won't even poop in my own apartment if someone else is there."

"Even if it's just your wife?"

We had hit a red light. I turned and looked directly at her.

"No."

"Wow," she said.

"I'm shy."

"Or extremely polite."

"I guess it's both."

"Have you always been like that?"

"Ashamed of my body and all its functions?"

"Yes."

"Yes. It's pathological."

We were near downtown, still on the Westside Highway.

"Pull over," she said.

"Why?"

"Because I want to make out with you."

I must have looked worried because she said: "Don't worry. We'll just make out."

"Just make out?"

"Yeah. Just once. Don't worry about it. I'm like a guy. You know, like a guy from the 1950s. I'll make out with you once, and then I won't call you."

I turned off at Clarkson, pulled over, and shut the car off.

Signs

As soon as I got home I snuck into the bathroom, searched for any marks of Annabel (red hair, lipstick, scratches) in the mirror, scrubbed myself in the sink, and tiptoed back out into the cramped hallway. The light in the boy's bedroom was out, but his computer, which had found a permanent home on the kitchen table, was still on.

I've never liked computers, but at that time, I didn't even know how to use one. Anything I wrote, I wrote on a bulky Underwood typewriter. A manual, no less.

When the boy had first come, he'd said he needed a computer for school. I told him he didn't.

"How am I supposed to write a paper without a computer?" he'd asked.

"James Joyce," I'd oh-so-cleverly replied, "wrote *Ulysses* without a computer. And I believe that Miguel de Cervantes wrote *Don Quixote* without one."

"That's not the way it is anymore. Everyone uses a computer."

"You can use my typewriter."

"It's not even electric! I can't turn that in! It'll look like some nut case wrote it."

I didn't believe him. I called the school. They informed me that he needed a computer. I hung up the phone and went to his room.

"You need a computer," I told him.

To his credit, he did not say "I told you so."

Soon afterward, we got Internet service over our phone line. Then someone—I think another parent at the television-shaped private school—informed me that it was easy to get pornography and that we should keep an eye on it. I asked the boy if this was true.

He said it was.

"Show me," I said.

And so into that primitive search engine he typed a three-letter word: sex.

"That's all you have to do?" I asked.

"Uh-huh," he said.

A minute later an image of an obviously underage Asian girl with a Heineken bottle in her vagina appeared on the screen. A group of old white men were watching her.

I was totally fucking appalled.

"No Internet," I said. "I don't know how to block this shit, so I'm cancelling it."

"But—"

"Non-negotiable," I interrupted. "Sorry, but I don't want you looking at this stuff. It's illegal, it's immoral, it's ugly, and I don't think it's good for you to see."

"What about parental controls?" he asked. "That way I can still get the Internet for stuff I need to research."

I felt like a Neanderthal confronting a nuclear bomb with a wooden club.

"You'll get around parental controls," I said. "So, no. No Internet."

A few months later, though, I recanted and hooked the computer back up to the phone line, but we insisted it stay on the kitchen table, where we could see it.

Dropping my stuff on a chair, I now involuntarily glanced at its greenish-grayish glow and read a document the boy had left open.

Taxes are reaching cataclysmic levels. Is Civil War imminent? Do we have to shed blood to reform the current system?

And then clumsily moving the mouse, I read more:

The government is afraid of the guns people have because they have to have control of the people at all times.

And:

The administration has claimed that Iraq has used weapons of mass destruction in the past. We've all seen the pictures that show a Kurdish woman and child frozen in death from the use of chemical weapons. But have you ever seen those pictures juxtaposed next to pictures from Hiroshima or Nagasaki? Remember Dresden? How about Hanoi? Baghdad? If Saddam is such a demon, and people are calling for war crimes charges against him, why don't we hear the same cry for blood directed at those responsible for even greater amounts of "mass destruction"—like those responsible and involved in dropping bombs on the cities mentioned above?

Behind me, the boy had come into the room. Lost in my reading, I hadn't heard him, and he'd startled me.

"What are you doing up?" I whispered, unconsciously moving my hand over my lips, like a guilt-ridden Lady Macbeth, looking not for blood but for lipstick.

"I couldn't sleep, and I got worried when I didn't hear you come in," he whispered back.

"Sorry. I was trying to be quiet."

"It's really late, isn't it? You're not usually so late."

"It was really busy," I lied.

"Oh..."

"What is this?" I asked, pointing at the wavering screen.

"It's just some stuff from an interview with Timothy McVeigh. He kinda makes a lot of sense, doesn't he?"

"He does," I admitted, "for a terrorist mass-murderer."

Like most people, I knew the basic facts of the case. McVeigh had bombed the Murrah Federal Building in Oklahoma City in retribution for Ruby Ridge, Waco, and the U.S. actions in Iraq during the first Gulf War, which he, McVeigh, had fought in. I dismissed McVeigh as a sick nut job, which he clearly was. But I didn't realize that he was only the most extreme example of a movement that was gaining momentum: an anti–federal government shift that included libertarians like the ageless Lyndon LaRouche, who had terrorized New York pedestrians since I was a kid.

In fact, LaRouche had set a table up two blocks away from our apartment and had badgered the boy into doing some work for them, which neither Lily nor I had any inkling of until one afternoon when I received a phone call from their organization asking where he was.

"Who are you?" I'd asked?

"We're calling for the boy," they'd answered.

"Yes, but who are you," I asked?

They wouldn't say and hung up.

Eventually, I got one of LaRouche's automatons to talk to me and I told them that if they ever called again or talked to the boy, I would bomb the fucking office—or something crazy like that—and they backed off. It takes a nut job to fight a nut job. But I'd never really understood why the boy had been interested in LaRouche in the first place.

Maybe it was because they were also outsiders. Maybe it was simply because they'd reached out to him. Maybe that was enough for a kid who found himself ostracized at his liberal school.

Lost in thought, I stared down at the still glowing screen and read the next quote.

The truth is, the U.S. has set the standard when it comes to the stockpiling and use of weapons of mass destruction.

Well, that's true, I thought.

"Is this for a school paper?" I asked.

"No. Somebody sent it to me."

"Who?"

"One of the Rossman twins."

"Which one?"

"I'm not sure. It's hard to tell because they share an email account."

"Not Kurt? The father?"

"No. One of the kids."

He could tell I was concerned.

"I thought you liked their dad," he said, sensing my upset.

"I do," I said. "I'm just a little concerned about some of his beliefs."

"So Kurt Rossman didn't send this?" I asked, still looking down at the greenish glow of the computer screen.

"No," he answered. "I told you."

The bedroom door opened. Lily, rubbing her eyes, entered.

"It's so late," she said. "What are you looking at?"

"Some Timothy McVeigh stuff that the Rossman twins sent," I said.

"Oh God," she said, pulling her robe closed.

"I kind of feel like I understand him a little," the boy said.

"You do?" she asked.

"Yeah," he answered. "I know he's got a pretty messed-up brain, but I think I've got a pretty messed-up brain too."

Despite the late hour, Lily's hackles were up.

"So you think it's okay that he bombed a federal building and killed innocent kids?" she asked.

"I didn't say that. I just said I understand him. I guess I'm just crazy, probably."

"You're not crazy," said Lily.

But the boy wouldn't hear it and began telling how he, like McVeigh, didn't fit in—how he was less attractive, less talented, and less intelligent than his fellow students. And how it didn't help that he had really, really shitty skin.

"You are not," said Lily, "any of those things, and certainly not less intelligent. And fourteen-year-olds are supposed to have shitty skin."

"I am less intelligent," he countered.

"That's not true," I said. "You are what is traditionally classified as Super-Duper Smart."

"Trust me. You're not at that school. It's a fucking top-rated private school in New York City. You should see how smart those kids are. I don't fit in."

"I can understand that," I said. "Some of them seem pretty obnoxious."

"You're so late," said Lily, glancing at the clock, and turning to me.

"It was busy," I said.

And then we were all quiet.

"What's that smell?" Lily suddenly asked.

"I don't know," I said as a chill went through me.

"It smells like some weird perfume," said the boy.

"No," said Lily, sniffing. "It's not perfume."

"I don't know what it is," I answered, staring back down at the glowing screen, reading McVeigh's words, and feeling the sense of an encroaching darkness.

Caravaggio

The music was turned up, the bar was packed, the café was full.

"I want to talk to you," she said, reaching for two red stirrers.

"Now?" I asked, topping the vodkas with tonic water.

"No. Later," she whispered, "when the regulars leave."

"What about?"

"I just like talking to you," she said. "Oh shit, I forgot."

"What?"

"I need an Orvieto."

And as I plunged my hand back into the ice bucket, the Loan Shark, sitting at the far end of the bar and barely visible behind the shrouds of smoke that hung in the air, pointed to the stereo speakers and cried out: "Is that Ben? Is it Benny?"

"You got it!" I shouted, grabbing the neck of the wine bottle. "Ben Webster with Sweets Edison!"

"And Hank Jones on piano," added Prez.

"Ah-ha!" cried the Loan Shark. "Oh Benny...oh Ben. Benny!" he said, as the tenor player unfurled a breathy series of perfectly placed triplets. "The best! The best! Not that this piece of garbage standing next to me would understand," he said, motioning toward a Wall Street guy who'd just bellied up to the bar.

"Are you talking to me?" asked the suit as he jostled for space.

"No. I'm not talking *to* you," said the Loan Shark. "I'm talking *about* you. There's a difference! Ah-ha! Nice country! All the garbage winds up here!"

But before the guy could respond, the Loan Shark stood, wrapped his knotted cudgel of a forearm around him, and ended the conversation.

"Don't worry," he said, taking the towel that hung from his thick bull-neck and wiping big beads of sweat from his bald, blockish head. "You're young yet. You'll learn. Now if you'll excuse me...I'm gonna go comb my hair. Nice to see you. I hope I never see you again."

Annabel—who thought that "the suits were just totally gross"—laughed, but the guy looked pretty pissed, so I made my way down to his end, got him his drinks, and apologized.

"I honestly don't know why you put up with that motherfucker," said Prez, as I came back to the service bar.

"The Wall Street guy?" I asked.

"No. That motherfucking dirty old Loan Shark."

"I take your point, Prez," said the Greek, lighting his cigar. "The man regularly impugns those around him and irregularly bathes."

"Frankly it's not a great combination," said the Critic, raising his eyebrows.

"I've got a soft spot for the guy," I said.

"That's because you've never had to use the commode after he's been in it," said the Greek, letting a long plume of smoke unfurl like a dragon's tail.

"I have," said Annabel, picking up her tray, "and it's pretty gross."

"So have I," I said.

"I shudder to think," said the Greek, checking his reflection in the mirror.

He had started out as an admiral's aide, a position that required him to care for the admiral's custom-made wardrobe. When he eventually left the military (after making gunnery sergeant) and started making good money, he'd traveled to London's Savile Row, where he'd purchased, under the admiral's expert guidance, a dozen suits, shirts, and ties from Dege and Skinner.

He liked to look good.

I watched his eyes as they shifted from the mirror and glued themselves to Annabel's ass. He had already sensed, I think, that something was between us, but even at seventy, he still wanted to stake his claim as the center of sexual attention.

When Annabel came back to the service bar, I asked if he'd ever hit on her.

"Yeah," she said. "Kinda. I mean, he's probably impotent, but one time he offered me a 'stipend' if I'd come over to his apartment and dance while he watched, and probably tried to jerk off, which is obviously just totally gross. But I didn't get upset or anything. Maybe I just have a thing for sad, old alcoholics."

"Me too," I said.

"But would you strip for them?"

"Probably. If the money was there, you know."

And then the Loan Shark called out for another drink—"Dewar's and water, no glass. Ah-ha! That's a tough one"—and it got later, as it always did. Around one o'clock, the Loan Shark left, the Wall Street guy and his model-thin girlfriend left, and the rest of the regulars slowly started filtering out, Annabel silently clapping her hands as they went. By two o'clock most of the regulars *had* gone, but the Greek—his red silk shirt like a red flame framing his great handsome head and gray curls, the cigar smoke practically pouring from his perpetually puckered mouth—was somehow still sitting erect, still leering at Annabel's ass and when she was absent, staring like Narcissus at his own image in the mirror. And just as I thought that the remaining triumvirate—the Greek, the Bishop, the Berliner—had drunk to the dregs their last drinks, in wandered the Painter, and before I could finish shaking his Sapphire martini, he was already holding forth on the art of Caravaggio.

"In fact," he was saying, as I placed his drink in front of him—he'd promised to have only one—"Caravaggio was hugely influential in his lifetime."

"Like Michelangelo?" asked the Berliner, pushing his cap to the side with a bathhouse insouciance.

"In the rooms, women come and go, speaking of Michelangelo," mumbled the Greek.

"Yes," said the Painter, "but he also created an entirely different way of looking at art."

Annabel, who had been waiting and waiting at the service bar, groaned audibly, twisting her torso and holding her legs tight together like a little girl trying not to piss herself.

"Can't we get them out of here?" she asked.

Grabbing the last three checks, I put them down on the bar. But nobody noticed because the Painter was talking about how Caravaggio had used a streetwalker as the model for his *Death of the Virgin* so that his work would have a "psychological reality." And when I tried to ask them to pay, the Bishop did not hear because he was asking the Painter if this use of "real people," this "change in painting" (the word change broken into two syllables—*chay-unge*) had to do with the Reformation?

I looked helplessly at Annabel; she helplessly at me—theological conversations conducted under the black cloud of alcohol could last for hours and hours.

"Didn't you call last call?" she whispered.

"Three times," I said.

"Ugh," she said.

"That's absolutely right," said the Painter. "It absolutely had to do with the Reformation."

"And the church was aghast," said the Bishop, playing a piano cadenza in the air. Trained classically, he often traced passages from Rachmaninoff to ornament his speech or to finish a thought when speech failed him.

"Oh yes," said the Painter. "Because these are real people. Real people suffering.'"

"Oh my God," whispered Annabel. "Are we as pathetic as they are?"

"No," I said. "We're worse."

"How?" she asked.

"We're serving them."

"I just want them all to leave," she whispered, leaning so close that I could feel her hair against my face. "I want them all to go."

The Greek called my name. His jealousy had roused him from his stupor.

"Pink gin," he muttered, pushing the empty glass defiantly in my direction.

Meanwhile, the bleary Bishop, now totally loaded on one too many bourbon old-fashioneds, was passionately telling the Painter that in his "own small insignificant way," he, like Caravaggio, had always tried to relate his sermons "to real life and to real people."

"Because if you *don't* relate it to real life," he said, as he executed an octave run with his right hand, "what does it matter? Of course, I don't have to explain that to you," he said, turning toward me. "You understand everything."

"That's right," the Painter was saying. "Exactly right. And he took these very real people and put them in this vacuum of darkness, with this raking and very theatrical light source. And I think he did that because if you *reduce* to the light and the dark and you focus *only* on the action you are portraying, you've increased the emotional tone of the painting."

"Talent," announced the Bishop, tracing out a figure in the bass with his left hand, "does what it can. Genius does what it wants."

I looked at the clock. It was quarter to three. It was enough.

"I'm sorry, so sorry to interrupt, "I said, "but I need to close out the register."

"Oh God. I'm so sorry…should I pay?" asked the Painter.

"If you could…"

"Yes, yes, of course," he said, digging for his wallet.

"Of course," said the Bishop, reaching for his own wallet. "We didn't mean to keep you."

"Oh God…oh Jesus…I'm sorry…I don't know what I did with my…" said the Painter.

"I'll pay for you," said the Bishop, putting money on the bar.

"Thank you," said the Painter.

"No change," said the Bishop. "That's all for you. I'm so sorry we were keeping you. Please forgive me my foolishness. I know not what I do."

And then his fingers played a disconnected fragment, a shard of a long forgotten piece in the air. His blue eyes watered, and he collapsed, completely crestfallen on the bar.

"You weren't keeping me," I said. "I just wanted to get started counting the register.

"Forgive me," he repeated, raising his head. "Forgive me." And then he blessed me with the sign of the cross and took my hands in his as the Greek, his head lolling back, muttered: "Pink gin, I'll take another pink gin…" while Annabel—my good angel and my bad—whispered, "Don't serve him or we'll never get out of here," while the Painter, though he was leaving, said plaintively: "If I could make just one last point, I would say that…"

"To be continued!" interrupted the Bishop, raising his right eyebrow for emphasis.

The Painter shrugged. Shyly, he said good night to Annabel and then apologized for keeping me so late.

I could see he was aching for her, and I felt terrible for him.

"You didn't keep me. I love listening to you talk about painting, and I think you're a fucking genius," I said, which was the truth.

He profusely thanked me and stumbled out. The Bishop, invoking his clerical authority, somehow maneuvered the Greek from his throne and shepherded him toward the door.

Outside, a car horn sounded.

Framed in the low arch, the Bishop blessed us both before vanishing into the night. Finally Annabel and I were alone—"in our own secret clubhouse," as she liked to say.

"You know," she said, "they come for you. They come because you let them talk. They come because you listen and respect them."

"No," I said. "They would come no matter what."

"It's weird. They're all so fucking smart."

"And erudite," I said.

"And so fucking talented. Why do they drink so fucking much?"

"Because they're so fucking smart and talented," I said, pouring her a glass of red, my hand shaking just a little.

"Are you nervous?"

"No. Why?"

"Because we made out the other night?"

"Maybe..."

"Don't worry," she said. "I told you. I'm like a guy from the fifties. I came, I got mine, that's it."

It was true. We'd made out in the front seat, she'd stuck her tongue in my mouth, she'd put my hand in her jeans, she'd come really fast, and then she'd hopped out of the car without taking care of me.

"You really are like a guy from the fifties," I said. "But you have a boyfriend—"

"Who's worse than the regulars. I don't know why I'm with him."

"And I'm married."

"I'm not looking for a relationship," she said.

"I know. But…"

"What happened to your separation?"

"We're trying to make it work because of the boy."

"Right…I forgot…you told me."

"And he's had such a fucking hard time."

"I get it," she said, as her body contorted again. "Ugh, ugh, ugh…"

"It's not that I don't want to…" I said, sounding like I was on a very bad soap opera.

"I get it…I totally get it…and I totally respect you…you love the boy."

"I do…I feel like he's mine. He's just skin and bones, like a little skinny puppy. He follows me everywhere. He still goes to the Laundromat with me."

"What kid wants to go to the Laundromat?"

"Wherever I'm going, he wants to go. It's been that way since we got him. He doesn't want to let me out of his sight. I think because he's worried something will happen to me like it happened to his father. When I get out of here late, he's awake, making sure I get home all right. And the dog is usually wagging her tail and pissing all over the floor.

"Last night I saw his light on, and I said, 'Hey, Millie pissed all over the floor.' He said, 'I took her out. I swear I took her out.' I knew he was lying, and I didn't even care. So I sat down on the edge of his bed, because I'd yelled at him the day before for forgetting to walk her, and I told him she was probably pissing the floor because she's so old and not to worry about it. After I told him that, he kind of broke down and said he was really sorry he lied, and he admitted he didn't walk her."

"So what did you do?"

"I told him it was okay."

"You did?"

"Fuck yes. 'Look,' I told him, 'kids don't walk dogs. I didn't.' 'But did you lie about it, like I just did?' he asked. 'Yeah,' I told him, 'of course I lied about it.

Kids lie to get out of trouble. Haven't you read *Tom Sawyer* or *Huckleberry Finn*? You're just doing what you're supposed to do. Don't worry about it. Go to bed.' And then he told me he loved me."

"I hope Lily realizes how lucky she is."

"Well…you don't have to live with me."

"No, you don't understand. She's lucky. So lucky."

A little later, after we finished our wine, I said I would walk her home. We walked mostly in silence.

I felt horrible. Not because what I told her wasn't true, but because on some level I knew that I was telling her how much I loved the boy because I wanted her to fall for me. Because I needed a woman to worship me, which Lily no longer did.

Sex

"I asked Vincent how big he thought you were," she said one night as we were cleaning up together.

"You did?"

"Yeah," she said, seemingly surprised that I was surprised, which of course, anybody in his right mind would have been.

"And what did he say?" I asked.

"He said you had good-sized hands, so he thought you were probably a pretty good size."

"Do you generally discuss penis size with Vincent?"

"Yeah."

"Do you realize that you're a bit of an oddball?"

"Kinda..."

That night I walked her home.

At 77th, we passed an adult store that had just opened.

"What's that doing up here?" she asked.

"I don't know," I said. "I guess they're getting pushed out of Times Square."

She asked if I wanted to go in, and together we browsed the sex toys, stopping to wonder at an unsheathed, fourteen-inch-long, massively thick dildo.

"It's just too big," she said. "Who would want that inside their body?"

"I would," I said, as we wandered toward the back.

"Yeah, baby!" she said, laughing.

"I'm sorry," I said, "but this is a lousy porno place."

"Why?"

"They don't have any booths in here," I said.

"What do you mean, booths?" she asked.

"When I was growing up," I told her, "they had these booths in Times Square."

"What kind of booths?"

"Booths with live girls in them."

"Did you go?"

"Once or twice."

"A year?" she asked.

"A day," I said.

"I set you up for that one," she said, laughing her laugh.

"You would go buy these tokens," I said. "Kind of like subway tokens. And you would go into this private dark booth—I think a token got you two minutes— and a little window would open, and you would see all these undressed women waiting.

"Really?"

"Really."

"Sounds hot," she said. "Then what?"

I had never told Lily or any other woman about this chapter of my New York adolescence, but Annabel really seemed to want to know.

"Well," I said, "you would point to the girl you liked, and she would come over to your window. Then she would point to her tits and say 'three,' and she would point down between her legs and say 'five.' Or maybe it was two and three. I can't remember."

"And you would actually touch them?"

"Yes…"

"And did they touch you?"

"No. Not usually."

"What do you mean, 'not usually?'"

"I mean, not usually."

"C'mon," she said. "You can tell me. Remember? I'm like a guy."

"Okay. One time, this black woman came over."

"Why did you pick her?"

"Because of her breasts," I said.

"Because they were big?" she asked.

"Really big," I said, remembering the streams of delicate blue veins branching out in intricate webs from her dark nipples.

"So what happened?"

"I gave her three dollars and started touching her tits. She wanted to know how old I was. 'Seventeen,' I said. And she told me that I shouldn't be in there. Then she wanted to know if I was touching myself. I said I was, and I asked her if it was okay. And she laughed and said, 'Yes, baby, everybody does that.' And then she told me that I was much more gentle then the other men, and she whispered into my ear, 'Do you want me to finish you off baby?' And I said I did. She reached her hand through the little window, all the way down to me, and I felt her hand close around me, and she said, 'That's a big dick for a white boy,' and as soon as she said that, I came."

"She said you had a big dick for a white boy?"

"Yeah...I didn't love the qualifier, but I was still pretty proud."

"Oh my fucking God! And then you came? You came in her hand?"

"Yeah. Just as my tokens had run out and the window was starting to close. She pulled her hand away so it wouldn't get caught, and I heard her whisper, 'Was that good, baby?' and I whispered back, 'So good,' and then the window shut all the way closed, and everything went dark."

"Oh my fucking God! Holy fucking shit!" said Annabel.

"Do you think I'm disgusting?"

"No. I think I'd like to be in a booth for you."

"You would?"

"I would..."

When we were outside again, she pushed me up against a wall and kissed me, pushing her tongue in my mouth.

When we got to her apartment, she asked if I wanted to come up. I said I didn't think I should. She told me to just come into the vestibule. "It's kind of like a booth," she said. I laughed.

We went in.

"Let me kiss you this time," I said, pushing her against the wall.

And then her tongue hot in my mouth; the harshness of the fluorescent light;

her lips so delicate I thought I might hurt her if I kissed too hard; her eyes closed tight; her moans; her smell; her shoulders tensing; her whole body tensing; her tongue deeper in my mouth, as if she wanted to crawl inside me; her hands reaching for my belt; her fingers clawing at my zipper, grabbing for me; my hands pushing her black tights down; the sudden white of her flesh; the shock of red between her pale legs; more of the smell of her—yeasty and sour, her teeth stained with red wine.

She was saying something about her neighbors. How they hated her. How they disapproved of her. One of her tits was slipping from her dress. Her pink-white skin, her pink nipple. "We shouldn't be in here," she was saying. "My neighbors hate me." And her back pressed against the wall, hitting most of the buzzers, and her body shuddering, and she crying out "Oh -my -fucking -God, oh God, yes!"; and the voices of some of those neighbors on the intercom, shouting at us through the small speaker, threatening to call the police, and demanding to know who was buzzing. And she grabbing my hand and pulling me through the door—I don't know how she found the keys in her bag so quickly—and then, like a stag in the wilderness, I found myself chasing her ass up five flights of stairs, stopping her at the top of each landing to rip off more of the tights. And all I could see as I charged behind her was her ass, her pink-white flesh, the red between her legs, her pigeon-toed walk, her fragile back, her bony ribs, her birdlike rib cage expanding with each breath, her narrow shoulders her red hair...her red hair...

And more fumbling for keys and into her apartment: a big room, high ceilings, spider web cracks on the walls, an old couch, blankets, pillows, things thrown everywhere, bookshelves stuffed with books and photographs, a stereo system, CD's all over the floor, magazines scattered on a glass coffee table, clothing everywhere, a man's bicycle, a big window, a courtyard, a tree branch scraping up against the window, nature, rain, and she pushing me down onto the couch. Our clothes coming off. She squatting over me with her hand on me, her red hair covering her face, partly covering her pink-white breasts, her delicate ribcage, her pink belly, the pink-red between her legs. And in the dark room, dark shadow. And she crouching, concentrating, lowering herself slowly;

her hand placing me, taking me inside; her face at my face, her fingers at my mouth. her hips moving on me, her eyes going dark. Dark, dark.

And then she was coming, clawing at me, telling me she wouldn't scratch me, telling me she wouldn't leave marks, and I don't know how long we were fucking, but I do know that the next night, as horrible and guilty and ashamed as I felt, I was back in her apartment.

On that second night, she dragged me into the bathroom—a city bathroom with one bare light, a pull-chain switch, an old sink with a rusted drain, a dirty cracked mirror, and molding falling into the sink. She opened the cabinet, grabbed some Vaseline and put it all over me. She bent over the sink and reached back with one hand.

"I'm not on the pill," she said, "so you can't come in my pussy." But she wanted to feel me come inside of her ass. "Tell me when you're coming and I'll come with you," she told me. Our eyes locked in the mirror. When I came, she started screaming.

When we finished she got into the shower with me. She washed me everywhere.

"So your wife won't know," she said. "See what a good mistress I am?" she said.

I tried to say something. She pressed a finger to my lips. She touched the lines between my eyes and smoothed the deep furrows in my brow, then said: "You don't have to worry about me. I don't want you to get caught. I'm not like other girls."

Together, we step out of the shower. She is toweling me off. My legs are shaking. She is helping me dress. She is wiping lipstick off of my lips. She is checking me for strands of her red hair. She is kissing me at her door. She is asking when I work again. I am stumbling back down the stairs. She is watching from her open door. The carpet is old, the stairs are warped, and the walls are crumbling like the walls of the Roman Coliseum. And then I am in the vestibule, temporarily blinded by the fluorescent light. And then I am out on the empty avenue, and I am walking, and I am praying that Lily is asleep.

The Crone

"Do you want a grilled cheese?" I asked, as the boy dropped his book bag on the table and slumped into one of the chairs.

"Sure," he said. "Thanks."

"Where were you? You're a little late. I was worried about you."

"Sorry. I was walking home from school, and this old woman stopped me. At first, I thought she was homeless. Her ankles were really swollen. They were almost kind of spilling out of her stockings. And her back was all rounded like a turtle's…and there were these wiry gray hairs sprouting from her chin."

"Like the beard of a Chinese sage?" I asked, turning on the stove and putting a pat of butter in the skillet.

"Yes," he said, laughing a little.

"It sounds like you ran into a crone."

"You're right!" he said, raising his eyebrows. "That's exactly what she was!"

I grabbed the cutting board and a serrated knife.

"Isn't it good to know that crones are still among us?" he said.

"It is," I answered.

"And she also had a very unusual hat," he told me.

"An unusual hat?"

"Yes. It was purple. Royal purple. And it was made of velvet. And she had this really nice speaking voice. I think she might have been British. Or maybe she was just really well educated. I couldn't tell."

Poking my head into the fridge, I grabbed a slab of cheddar.

"What did she want?" I asked.

"She lived on 108th; she needed help with her cart."

"That took you a long time," I said, cutting four hunks of bread and slathering

169

them with whole-grain mustard.

"It took almost an hour to travel three blocks."

"An hour to travel three blocks?"

"Yup. I'm not even exaggerating."

"I believe you."

"And her apartment," he said, "was on the fifth floor."

"A walk-up?" I asked.

"Yeah."

"Boy, you really got screwed on that one."

"Yeah…and the stairs were covered in this crazy worn, deep carpet—I think it was a shag carpet. And it muffled the sound of our footsteps, and all the hall lights were out. So it was really spooky. I felt like we were two ghosts. And when we started to climb it got kind of weird."

"What do you mean 'weird?'"

"The higher we went, the more it felt like the stairwell narrowed. I don't know why, but it seemed like the stairwell was constricting. Like it was a blood vessel or something. Like it was a living thing. And the crone's cart weighed a ton. I was sweating like crazy. And by the time we reached the third floor, the stairwell barely seemed wide enough to walk up. I felt like I couldn't breathe. And by the time we got to the fourth floor, I could feel my elbows brushing against the banisters. It just got narrower and narrower and narrower. And finally it got so narrow that on the last leg of the climb I was almost tempted to turn sideways. And I'm not exaggerating."

"I believe you."

As I watched over the sandwiches, he told me the rest.

Behind him, the crone was maneuvering like a mountain climber, grabbing for a foothold, a toehold, anything she could find. At one point, he thought she might be crawling up, but he didn't look back because he didn't want to embarrass her.

Finally they reached the fifth-floor landing.

When she unlocked the door, he saw that there were no curtains or shades on the windows, and the sun flooded into the apartment. His pupils, reduced to pinpoints from the darkness of the stairwell, took several minutes to adjust. She asked him to wait while she put her groceries away.

The apartment looked like it had been bombed. There were two rusted chairs in the living room and nothing else—no table, no couch, no shelving. The linoleum floor was badly worn.

On the walls, the paper had peeled away, revealing layers and more layers. In one spot that he studied, a geometrical pattern gave way to a layer of flowers, which gave way to yet another layer of eggshell blue. And underneath that layer were still more layers. In all, he counted thirteen.

"I felt like an archeologist working at one of those sites where only fragments of a city remains," he said. "Someday all of New York will be like her apartment. Someday it will be destroyed like Mohenjo-daro or Carthage. War will come. Or the oceans will come and destroy it, and then, when the sun burns hotter, the waters will recede and some future man will sift through our remains."

After finishing up in the kitchen, she returned with two cups of tea and asked him to sit with her for a while. Her elegant voice, with its British accent, echoed in the empty room. He noticed that she drank from her cup with her pinky daintily pointing outward.

"People hold onto civilization no matter what, don't they?" he said.

"You mean like orchestras performing while London was being bombed?" I asked.

"Yes, that's what I mean," he said.

They'd talked for a long time, the crone and the boy, but he couldn't remember one word of what they'd said to each other. It was as if he had been talking to a ghost. He wondered if he'd imagined the whole thing.

"Maybe I went crazy for a couple of hours," he said.

"No," I said, "I don't think you went crazy."

"But it's in my family."

I thought of his mother locking him in the room with no light and no food. I worried that the crone had unnerved him.

The sandwiches were done. I put one on a plate for him.

"I guess I just hate seeing people old and alone," he said, sitting down to eat.

"It's good you went," I said.

"You should go into people's apartments," he said. "You should see how they live. You learn things."

The next morning I sent him off to school and went to the roof to drink my coffee.

Looking up, I saw the silver belly of a plane, low and glinting in the sun.

A minute later, black plumes of acrid smoke rose from the southern tip of the island.

Nobody seemed to know what had happened.

And then there was another plane.

I ran the twenty-six blocks to his school.

In the front hall, a kid in a soccer shirt was sobbing. Kurt Rossman was standing outside one of the classrooms, ranting. I managed to avoid him. The boy was with Asma. She said her father was on the way. I called Lily. She came and met us. People were already in the streets, flowing uptown. I kept the boy close. When we got upstairs Lily made what calls she could. We spent the rest of the day glued to the television set.

The FAA shut the airports; bridges and tunnels were closed.

Bush spoke from Barksdale, Arizona. He quoted the 23rd Psalm and then disappeared. It was rumored he was in the air. It was rumored that Cheney had gone underground.

Everything south of Canal was evacuated.

The bar was closed that night; the next, I was back at work.

How did you find out? Where were you when it happened?

Those were the questions.

"I was driving into the city," said the Bishop, "from Brooklyn...and I saw, out of the windshield...I thought it was a special effects thing...for a movie... and then the other plane..."

He broke off and wept. The Berliner went to him and comforted him.

"Guys we played softball with," someone else was saying, "in the Homeowners League...and their sons....gone...Manhasset people..."

The Greek, who'd worked on Wall Street for years, said nothing.

Someone else had seen people jumping.

"I can't...imagine..." the Bishop was saying

"There was nowhere to go," said the Berliner.

"The staircases were impossible," said the Czech.

"Go into the smoke and let the smoke—"

"But the fire..."

"Six of one...half dozen of the other," said the Cop, staring straight ahead.

"The panic...you can't think," explained the Secret Service guy.

The pictures of the missing went up.

The law enforcement guys looked haunted.

Some were working the pit at Ground Zero.

In the bar there was lethargy.

Television briefings pushed aside the conversation and the music.

Rove defended Bush's disappearance. Ashcroft said that the FBI was investigating a flight school in Florida. Rumsfeld obfuscated. Wolfowitz slithered. Cheney growled. Condi and Colin looked suitably grim.

Fifty thousand reservists were called up.

Afghanistan's border was closed.

George the Second spoke from the rubble.

"You're either with us or against us," he said.

The world was divided into black and white.

The bar followed suit.

"We allowed it to happen," the Painter whispered. "There's something that's not being stated. Something they're not telling us."

"He's right," said someone else.

Cheney was an evil man. Capable of anything. And Building Seven—if it wasn't hit, why did it fall?

"Thermite," said the Painter.

He had a friend who was a physicist, and the physicist said it was impossible for those towers to come down. It was an inside job. It had to be.

Those were the whispers.

"Why do they hate us?" someone else asked.

"How about the bombing of Beirut in 1985?" said the Critic. "How about Israel's occupation of the West Bank and Gaza? How about Clinton's bombing of the Al-Shifa pharmaceutical plant in the Sudan?"

"It was one fucking pharmaceutical plant, and they had a chance to get Bin Laden," said the Secret Service guy.

"That one fucking pharmaceutical plant made ninety percent of the country's pharmaceuticals. And after they bombed it, over ten thousand people died from infectious diseases."

"Where are you getting those numbers?" asked the FBI guy. "From Radio Managua on the Potomac?"

"What is Radio Managua on the Potomac? I'm almost afraid to ask."

"NPR," said the Secret Service guy.

"Charming. Look, the point I'm making is that our government is at least partly to blame."

"So we deserved it?" asked the Cop.

"Of course not. I'm not saying that," said the Critic. "It was a fucking atrocity. A heinous act. But they're not bombing Switzerland; they're not bombing Norway. So obviously we need to change what we're doing. And if we do attack them, we'll be playing into Bin Laden's hands because we'll be mobilizing thousands of other terrorists."

"I'm sorry to tell you this," said the Cop to the Critic, "but there are bad guys in this world. There are angels too. But there are bad guys in this world. And I've dealt with them. There is evil. And nothing our government did justifies ramming two planes filled with innocent people into two towers filled with more innocent people. And we don't get to do nothing. You can't make an intellectual argument for doing nothing because it's not an intellectual argument. Because when somebody is trying to kill you, there's a second brain that takes over. Not the brain that's in your head, the brain that's in your stomach.

"When I was getting shot at in Vietnam, nobody had to tell me what to do. As soon as those bullets started coming I was burrowing like a snake into the ground using muscles I never knew I had. And when I came back up, I came up firing. But if you've never had to use that brain—that second brain—you don't know how to respond to this. I do.

"It's pretty simple: they're evil. They hate us. They want to destroy us, and we have to defend ourselves in any way that we can. Watch the television, if you don't believe me," he added. "They're celebrating in the streets."

"Bomb them back into the fucking Stone Age," said the FBI guy.

"Turn the desert into glass," said the Secret Service guy.

"Go into Tora Bora and smoke 'em out," said the FBI guy. "Smoke 'em out."

Annabel, who had come to the service bar, rolled her eyes.

Nobody else spoke.

When I got home, the boy was awake and at his computer.

"What are you doing?" I asked.

"Just researching some stuff," he said, "for a thing I'm writing for school."

"About what?" I asked.

"About this country."

"Oh?"

"Yeah. I think people are going to go a little crazy, and a lot of these websites say the government is going to take away a lot of our freedoms. It's probably a good idea to keep some food and water around, you know?"

"You're just like my dad was," I said.

"How?"

"He was a dyed-in-the wool survivalist who kept thirty thousand dollars in a sock and iodine tablets in his wallet in case Indian Point blew."

"I don't think that's so crazy."

"Maybe not."

"I guess I'm just worried about a lot of stuff."

"A lot of people are," I said.

"And bad stuff happens, you know."

"It does."

"Do you think our government knew this was coming? Do you think they let it happen?"

"No, champ. I don't."

"I don't know. Apparently there was a lot of stock market activity leading up to the attacks. A lot of trading volume. And some people are saying that the U.S. military was told to stand down."

"Stand down?"

"Yeah. Kurt Rossman thinks NORAD might have issued a stand down order."

"What's NORAD?"

"North American Aerospace Defense Command."

"Oh…I didn't know that."

"But do you think they were told to stand down?" he asked, looking so sad and so scared and so worried and so much older than he was.

"No," I said, running my hand through his hair. "I think Kurt Rossman is a really smart guy, and I think our government does some really shitty things. But no, I don't believe that our military stood down. I really, truly don't believe that."

Then I told him it was late and that he should go to sleep.

Reluctantly, he rose from the table and shuffled down the hallway, the weight of the world on his skinny shoulders.

In *The Odyssey*, Homer says that there are two gates that our dreams pass through: one made of polished horn and the other of sawn ivory. Through the gate of ivory come deceptive dreams; through the gate of horn, the prophetic and true.

In our modern age, I think of King's dream of going to the mountaintop and Kennedy's dream of going to the moon as being collective dreams that blew in through the gate of horn.

Those were the dreams I grew up with.

But the dreams we dream now—of terror and falling towers—are dreams that come through the ivory gate: false messages from false gods, delivered through the false gate to a sickened collective unconscious.

And I wondered, as I heard him shut the door to his room, what his dreams would be and which gate they would travel through.

I wondered if he saw in his mind's eye those unremitting dystopian visions of the future that were so soon to haunt him or if he dreamt instead of the distant past, of those beginnings of man that he so loved to study, before he turned his mind toward doomsday scenarios and cataclysmic endings.

PART THREE

Callicoon

The day after the Twin Towers fell, Laroche managed to get through on a landline. He wanted to come to the city to see Sparrow, but he was in the hospital with pneumonia.

"They got me all stuck with IVs and tubes," he told me. "And they've got this drain on the right side of my back to draw out all the fluid that's in there. So I guess I'm not going anywhere anytime soon."

He began calling every night. Usually around six.

Sometimes he called in the morning too.

He was worried about how the attacks had affected the boy—worried because "it" ran in the boy's family.

He didn't say mental illness, but I knew what he meant.

I was worried too—worried about the McVeigh stuff I'd been finding on his computer and worried about his growing belief, nurtured by Kurt Rossman, that NORAD had ordered the U.S. military to "stand down." But I didn't want to give Laroche any ammunition if he was still looking for a reason to take the boy back, so I told him that we were keeping a close eye on things and that I thought he was handling it pretty well.

In the background, I could hear a hospital monitor beeping.

"Well…in war," he said, after pausing to catch his breath, "when something happens, sometimes you think you're okay, and then later, you realize you're not."

Lily, sensing my alarm, came closer so she could listen.

"And from what I read in the paper," Laroche continued, "it's still pretty bad down there."

There was no sense in denying the undeniable.

"It is pretty bad," I admitted.

There was another pause, another labored breath. I girded myself for what was coming next.

I thought that Laroche was about to tell me that he'd known from the beginning that New York City was a dangerous place, where all kinds of evil visited. I thought that he might threaten legal action. That he might try to use the attacks to get custody for Lavinia or for himself. But he didn't.

"Did you lose anyone?" he asked.

"No," I said.

"That's good...and Lily...she didn't?"

"No...we were lucky... thanks for asking."

"Well...once I get out of this damn hospital, do you think the boy might want to get away and spend a couple of days with me? A weekend up here?"

"I'm sure he'd like that," I said.

"I think he'll like the new place."

About a year before, Laroche's mother had died, and he'd found he couldn't live in the house they'd shared. Too many ghosts, he said. He'd moved to a small town called Callicoon in upstate New York near the Delaware River.

"He can fish or hike in the woods here. And we have a bowling alley and a movie theater," he told me.

"When are you thinking of coming to get him?" I asked.

Lily, who'd been listening in, started mouthing "absolutely not."

"Maybe middle of October..."

"I think that would be okay."

"Can you drive into the city yet? Or do they still have the bridges closed?" he asked, while Lily angrily whispered, "No, no, no."

I put my hand over the receiver and shushed her.

"The bridges are open, Claude."

"Well, middle of October. Like I said, I think I'll be fine to come down and pick him up. If it's all right with Lily."

I couldn't say no to him.

"I'm sure it's fine with Lily," I answered as she continued her silent protest, "and I know the boy would love to see you."

"All right then…I'll talk to you soon."

"Take care, Claude," I said, and I hung up.

Lily was pissed.

"He wants to take him to Indian Leap?"

"To Callicoon. His new place. For a weekend."

"When?"

"Middle of October."

"I don't think that's a good idea."

"What am I supposed to tell him—he can't see him again?"

"No," she said, "of course he can see him, but he can't take him away from here. Not now. I don't trust him."

"Look, I don't love the guy either, but I don't see how we can tell him no."

"I do," she said, sticking out her chest.

"I'm sure you do," I admitted.

"You can't stand that man."

"I think he's changed."

"You just want everybody to like you."

"That's not fair. It's true, but it's not fair."

"What are you guys arguing about?" said Sparrow, who'd just wandered into the living room.

"Claude wants to take you upstate for a weekend in October," said Lily, putting her hands on her hips like a hausfrau.

The fight lasted about an hour.

She accused me of "colluding" with the boy, "undermining" her authority, and being a "total wimp." I stood there like a punching bag.

The boy, who wanted to go, won.

A month later, I was waiting in front of our building.

It was fall. The trees that lined 106th were turning, the gang kids were swarming, the angel, dirtier than ever, was watching, and the preacher, his briefcase filled with Bibles, was chanting, "Halleluiah! Halleluiah! Halleluiah!" and "Praise God! Praise God! Praise God!" and "He loves you! He loves you! He loves you!"

An old Buick—the driver invisible behind tinted windows—pulled in. Then the driver's door was pushed open, and the rubber tip of a metal cane tapped tentatively at the pavement. A moment later Laroche poked his head out, and I smelled that particular smell that comes from old people's cars.

He got out slowly, clutching his ribs—I imagined—where the tube had been. When he finally got to standing, he blinked slowly in the sun. His mouth hung open in confusion. The formerly fleshy skin was now pulled tight over the bones of the face.

The man I'd fought with in front of Orin's house and in the lawyer's office was gone. Then, he'd been old; now, he was feeble.

"How was the traffic?" I asked.

"Not too bad…made pretty good time," he said, swiveling his head slowly to take in his surroundings.

"What floor are you on?" he asked.

"The fifth."

He nodded and we started toward the stoop.

The gang kids, seeing him struggle, parted. The front of the building looked especially filthy, the vestibule worse. There were garbage bags piled under the stairs and most of the tiles were broken or missing. Somewhere above us, a dog was barking.

This was the New York apartment of his nightmares, not the one I described at the meeting with his lawyer. But he barely seemed to notice.

We began climbing. Laroche was stopping on each landing, clutching at his ribs and struggling for breath like a fish out of water. I asked if he needed help. He refused. Above us, sunlight came from the transom, illuminating the curls of his thinning white hair.

When he finally got to our floor, I pushed open the door, and he felt his way down the poorly lit hallway with his cane. In our living room there was light.

And the boy.

When Laroche saw him, what seemed like an internal sob shook his body. But he fought it back.

"You got big" was all he said.

"I did?" asked the boy.

"Oh yeah," said Laroche as his eyes watered.

He dabbed at them with a handkerchief.

He apologized.

"I'm sorry…I was just so worried…"

"I'm okay," said the boy.

"I was so worried," he repeated, turning toward Lily as if to explain.

The boy went to him and hugged him in that sweet way that he always had, and Laroche took him in his arms and sobbed openly. I saw the man's tenderness, and I saw why the boy loved him, and I felt that I had been wrong about the man.

Lily saw it too. She welled up.

She brought us tea.

It was getting late. The light was going, and I was worried about his driving. He said he'd be fine if he could just rest for a bit. The drive wasn't long. Two hours at most. He'd take the boy and bring him back Sunday evening.

Sunday, I came home from work early. Lily was up in arms.

"I'm just asking you what you did?" she was saying to the boy.

"I can't tell you," he answered, agitated and pacing in the living room.

"Can't tell me what?" she asked.

"Nothing."

"What do you mean 'nothing'? What is it?" she asked.

"Let's just drop it. Okay?"

"You can tell me."

"I can't tell you."

"Can't tell me what? What can't you tell me?

"I can't fucking tell you," he shouted, "because I know you'll be upset, because I know how you are about these things!"

"What things?" she asked.

"What things?" I asked.

"Nobody did anything to you…did they?" asked Lily, who was completely freaked out.

"You mean," he asked in a mocking, textbook tone, "like a teacher, or a relative, or a trusted friend of the family?"

"Yes," she said.

"Jesus Christ."

"What?"

"I know that you and Lily think Claude did something to me—"

"I didn't think that," I interrupted. "Never, never, never."

"That's a lie," he said. "I know you both think bad things about Claude because I heard Lily making some joke about how he took off my Dad's shoes one night when he was drunk and passed out. And I heard her going on and on about how weird Claude is and what a deviant he is. *Deviant*. That's the word she said. I heard her say that to you. You think it's nice to hear that kind of stuff?"

"No...I don't..." I said.

"Well, it's not that big of an apartment, and I hear stuff, and to tell you the truth, I kind of thought you wanted me to hear it," he said, pointing at Lily.

"I didn't want you to hear it," she said. "That's ridiculous."

"I'm sure she didn't want you to hear it," I added, although I wasn't so sure.

"I don't think she should joke about it or talk about stuff she doesn't know anything about," he said, turning to me.

"You're right," I said. "And I shouldn't either."

He was furious. He wouldn't look at us. He ran into his bedroom, and I followed. He was on the bed. I stood in the doorway.

"He is good to me, and I don't like her making fun of him just because he doesn't agree with her politically and he doesn't do yoga or any of that crazy Forum-shit she does," he said.

"You're right. He's a good man, and he's been very good to you."

"Well, do you think he did something bad to me?"

"No. I was just worried," I said, sitting next to him on the small bed. "Some of the things he's done have worried me."

"Like what?"

"Like telling you about the Korean War and showing you the photographs.

I was worried you were too young to hear about that."

"Well, I think it was good to hear about that stuff. Wars have to get fought sometimes. Right? Like World War Two. Right?"

"You're right," I admitted.

"And people," he continued, "die…"

"They do," I admitted.

"They die or they get wounded, and they do it to keep people like us safe, and we don't seem to give a damn about them. Nobody seems to give a shit. I never hear anybody at school saying anything about the guys we just sent over to Afghanistan. They just sit there in their fancy private school and take everything for granted. I mean…Claude has been in pain his whole life because he went and fought for something he believed in. And now people like Lily make fun of him, and I'm sorry, but I think people are selfish and stupid, and it's just fucking ridiculous to make false accusations about someone who served his country like Claude did, especially if you don't know what really happened. But let her be that way…let her be that way…I guess…"

"You're right," I said. "You are right. It was unfair, is unfair of me, or Lily, to assume he did anything inappropriate. Our job is to try and protect you, but sometimes our judgment isn't so great. And so, I'm sorry. I know Claude means a lot to you."

"I mean, for chrissakes," he cried out, "I was over there for dinner five times a week…his mother cooked for me…they really took me in when nobody gave a shit."

"I know," I said, putting my hand on his back. "You told me."

"So can you tell Lily to fucking knock it off?"

"I will. She'll knock it off, and so will I."

"I'm sorry I got so angry," he said, sitting on the bed next to me and nodding his head like a sweet bird.

"Fuck that. You were pissed, and you had good reason. You don't have to be sorry. But I would like to know what it was that you thought you couldn't tell us."

"You won't be mad?"

"No. I won't be mad."

"Promise?"

"Promise."

"We went shooting. That was all."

"Shooting?"

"Yeah…"

"Where?"

"To a range."

"In Callicoon?"

"Across the Delaware on the Pennsylvania side. It was kind of on top of a mountain over there."

"What did you shoot?'

"A rifle. A twenty-two caliber. And a handgun. A forty-five caliber service revolver. Claude showed me how to load them. And all this safety stuff. He just wanted to teach me how to shoot, and I thought it would be fun."

"Was it?"

"Yeah…you're not mad…or upset?"

"No." I lied.

"And I think it's good stuff to know. After what happened here, who knows what's going to happen next. Right? I mean, there are some pretty bad actors in the world…unfortunately."

"There are," I admitted.

"I know Lily doesn't like it to hear it, and the kids at my school don't like to hear it, but I think we have to eliminate the threats."

Listening to him talk about "bad actors" and "eliminating threats" troubled me.

I'd had the same reaction when he'd asked me if I thought NORAD had told the military to stand down.

They didn't sound like his words or his thoughts.

And though he was still sitting on his bed talking to me, his mind seemed to be racing uncontrollably.

I felt that he was becoming someone else—someone whom I didn't know.

And he looked so afraid.

The Note

It was Saturday night, it was crowded, and it was loud.

"There's a note for you downstairs," said Annabel, who'd just fought her way to the service bar. "I put it in your left pocket."

"Okay," I said. "I'll go look in a minute."

She leaned closer. "Isn't that that actor?"

"Where?"

"Right over there. Telling the joke."

"Oh yeah."

"The left pocket," she repeated, lifting her tray over her head and squeezing back through the crowd.

"So he changes his name," the Actor was saying, "from Sydney Goldfarb to Horace Pembroke the Third, and they let him into the country club. The first day there, he's teeing off, and he shanks the ball and says, 'Oy vey—whatever that means...'"

Contessa squealed with laughter. The Cop, who was hard of hearing, asked him to repeat the punch line. Then he laughed and turned toward the Bishop, who was drinking rye and discussing church politics.

"Oh, it's very interesting," the Bishop was saying, "but in the end, you see, it didn't matter because the bishops had all agreed in advance who it was going to be."

"That's politics for you," said the Reporter, shrugging his shoulders and pushing his glass toward me, while the Greek, who was reclining in his chair and blowing great rings of smoke, nodded his gray-curled head in agreement.

Next to the Greek sat the Berliner, and next to the Berliner the Czech, and next to the Czech the Painter, who asked me, as I made his martini, if I'd ever seen *The Friends of Eddie Coyle*.

I hadn't.

"You should," said the Painter.

"Absolutely fantastic movie," added the Reporter, stirring his scotch counterclockwise, "about a small-time crook who's being run by the FBI. And there's this other guy," he continued, "who seems like a nobody. He's just a bartender. But it turns out he's the nexus of the crime ring. So they take him out and kill him. And that's how it ends. With the bartender bleeding to death in a ditch somewhere."

"I hope that's not how I end up," I said.

"As you sow, so shall you reap," said the Greek, a plume of smoke punctuating his pronouncement.

"Robert Mitchum," added the Painter, "plays Eddie Coyle."

"Now that was an actor," said the Loan Shark, twirling his fingers in the smoky air. "Not like these pieces of garbage today who call themselves actors."

And next to the Loan Shark, just a little farther down the bar, the Secret Service guy was telling a dark-haired, very neurotic woman who taught art at P.S. 75 about how he'd met Castro, as she compulsively doodled on a napkin.

And next to the Art Teacher, at the far end of the bar, the Critic was talking to a bleary-eyed blonde, who looked doubtful.

"That was Captain Beefheart's real name?" she slurred.

"That was his name," said the Critic, lighting a Parliament, the brand Lily had smoked in college.

Someone turned the music louder. Louis's horn blared like Gabriel's. More people pushed in. The Blonde pushed back. The Bishop told everyone to behave or he'd send them all to their rooms. The Actor laughed his big baritone laugh. More people poured in. And as they pushed toward the bar, hands waving money or empty glasses, it seemed like everyone was swaying together in one big mass, and the floorboards seemed to be buckling from the weight. The smoke hung in clouds, and the whine of the smoke eater was like an engine's whine, and there was shouting and unnatural laughter, and the undifferentiated drone of drunken voices. As the bar rolled over invisible swells and surges, I thought of the sea at night. And of storms.

Red at night, sailor's delight; red in the morning, sailors take warning.

At the end of the bar, looking flushed, expectant, and happy, Annabel appeared.

"Did you read the note?" she asked.

"I haven't had a chance. It's so fucking busy."

"Read it, read it!"

"I will, I will!"

But for the next hour I couldn't.

The Critic was telling the Blonde about the time he interviewed Joey Ramone, the Painter was talking about Thomas Cole, the Reporter was telling a story about Syria, the actor was telling Contessa joke after joke, and the Bishop was discussing the existence of God with the Berliner, who was discussing the disappearance of bathhouses with the Czech, who was asking some of the law enforcement guys whether or not they thought there could be another attack. And then it was later, almost one o'clock in the morning, and the law enforcement guys looked grim, telling the Czech that it was probably just a matter of time before something else happened. Maybe something even worse.

Annabel, exhausted from the night but still smiling, came back to the service bar.

She wanted to know if I'd looked in my left pocket yet.

There were only a few people left—the Bishop, the Painter, and the Berliner. So I went to the small door at the end of the bar, ducked under the low frame, and went down the dark, rickety stairs that led to the basement.

At the bottom to the right, there was a walk-in freezer made out of wood. It must have been over a hundred years old. Next to the walk-in was a battered metal table where the Chinese cooks did their prep work. To get to the back, to the liquor cage, where I hung my coat, you had to duck under a pipe.

Down there in the quiet, I reached for my jacket and rummaged around in the left pocket.

The note had been folded into a tiny little square.

The writing was in red pencil.

I'm pregnant, it read.

When I came back up, the Bishop told me I looked like I'd just seen a ghost.
He and the Painter and the Berliner left soon after that.

Still flushed, Annabel came to me.

"Are you happy?" she asked.

I couldn't talk.

"You're not?"

"No. It's just…"

"It's just what?"

"It's just that…"

"Just that what?"

"The boy…"

"But you're so unhappy."

"I am…I am unhappy…"

"Isn't it incredible?" she said, putting her hands on my face and concentrating all of her being into my being. She kept talking. I knew that because I could see her heavily lipsticked lips moving, but I couldn't hear her.

I couldn't talk. Couldn't answer her.

I watched her face fall, watched her façade drop.

In a million incremental steps, I watched her harden.

"You were inside of me," she was saying. "You were inside of me…so don't tell me you don't want…don't tell me that…"

"I'm not saying that—"

"You are."

"I'm not."

"I can see it…I can see it in your eyes."

In a fury, she stormed out.

Behind me, in the hall, the Chinese night porter had dutifully begun his mopping.

There was a phone on the wall by the host stand.

I called Pierce.

As was his wont, he began legal proceedings, playing prosecutor and judge and only occasionally taking over the role of my defense.

"Let me get this straight. You're fucking a girl who's obviously nuts, she has a boyfriend, she's not on birth control, you're not wearing a condom, and you come inside of her?"

"She said she knew her body really well, her cycles, you know, because she's a dancer."

"So basically, you're a total fucking moron who's created a pretty fucking big problem for himself."

"Exactly."

"Got it. Let's work from there."

"Good."

"All right. So if you stay with Lily because of the boy, this unborn child won't have a father, which isn't good, because as we already know, Annabel isn't the most stable girl in the world, is she?"

"No."

"When her boyfriend finds out, he'll leave her, and she'll be a single mother working as a waitress and living in a trailer."

"I don't know that she'll be living in a trailer," I said.

"Don't interrupt me, counselor."

"Sorry."

"On the other hand, if you leave Lily and move in with Annabel, Lily will never speak to you again, and you'll end up abandoning a kid who depends on you and who's already had to deal with more shit than any kid should ever have to deal with."

"Right."

"And forgetting for a moment the emotional mess you've created, there's no way in the world you could financially support two kids."

"That's correct."

"And even if you did move in with Annabel, you have no idea whether or not that relationship would work out because you guys have never really been together. Maybe you'd end up hating each other. Maybe you'd end up even more unhappy than you are with Lily."

"Possibly."

"So you've totally fucked yourself and have managed to undermine your sole accomplishment: taking this boy in and devoting yourself to his well-being."

"Exactly."

"Fine. Now that I have all the facts, I think we can move forward."

Pierce did have all the facts, but facts are rational. I wasn't being rational and hadn't acted in a rational way. I was forty-three. I had a job I hated. I was in a bad marriage. And what I wanted was a woman who wanted me. And what I wanted was a child. A child of my own. And wrapped up in this big problem, as Pierce had put it, were those things that I wanted.

And those things had nothing to do with the facts.

At quarter past four, Pierce reached his verdict.

The facts had won.

She needed to be talked out of it.

Certainly, as the son of an ethicist and prominent Catholic scholar, Pierce must have been conflicted. But despite whatever inner confusion he may have harbored, he began, later that week, to call Annabel, and he began to advance the argument, as gently as he could, that she not have the baby.

It must have been a very distasteful role.

My days were like this. Depressed and exhausted from my nights at the bar, I slept late. Around noon, I got my coffee from the bodega and walked the dog in Riverside Park. At three, the boy came home, and I helped him with his homework. Then I went to work. If Annabel wasn't working, I called her at the end of the night from the bar to check in. Or, if I was at home, I'd tell Lily I was going out to walk the dog, and I'd call her from a pay phone.

"Your friend Pierce already called me," she said one night.

"He did?"

"Yes, he fucking did. He doesn't think I should have it. Did you tell him to call me?"

"I didn't," I said.

"Well, I'm having this fucking baby," she said.

"Okay, all right," I said, feeling that now-familiar nausea, racing heart, and clammy sweat all over my body, thinking into the future, into that dark, unimaginably painful moment when I would have to tell Lily and the boy that I had impregnated one of the waitresses and that I would be moving to Alabama to work on a feed lot—or something like that.

"Are you still there?" she asked.

"Yes. I'm here," I said, though I was far away.

"Is this something you want? You never tell me what you want. I don't think you ever tell anyone what you want."

"It's not that I don't want it. It's the timing. It's the boy. I can't leave him right now. And I don't think you should do it alone. I think it would be difficult," I said, hating the sound of my hollow voice.

"But, you're not answering me."

"I'm not?"

"No..." she said, elongating the word with her southern drawl, which had suddenly surfaced, making me think again of how we would probably have to move if she had the kid.

"You're not answering me. Do you want this baby?"

"I want it but not now."

"Ugh," she cried. "That doesn't help me."

"What did Pierce say?"

Why was I abdicating?

"You know what he said because you told him to call!"

"I didn't ask him to call. He cares about you, he cares about me, and he's concerned."

"That is such fucking bullshit!"

"It's not."

"Oh, come on. It's fucking bullshit!"

I suddenly realized just how cold it was; the wind was whipping off the Hudson. And my emotional state was spooking the dog, I think.

"Are you there?" asked Annabel.

I'd told myself I couldn't because of the boy. Was that true? Maybe I did want the baby. Maybe it would be a good way to get away from Lily.

"Are you there?" she asked.

But the boy, I thought.

I could hear her crying now on the other end of the phone. My impulse was to leave. To go anywhere. California. Canada. Cuba.

"I'm here," I whispered. "I'm here."

"I don't know what I'm going to do," she said.

"It's just that the boy's been through so much…" I said.

"I know."

"And I worry that if I left him…right now…"

"I know."

"So I couldn't be with you…right away…and I worry…about you being alone…with a baby and working a restaurant job…"

"I know…that's what Lenore said. That's what Lois said. That's what Pierce said. That's what everybody says."

And every time she leaned toward not having the baby, I softened. I softened because I knew she was sacrificing, on some level, for the boy, whom she didn't even know. At those moments, she just seemed like the most amazing fucking woman, and I was convinced she was my true love. I just wanted to leap into a new life and have a baby with her even if it meant drinking Jack Daniels with her family, going to tractor pulls, and working in a slaughterhouse, or feed lot, or whatever it was they did down there.

"Ugh," she was saying, "why does it have to be such bad timing? Why does it have to be so complicated?"

"I don't know," I was saying, my voice sounding hollow again.

And of course, because she was so fucking attuned, she heard the hollowness. And she turned again.

"I don't know," she said. "I don't know what I'm going to fucking do. But you tell your friend to stop calling me. You tell that heartless fucking asshole who could give two shits about anybody other than himself to stop. You tell him," she said, crying again. "You tell him, you fucking tell him, to fucking stop."

"I will."

"You tell him," she said, still crying.

I had never felt lower.

When I got back from my walk, Lily wanted to talk.

I thought she knew, or suspected, but she didn't.

The school was worried about an essay the boy had written, and they'd called us in for a meeting.

Red Flags

The guidance counselor was named Shelley and she had on her desk several of Sparrow's papers. She felt they were "potential red flags."

I wanted to know which essay in particular.

"This one," said Shelley, pulling out an essay on libertarianism.

"Does it raise a red flag if the student's politics don't hew to the liberal politics of the school?" I asked.

"Are you a Republican?" she asked, looking at me suspiciously over her reading glasses.

"I happen to be a Democrat. That's not the point. What I want to know is if the school is upset about him not following liberal orthodoxy, or if the papers show a genuine psychological problem."

"Obviously it's a problem. We know that and we're worried too," said Lily.

"Have you read these papers?" asked Shelley, fanning them across her desk.

"I read all of his papers," I said. "And I'm worried too. And I think therapy would be great for him."

"Then why are we arguing about politics?" asked Shelley.

"Because I don't like having my kid ostracized for not having the same beliefs as everyone else. Because I don't like other kids putting up posters of him dressed as Holden Caufield and mocking him."

"That was three years ago," said Lily. "He needs help, and you agree he needs help. Why are you being so defensive?"

I was being defensive. In fact, I was a mess.

I thought the guidance counselor was being obnoxious, but she was right.

I apologized.

"What do we do next?" asked Lily.

Shelley thought we should see a social worker. She recommended the Jewish Board for Family and Children's Services.

The next week, we went.

The social worker was a young Latina woman, named Anna. She listened intently. I liked her much better than Shelley.

"So why don't you start by telling me why you're here?" she asked.

"Because they're worried about me," said the boy.

"Why are they worried?"

"I think they're worried that I'm worrying so much," he said, laughing.

"And what are you worried about?"

"The country. The world. A lot, I guess."

"And what worries you so much about our country?"

"A lot. I just don't like our culture. Or the direction we're heading in. And they're definitely trying to take away our freedoms, our rights, our civil liberties."

"Who's they?"

"The government."

"Are these things you discuss in class? Or read about in the paper?"

"We've talked about the Patriot Act in social studies, and the *Constitution*; the other stuff I read about on the Internet."

"What's the other stuff?"

"I've been reading a lot about Ruby Ridge...and about what happened at Waco..."

"That's what we're worried about," said Lily.

"You're worried about the time he spends on the Internet?"

"Especially this Timothy McVeigh stuff."

"And why are you upset about that?" asked the social worker.

"Because I feel like he's identifying with McVeigh," said Lily.

"I'm not identifying with him! Jesus! I just thought he had some pretty good points. He was a soldier in Iraq in the first Gulf War, and he saw what we did there, and he thought it was immoral, which is something I thought you would agree with."

"He's a terrorist," said Lily. "A terrorist who killed children."

"He didn't know there were kids in the building! Think about it! Why would they put kids, why would they put a daycare center, in a federal building? Why? Answer that. Okay?"

"Why do you think?" asked the social worker.

"Because if you put kids in a building, you can say that anyone who attacks you is an animal. It's a human shield."

Lily threw her hands up. "I don't think that's what happened. I'm sorry, but I don't think they put kids in the building for that reason. And this is exactly the kind of conspiracy stuff you're getting on the Internet—"

"Right. Great. I'm a conspiracy freak. Then you can dismiss me too."

"Lily…" I said.

"An asteroid is going to hit us!" she shouted. "David Koresh is a hero! HIV is a hoax—"

"Asteroids come near us all the time! HIV *is* a hoax! There's a book—"

"Lily!"

"Everything is a conspiracy," she continued. "The world is coming to an end. They're will be civil war and chaos—"

"Things are really bad! I'm not just making stuff up! Bad things happen!"

"I know that," said Lily, her face hardening.

"And there probably will be civil war and chaos. Okay? There are a lot of angry people out there. And we do have a really shitty government. Look what they're doing right now in the Middle East. Look at what they're doing to the *Constitution*. Jesus H. Christ! You think everybody who disagrees with you is an idiot."

"That is not true."

"Well, I happen to know some stuff. Okay? I happen to know a lot about geology. I've been reading about it my whole life. Okay? So I think I know a little bit about fossils and fossil fuels. And I think that we'll probably run out of oil pretty soon. I mean, it's a limited resource, and there are a lot of people on the planet. And I think that once the oil runs out, the shit is going to really hit the fan. And I wouldn't count on our government to do jack shit to help us. And I think they're shredding the *Constitution*. And I think what they did at Ruby

Ridge was wrong, and I think Janet Reno is a fucking criminal, and so do a lot of other really intelligent people. Does that make me a fucking conspiracy freak? I'm sorry," he said, turning to the social worker.

"What are you sorry about?"

"I didn't mean to curse."

"It's okay. You can say whatever you want in here."

"Okay. What I'm trying to say is that I don't think it's crazy to say that we're going to see things really start to fall apart."

"This is what I'm worried about," said Lily. "This is exactly what I'm worried about.

"What kinds of things are you worried will fall apart?" asked the social worker.

"The grid."

"The grid?"

"The electronic grid. Which means bank accounts, cell phones, computers—all that stuff. It's all gonna go. Who knows? Maybe we'll even end up using ham radio again."

He let out a laugh that sounded forced and unnatural to me.

"Of course, we'll probably have to hook them up to generators."

"The ham radios?"

"Yeah."

"And do you think this will happen soon?"

"Yes."

"He's writing a book about it," I said. "And it's pretty damn good."

"I don't think it's any good at all," said the boy.

"Did you start it on your own?" asked the social worker.

"No. It's for an English class project, and I've only done two chapters. I don't think I'll be able to finish it or anything like that."

"That's a lot," said the social worker.

"It's really good," I said.

"It is," agreed Lily. "He's a very talented writer."

"What's it about?"

"Well, in the first chapter, the government sees the shortages coming, so they decide to strategically abandon the poorest parts of the country. Places like where I'm from. Places like Indian Leap."

"Indian Leap?"

"It's in Massachusetts. Near Springfield. It's small and it's a pretty crappy place, so you wouldn't know it."

"Crappy how?"

"There's a lot of poverty. And drugs and crime. The people don't have a lot of hope, really. So in my first chapter, like I said, the government decides that the only way the country can survive is if they cut off the poorest parts. Take them off the grid. And Indian Leap is one of the places they cut off."

"It sounds really interesting."

"It is," I said.

"And what's in the second chapter?"

"The second chapter is called 'The Masses.'"

"It sounds like a great title."

"It isn't original. We're reading about Karl Marx in social studies. I took it from his book."

"You're reading Marx in high school?" asked the social worker.

"In German," I said.

The social worker's jaw dropped.

"He's kidding," said Lily.

"What's that chapter about?" asked the social worker.

"It's about the town and the people in the town. The people are kind of oddballs. When I read it in class, the other kids laughed, probably because the people I wrote about are such weird characters, because they're based on the people I remember from being a kid. But there's this one family that's pretty normal. The father is a steelworker. He's the one who decides to fight back against the government. He gets everyone to band together. He's the hero."

"What makes him a hero?"

"He cares about the common man. He treats everybody with respect. He loves his kids. He's a blue-collar guy, but he's smarter than everyone else. And he doesn't look down on anyone. Kind of my ideal guy, I guess. The kind of guy who steps up when people need him."

"And who is he based on?"

"The steelworker?"

"Yes. Is he based on someone from Indian Leap?"

"No. I based that character on my uncle."

"What's wrong?" asked Lily, looking at me.

I felt like a fraud.

"I didn't know you based that on me," I said.

We were out of time.

The social worker asked the boy to wait outside. Then she talked to us for a few minutes. Lily wanted a diagnosis.

"Obviously, he has a lot of trauma to process. Given what he's been through, he might even have post-traumatic stress disorder. I do think we might want to send him for a psychiatric evaluation."

"So he'd stop seeing you?" I asked.

"No. He'll continue to see me, but he's dealing with a lot of anxiety, and I think it might be good to help him with that."

"With medication?" asked Lily.

"Not necessarily. It might be enough to just change some of the behavioral stuff. If he's spending a lot of time on the Internet and it's causing him anxiety, maybe we can talk about limiting his time on it. Let's wait and see."

She gave us the psychiatrist's card.

His name was Richard Greenberg, and he worked at Bellevue Hospital.

On the way home, the boy and Lily had a bad fight. He felt she'd humiliated him in front of the social worker. She said she was being honest. I said they were both right.

When we got home, she turned on me. I hadn't said enough. I'd taken the boy's side. I was flirting with the social worker.

That week was a bad week. I felt like something inside of him was changing. He kept to his room. He wouldn't talk to Lily.

On Wednesday night I came home late and saw a strip of light under his door. I knocked and went in. He was reading a U.S. Army manual on how to survive in the wilderness. He put the book down and looked up at me.

"I don't want Lily to go with us tomorrow. Is that okay?"

"Why not?"

"I just don't. Can you take me?"

On Thursday, I picked him up at school, and we took the subway downtown. Big brown blocks of buildings, seemingly devoid of life surrounded the hospital.

At 28th we walked through the wrought iron gate.

Inside the entrance there was a large photograph of the first public amphitheater for clinical teaching and surgery—doctors in black coats hovered over an invisible patient, and rings of smug, disinterested medical students rose behind them. I thought of *The Inferno*, the rings of observers like Dante's rings of hell.

My stomach was unsettled. I needed to use the bathroom. I told the boy to wait. Squeezing past the crowd of people waiting to be seen, I pushed the door open and headed for the single stall in the back. The tiles were that sickly, distinctly institutional shade of green. The toilet seat was up. It had not been flushed. There was toilet paper on the floor and a broken nail clipper. The smell was a mixture of shit, piss, stale sweat, and unwashed flesh. It was so pungent I nearly vomited.

I squatted over the bowl trying not to touch it.

On the green door, someone had scrawled the names of Hector Lavoe, Tito Puente, Eddie Palmieri, and Willie Colon, and underneath those names were the words *en mi corazon, hasta la muerte*. In my heart until the death.

When I finished I got the boy, and we followed the color code to the second floor to the psychiatric unit. The elevator had a metal floor and metal walls. I was told to wait while he was being evaluated.

Restless, I wandered the halls and looked at the paintings on the walls. A lot of them were abstract, with floating shapes and geometric patterns. Most were hideous. At the end of one of the halls was a Miró called *People at Night Guided by the Phosphorescent Tracks of Snails*, and I thought, is this the kind of painting that calms and soothes the troubled, the panicked, and the unhinged?

Who knows? Maybe the crazy are happy to know that they are not alone in their strange perceptions.

Opposite Miró's *People at Night* was Monet's *Morning on the Seine Near Giverny*, which struck me as being just as potentially destabilizing.

From behind one of the doors I heard screams. I looked up at a clock. The hour was coming to a close. The last painting I looked at was of an elegant man, mustachioed, wearing a white linen suit and white summer hat. Seated out of doors at a wooden table, the man was pensively sipping his coffee. Nearby, a woman in a hammock, perhaps his wife, slept in the shade of two great oaks while an old servant worked in the garden.

A life that no longer exists, I thought. A life that nobody in these ugly halls and padded rooms will ever have. A life of financial abundance, with the luxury of time for pensive reflection in the backyard of one's summer home.

I looked back up at the clock: ten minutes until four.

I went and knocked on the door.

The psychiatrist came out and shook my hand.

He had a potbelly, a moustache, and big lips that flapped when he spoke. I thought he looked like a walrus. He waved me in. It seemed like the session had upset the boy. He was wild in the eyes. He was not himself.

"He thinks that *they* are coming after him," said the psychiatrist, motioning for me to sit. "He's not sure who *they* are, though he thinks that *they* are the federal government."

"It could be a different organization," admitted the boy.

It seemed like he was having a break right in front of me. His fear was distorting his features. Making him less recognizable.

"There's definitely some paranoid ideation here," said the psychiatrist, as if the boy were not in the room. I wanted to punch him in the face. To bloody his nose and flapping lips. I felt he'd done something to him.

The boy looked at me questioningly.

I wanted to hold him and say, "Who is this man between us? Who is this walrus in a suit and tie between us? Who built this building? Who made this part of the city? Who paved over the farms and destroyed the abundant rivers that were here? Who made this ugliness? Who put these demons in your sweet and brilliant mind?"

The walrus was still flapping his lips. His breath stank. He was saying something about starting with a mild antianxiety. He was saying something about a clinical trial.

And I wanted to say, "I don't want him in a clinical trial. I don't want him to be an inpatient, an outpatient, or a statistic. I don't want him in here. I don't want him on pharmaceuticals. I don't want him wandering the city at night, guided by the phosphorescent traces of snails. No. I want him sitting in his backyard, contemplating literature, or life, while his wife sleeps nearby in a hammock.

"I want him drinking coffee in a garden in the morning, with his children at his feet, contemplating the stars in the backyard at night with his wife on his arm.

"Anywhere but here.

"Anywhere."

Ritmos Calientes

The place was packed with people, filled with smoke, and louder than I'd ever heard it.

"Cal Tjader! Willie Bobo! Mongo Santamaria! Pancho Sanchez! Chombo! Chombo Silva!" shouted the Loan Shark. "Am I right!?"

"You got it!" I shouted back, over Tjader's churning rhythms.

"They don't make them like this anymore! These are dinosaurs. Dinosaurs!"

"And don't forget Vince Guaraldi on piano," said the Critic.

"Thank God we have the recordings!" shouted the Loan Shark, drumming his fingers on the bar. "Now I can't leave! Another Dewar's, please!"

"And I'll take a pink gin," said the Greek.

"Pink gin?" asked the Cheshire Cat.

"Gin with bitters," said the Greek. "Britain's Royal Navy."

"I got a cousin in Mississippi who drink hisself a mint julep," said the Cat.

"I'm not sure I see how that's relevant," said the Greek.

The band stopped, and Tjader played two bars of a montuno on his vibraphone.

"*Guachi Guaro!*" sang the musicians, and then they kicked back in like a well-oiled machine.

"Gosh, this is pretty neat stuff," said the defrocked Priest, as the Contessa smiled her red-lipstick smile, raised her hands to the ceiling, and started shimmying her big Italian hips.

At the other end of the bar, the law enforcement guys ordered a round, and I brought them their drinks. The Contessa ordered a Ketel. The Cat wanted another Absolut, rocks. The Critic wanted a spritzer. The Greek stirred his pink gin.

"The Contessa is on our tab," said the Berliner. "She is a fantastic creature. Have you heard about her seven husbands?"

"I was number five," I said.

Still dancing, shimmying, and trailing cigarette smoke as she twirled, she shrieked with delight.

"Honey, if you had been number five, there would have been no six or seven. If I had you, I would have never let you go."

"Ditto," said the Berliner.

"What about me?" said the Czech.

"What about you?" asked the Berliner from under his leather cap.

"*Shee-it*, motherfucker. I wanna be just like you when I grow up," said the Cat, grinning.

"*Guachi Guaro!*" sang the band.

To my left, through the crowd, I could see Annabel struggling toward the bar for drinks. She looked grim. Behind her, the comics were clumped together, trying to outdo each other with bits—their laughter mixing with the cry of Chombo Silva's saxophone. The Loan Shark, dancing the length of the bar like a polar bear, watched them for a moment and twirled his fingers in the air.

"Nice country," he said before heading toward the toilet.

Annabel stood at the service bar with her tray. She needed two white Bordeaux, a bourbon Manhattan, and a Bloody Mary.

"What's wrong?" I asked.

"Lois just told me that she didn't think I should be with you. Or work here. I mean, I'm fucking working and she tells me that."

Lois was a lesbian comic. I thought she was very funny. She hated me.

"I'm sorry," I said, as I grabbed for the sweet vermouth.

"And Lenore said the same thing to me when I saw her today. She thinks I'll get hurt. She thinks I shouldn't have it. She thinks it's a huge mistake."

Lenore was a songwriter who lived next door to Lou Reed. He'd heard her play and thought her stuff was really good. They'd ended up shooting heroin together.

"I feel like they're all ganging up on me."

"That's shitty."

"Yeah. And Lana doesn't think we should be together either."

Lana was an ex-model who lived with a well-known modern artist who made collages out of stock photographs, pornography, and "hypertext."

"When did you talk to Lana?" I asked, grabbing the cold neck of the Bordeaux.

"I had lunch with her and her asshole boyfriend yesterday."

"Does the boyfriend also have an opinion?"

"He thinks I should quit this job and stop seeing you."

"So it's unanimous," I said, jamming the Bordeaux back in the ice.

"But we can't trust his opinion."

"Why not?"

"Because his stuff totally sucks."

"He's a talentless asshole," I admitted. "But your friends are probably right."

"No they're not! What the fuck do a lesbian comedienne, a heroin addict, an ex-model, and a totally gross guy who makes collages out of porn know about us?"

"The sources are suspect," I said, which made her smile.

"They don't understand. It's like we're in our own little clubhouse. It's like we're outside of everything."

Out of the corner of my eye I saw the defrocked Priest snatch a grape from the fruit bowl.

"Please don't eat those."

"Sorry, chum."

The Critic ordered a spritzer.

I finished Annabel's drinks. She leaned toward me and put a hand on my face.

"I know they're right. But I want to be with you," she said.

"I know," I said.

The Critic repeated his order. He was drinking fast. He was very drunk.

"I heard you the first time," I said without turning from her.

Her hand was still on my face. I could feel myself getting lost. I don't know how else to describe it. I wanted to tell her to stay in the back of the restaurant. In the café. Away from all the smoke. I wanted to tell the comics to move, or leave. I wanted to tell them that if they knocked into her, I'd kick the shit out of them. I wanted to tell her her friends were wrong. I wanted to be alone with her.

"*Guachi Guaro!*" sang the band.

"What does that mean?" she asked.

"It doesn't mean anything," I said.

Tjader kicked into a higher gear. The comics were laughing louder. The defrocked Priest was ordering a drink for the Czech. "No. I can't," the Czech was saying. "I have to work tomorrow."

"Get us a whole round on me, chum," the defrocked Priest was saying.

They frantically waved their hands at me to signal that they were done.

Some guy—a tall slim black man wearing a pork-pie hat and tortoise-shell glasses—took out a harmonica and started playing along with the music. It was grating. I asked him to stop.

"Chum! Where's Lev's martini?"

Getting angrier, I turned on the Priest. "He doesn't want another one," I said.

"Well, I happen to think you're a pretty neat guy," said the Priest, blushing, "but that's just me talking."

The slim black man in the pork-pie let loose with an intense, upper-register wail on his harp.

The Critic covered his ears.

"That is crazy making," said the Art Teacher, doodling on her napkin.

A bunch of suits were trying to get my attention.

Annabel was still at the bar, the four drinks on the tray.

"Can we talk later?" she asked.

"Yes," I said.

"Hey baby," called the Cat. "Have you seen that movie *Crash*?"

I told him I hadn't.

"You should, motherfucker," said the Cat. "It's like what we used to call a blue triple-X. The lady in it, she something else. Heh, heh. If God invented somethin' better than pussy he keepin' it to himself."

"Hey, chum! Can we get another martini for Lev?"

"He doesn't want one. And leave those grapes alone."

"What, chum?" asked the Priest.

"Leave those grapes alone!" I shouted.

"Sorry, chum."

"They're for the drinks."

"Right, chum."

Annabel had come back to the service bar. Her table wanted a blackberry-banana daiquiri. It was a drink that Vincent did, and it was a pain in the ass to make: ice, fresh lime, simple syrup, rum, bananas, and blackberries. While I was making it, the suits ordered another round, the Cat wanted his vodka "topped off," the Loan Shark wanted another Dewar's, Prez wanted his Stoli, the Priest wanted his vodka-half-tonic-half-soda, and Contessa wanted her Ketel. On a good night, she could go through a whole bottle.

The Bishop walked in dressed in full clerical regalia.

Everyone applauded. He bowed.

"*Guachi Guaro!*"

It was getting louder.

The Bishop found a seat next to the Painter.

"How can you hear yourself think in here?" he asked, fingering his heavy cross.

"You can't," said the Painter.

The guy in the pork-pie hat was wailing again on his harmonica, the Bishop was apologizing to the Painter about being so late, and the Greek was smoking his cigar, considering a cognac. Annabel was still waiting for the drink.

"Chum, Lev could still use that martini," said the Priest.

"He doesn't want one," I said, working the spoon down into the whirring blender. "He doesn't fucking want it!"

"Hey, I'm on your side, chum."

There was a wail from Tjader's horn section, and the timbale player kicked off the next chorus. The stereo had been turned up even louder. The comics were doubled over and howling. The suits were arguing about the NFL draft. The Berliner said something I couldn't hear, and there was a screech from Contessa. I could feel the rumble of the uptown local.

There was a smell of burning rubber and a grinding whine from the machine—the sound of metal on metal. I had worked the spoon too far down and had ruined the blades. I threw the blender down onto the floor. It smashed into pieces. The guy in the pork-pie started wailing again on his harmonica.

"Put that fucking harmonica away before I shove it up your fucking ass!" I shouted.

"You can't talk to me like that!" he said, leaning over the bar and getting in my face. "I got a right to play my blues, you cracker motherfucker."

I came out from behind the bar. He grabbed a stool to swing at me, but it fell feebly to the side. He was tall but not strong, and he was wasted. I grabbed him by the shirt collar. His glasses had fallen half off his face. The law enforcement guys came through the crowd and told me to take it easy. They told the tall thin man in the pork-pie hat to leave.

The defrocked Priest was flushed.

"Sorry, chum. Hope I didn't throw you."

I didn't answer him. I went back behind the bar. I tried to regain my composure. I was out of ice and went down to the basement to get some. Annabel went with me. When I came back up, Lily was there. She never came in. That night, she did. She was standing next to the Priest. His back was toward me.

"You'd better take a number," I heard him saying as I came up with the bucket of ice. "There's quite a long waiting list for him."

"Is that right?" I heard Lily say.

The Berliner must have known. He tried to shush him.

But the defrocked Priest kept talking: "Oh yes. He's down there right now with a cocktail waitress."

When he saw me he said, "Hey, chum. You've got another fan here."

When Lily saw Annabel come up behind me, she ran out. I told the night porter to watch the bar and followed her. I caught her at Broadway. We argued on the meridian as the traffic flowed by and the subway rumbled underneath.

"I'm not sleeping with her. That guy's a fucking drunk, and he doesn't know what the fuck he's talking about."

"You expect me to believe that?"

"He's a jealous faggot, and he should keep his fucking mouth shut."

"Since when do you call people faggots?"

"I'll call him whatever I want to call him."

"And fuck whomever you want to fuck, apparently."

"I told you not to come in here."

"Because you don't want me to see who you're fucking?"

"Because I'm working."

"How stupid do you think I am? It's ridiculous. It never occurs to anybody that I might be your wife, because they don't even know you have a wife."

"I don't want them involved in my personal life."

"Do you want to leave me?"

"I'm not sleeping with her."

"You take a shower almost every night you come home. You don't even try to touch me anymore."

"Because you never want to fuck!"

"So you fucked somebody else."

"I didn't."

"Why are you lying to me?"

"I'm not lying!"

"You're right. I don't fuck you. I'm sorry. But are you sleeping with her?"

"No!"

"I don't believe you."

"Then don't fucking believe me."

"Get another job. I don't want you around her."

"We need the money."

"You could make the same money doing something else."

"How?"

She turned away from me.

"Where are you going?" I asked.

"Don't touch me."

"Look. I have to go back in and finish. Take some money for a cab."

"I don't want that money," she said heading north and leaving me alone on the meridian.

I had to go back in. I went back across Broadway, nearly got hit by a cab, tripped on the fucking curb, ran up the sidewalk, down the steps, pushed the door open, pushed through the crowd, and went back behind the bar. The night porter had no idea what he was doing. People needed drinks. Annabel was where I'd left her. The comics were still laughing. Cal Tjader was still playing on the stereo. The Priest was standing between the Berliner and the Czech.

"Sorry, chum. I guess I messed up pretty bad," he said.

"You sure did, you fucking dicksucker," I said.

"Don't..." said the Bishop. "That is beneath you."

"Making me listen to your bullshit night after fucking night, buying people drinks when you can't even pay your own fucking check."

The Priest flushed and opened his wallet.

"Stop it," said the Bishop.

"Chum, I can settle up..."

The wallet was empty.

When I got home, I opened the door as quietly as I could. I looked for the strip of light under the boy's door. It wasn't there. Lily and the boy were both up.

They were sitting together at the kitchen table. The computer was off.

"I told him we're separating," said Lily.

The boy wouldn't look at me. I could see he'd been crying.

"That's not true," I said.

"It's true," said Lily.

"It's okay," said the boy. "People go..."

"I'm not leaving," I said. "Nothing is changing."

"It's okay," said Lily.

"It's okay," said the boy.

I sat down at the table with them.

I felt like crying, but I didn't.

"I told him you're not happy here. With me," Lily said.

She looked very small.

"That's not true," I said.

I looked at the boy's hair. He liked it when I cut his hair. I'd cut it the day before on the roof. It always looked terrible when I cut it. Like a bird molting.

"I did a shitty job on your hair," I said.

"I think you did a great job," he said.

I put my hands in his hair and grabbed him to me and told him I was so sorry, and I fell apart.

In the Dark

The next morning I had to go see Vincent. It was a studio on the top floor, above the bar.

I knocked.

"My man, my main fuckin' man. It's open. Come on in."

The apartment was decorated with Navajo rugs, pre-Columbian pottery, and a reproduction of Caravaggio's *Death of the Virgin*. The wine rack was stocked with Bordeaux and Burgundy; the bookshelves, packed with art books, cookbooks, military histories and dictionaries; and a nylon string guitar hung on the exposed brick wall. In the middle of the main room, there was an antique table with three chairs: a king's chair, a lawyer's chair, and an elegant chair—as he described them. And on all four walls, mirrors had been hung at odd angles.

It was tasteful, dark, and disorienting.

"Out here, my man!"

He was on the deck, surveying his potted herbs and plants, and swirling ice in two burgundy glasses.

Squinting, I made my way into the blinding sunlight.

He was tall, broad, and sinewy. He was wearing a mostly unbuttoned black silk shirt, white pants, and a white military belt. His black sandals were custom-made.

"How did you like that Cal Tjader tape I made for you?" he said, as he tossed the ice from the glasses to the courtyard below.

"I loved it."

"I knew you would," he said, reaching into his pants pocket, "so I made you another one. All Cubano. Quarteto Patria. Septeto Habanero. Orquestra Aragon. It's a little too rich for the average donkey."

The names of the groups were written in red ink; the songs in black.

"Thank you. I love this stuff."

"That's because you're not the average donkey."

"Thank you."

"You're welcome, you polite prick," he said, ducking through the door and leading me back into the darkened room. With exactitude, he set the chilled glasses on the table.

"Now sit the fuck down in the king's chair while I get us some wine."

"None for me, thanks."

"Why not?" he called from the kitchen.

"It's nine o'clock in the morning."

"So what? Why be like all the other donkeys?" he said, coming back in with a sweating green bottle cradled in his hand. "This is Puligny motherfucking-Montrachet."

"Expensive?"

"Who gives a fuck how much it cost, you penny-pinching Jew," he said, cutting the foil and digging the screw into the cork at a ninety-degree angle.

He pulled and poured. "Look at that color," he said, holding his glass just above shoulder level and toward the shaft of light that came through the open door. The wine was yellowish and grassy.

"Taste it. How is it?"

"It's delicious."

"I know, my man. See, if you want to learn about wine, you have to drink the best. That way you can see what the lesser wines are trying to do and where they come up short. You want to know sculpture, you look at Michael-faggolo. You want to know fresco, go to Italy and look at *The Last Supper* by my man Leonardo."

"I've never been."

"Never? My man, go! Go to the Convento di Santa Maria Delle Grazie in Milano. Go while you can still get a good hard-on. Go there, my man, and drink the wine and eat the food and see that beautiful fresco."

He stuck his nose deep into his glass and inhaled.

"Jesus and his twelve apostles were dick-sucky-pooh," he said, after he'd exhaled. "I know it. Twelve guys out in the desert together? He probably gave Matthew a little quick-dick. Peter and Paul too. Judas was straight. That's why he betrayed them."

"Interesting theory," I said.

"Oh, that is beautiful," he said, tasting the wine. "Now tell me what the fuck happened down there last night?"

"Delilah's pissed?"

"My man, she's got a sandstorm in her pussy she's so pissed."

"Shit. I'm really sorry. It was busy. It was packed. Some guy was playing his harmonica down there and pissing everyone off."

"Who?"

"I don't know who he was."

"Some piece of tar paper?"

"He was black."

"I figured it was some nigger."

"How can a guy who loves black music be so racist?"

"My man. I hate everybody. The rice and beans, the white trash that don't burn, the lampshades. It's my grandmother's fault. She was a Polack who hated everybody. She was part-chosen herself and still, she hated Jews. I swear to God, I'm brought up with nothing but prejudice. I apologize. What happened next?"

"I told him to stop. He kept playing. I told him again. He kept playing. It got busier. I lost my cool. I told him to stop playing or I'd shove it up his ass."

"Good. Then what?"

"He accused me of being a racist."

"Fuck that fucking lowlife. Then what?"

"He started to play again. I grabbed him by the collar and threw him out."

"My man, you must have grabbed him pretty hard, because you ripped the collar and he called Delilah, screaming bloody murder. She wants you to apologize and pay for a new shirt."

"I'll pay for it."

"And when he comes in, make nicey-pooh to him. Okay?"

"Okay."

"I'm gonna put on some music. You like gospel?"

"I love it."

"This is the good shit. Dixie Hummingbirds, Soul Stirrers, lotta good shit."

Sam Cooke's voice filled the room, and I started to feel good.

"Then what happened?" he asked.

"The Priest was trying to buy drinks for everyone."

"Simon, who wants to suck a dick?" Simon, fittingly, was the defrocked Priest's name. "He can't even pay for his *own* drinks."

"I know. I ignored him."

"Good. Then what?"

"I was making a blender drink. He was distracting me, and I dropped the spoon too far down into the blender and broke it."

"Simon suck-a-dick distracted you?"

"Yeah. And then I was so pissed I threw the blender against the wall."

"Was he hitting on you?"

"No. Just annoying me. It was my fault."

"Don't defend that dicksucker. It wasn't your fault!"

"Sorry about the blender."

"Who gives a fuck about the blender?"

"This wine is really fucking good, and this music is really fucking good."

"I know, my man. I knew you'd like it. What happened next?"

"I ran out of ice. I went downstairs. With Annabel."

"She was a dancer, you know. A serious dancer."

"I know."

"She's got a nice dorsal fin, and she's a good kid."

"Dorsal fin?"

"Ass."

"She does."

"You should give her a little quick-dick."

"I did."

"Good. She needs it and it's good for you. So you go downstairs for ice.

Then what?"

"While we were down there, my wife came in. When I came back up, I heard Simon talking to her."

"Oh, shitsy-pooh. What was he saying?"

"He was telling her that I was downstairs with one of the waitresses. He said we had a thing going and that she should take a number."

"He said that to your wife?"

"Yeah. And then she ran out crying."

"And that was when you called him a dicksucker?"

"Yeah."

"Good. He deserved it. Don't worry, my man. I'll talk to Delilah and straighten it all out."

I'd drunk all my wine. The Dixie Hummingbirds were singing "The Last Mile." I was feeling a bit blurry.

"I'm sorry," I said.

"Don't be," he said, pouring me more.

"I don't think he did it on purpose."

"Of course he did it on purpose. Everything's on purpose. His marriage is fucked up, so he wants to fuck up your marriage."

"Yeah. And it was bad. Bad timing."

"Why was it bad timing?"

"Because I'm raising my nephew and he's having a rough time. I don't want to, you know, split with my wife and leave him."

"I forgot. I forgot about the kid. Good kid, right?"

"He's a *great* kid. He wants to be an archeologist."

"Tell him if he's gonna be an archeologist he's got to steal. You only make about twenty thousand a year, so if you find an antiquity, you take it. Go to any museum, it's sixty-five-percent forgeries. The Popey-poohs stole all the good shit. They got Phidias right there in the Vatican. They stole everything. Pissed off the dune-coons. Personally, I like Aztec, Mixtec, Toltec. All the tecs. But the best is that Olmec shit. You know those Negroid heads that come out of there? As tall as you and I. Olmec slaps the fucking piss out of the Mayan shit. I got infatuated with it. I'll talk to your nephew. Is he gonna go to college for that?"

I looked down. I'd finished three glasses of wine, and I felt drunk.

"I don't know. He's having some trouble."

"What kind of trouble?"

"Some psychological stuff. The school social worker sent him to Bellevue for an evaluation. They're worried because his mother was schizophrenic. And he's having what they think are some paranoid delusions."

"Oh shit. And now, thanks to Simon suck-a-dick, you got your wifey-pooh angry at you?"

"Yes."

"And little Annabel is probably pissed off too."

I don't know why I told him. Maybe the wine. But it just came out.

"And she's pregnant," I said.

"Oh fuck…"

"Yeah."

"She shouldn't a done that to you, my man."

"I don't think she did it to me."

"She tell you she was on the pill?"

"She said she knew her cycle. She said it was okay to come inside her."

"Oh my man, she shouldn't a done that."

"I should've been using a condom."

"Why? I hate condoms."

"Because I'm married, and this kid is depending on me."

"Stop blaming yourself for so much shit! I can see exactly what happened, clear as day, my man. She got that alcoholic-comic boyfriend who can't get a good hard on; her clock is ticking; she wanted a kid; she trapped you. I would make her get rid of it. That's what I would do."

"Maybe I want her to have it. I don't know."

"You have to know. Who the fuck else would know?"

"A part of me wants it."

"Okay. Have it."

"But then I lose the kid I'm raising now."

"Why?"

"Because I'm the only one he trusts, and if he finds out I fucked around on Lily and got a waitress pregnant, I'll be a fuckup like everybody else in his life. And I'm really worried about him right now."

"What is he: sixteen, seventeen?"

"Seventeen."

"Then he ain't a kid anymore."

"He's a young seventeen."

"My man. Next year, he's eighteen. He'll be okay."

"I hope so. I really fucking do. But right now he's got a psychiatrist at Bellevue evaluating him for post-traumatic stress disorder, and they're talking about putting him in some clinical trial. I don't know what the fuck I was thinking."

"You weren't thinking. Your dick was thinking."

"I fucking fucked up."

"My man, don't be so hard on yourself. Look, your marriage was no good; you were discontent; you left. Then you got back with her for the kid. You did your best. It didn't work out. Right?"

"Right."

"Okay. So if you want to be a stand-up guy, you can still be a stand-up guy. You want to have a kid of your own with Annabel, have a kid of your own with Annabel. But do it now, because she ain't getting any younger and you ain't getting any younger."

"What do I tell the boy?"

"He don't have to know right away. Live with the wife until the kid gets straightened out. And when he turns eighteen and goes off to college, you move in with Annabel. Pick up eighteen extra shifts to pay for the whole mess if that's what you want. It'll take some balls, but you got more balls than a pinball machine. See, I never wanted a kid because I never wanted to perpetuate myself, but if that's what you want to do, do it."

He took out a moist little brick of something brown and put it on the table.

"C'mon, my man, you need to get high and relax a little."

"Nah. I can't. Thanks."

"Jesus! That Jew guilt has your brain in knots. Get fuckin' high!"

"I'm good with the wine."

"C'mon, Rabbi! All mother-fuck-face-week long you got to deal with the donkeys down there. The Library of Losers. And now you got a whole lot more shit on your shoulders, and you're not going to relax a little? Well, mother-fuck-that! Have some fun and get fuckin' high, my man! This is good hash."

The hash was very strong. I got very high. When we finished the Montrachet, he opened a Clos de Mouches. The afternoon wore on, and I got hungry. We ate jellied pig's feet he'd picked up in Chinatown. They were good with the wine. Later, when the sun went down, he fried some sausage links in pork fat and opened a bottle of Burgundy. The sausages were good, and the wine was good. I was drunk and high and felt good.

Then he brought out the coke.

It had a pinkish tint. He said it was pure.

I had done it a couple of times before and swore I'd never do it again.

It was getting dark. I was very stoned on the hash. Mahalia was singing, "Get a little higher."

He told me to do a line and I did.

"How do you feel?"

"Good."

"I know. This ain't that Hundred and Twenty-Fifth Street drip. How do you feel now?"

The intensity of the rush pulled me up from my chair.

"I feel...very focused," I said. "I feel good."

"Good. I hate to see you so depressed."

"Yeah..."

"You're goddamn right, 'yeah.' That's why I hate the Jew in me. Jews care about everyone else in the world, but they have no idea how to take care of themselves. You gotta start concentrating on you. You gotta know yourself. What turns you on. What you want. Not what everybody else wants. What you want."

He went back to the stereo and put on the Dixie Hummingbirds.

The apartment was dark. I sat back down and listened.

When I was a kid I used to go digging in record bins for gospel. Or I'd listen to the low end of the radio late at night, looking for the Dixie Hummingbirds, or the Soul Stirrers, or Marion Williams. Now James Walker was singing, "I'm not worried, I'm not worried," and I found myself grateful that there was still a voice left like that in the world. It sounded like there were briars and brambles and dirt and earth in his voice. It was a voice that grabbed me by the balls, worked its way up through my belly, laid claim to my heart, and then shot up through my throat, leaving trails of salty tears on my face.

I looked over at Vincent. His eyes were brimming over.

"I know, my man. It hurts me too. Nobody appreciates this. I put it on, the barstool-sniffers don't even notice it."

At ten o'clock I called Lily. I told her I couldn't come home because I was drunk and didn't want the boy to see me. She asked if I was with the girl from the bar. I said I wasn't.

When I got home four hours later, she was waiting for me. She looked small, hard, and distant. I admitted I'd smoked some hash. I told her it wouldn't happen again. She said she thought I should move out. I said I wasn't going to. I thought we needed to stay together at least until the boy went to college.

That night, I slept on the couch.

The Comic and the Clinic

When I woke up it was almost noon, and I was badly hungover. I went to the window and pulled the shade. The streets were black, shiny, and wet; the buildings shrouded in fog. I went down to the bodega for coffee and a roll. The coffee was bitter and strong. The roll helped settle my stomach. I stood under the red-and-yellow awning and thought for a while. Then I began walking down Amsterdam Avenue toward Annabel's apartment.

Crossing 103rd, I saw, under a big colorful umbrella, a woman walking with her little girl. The girl had big saucer eyes and brown curly hair. She was wearing a pink leotard, white tutu, and red rain boots. Every ten yards or so, she would stop and try a pirouette or a jump, or, standing on her tippy-toes, she would stretch her arms toward the sky and stick her tongue out to taste the rain while her mother called for her to come back under the umbrella so her costume wouldn't get wet.

At 96th, I watched as they headed west, the girl jumping up and down like a little Mexican jumping bean, splashing in whatever puddle she could find, and the mother reaching for her hand, telling her to hurry. I watched them until they were out of sight and then kept walking south, sipping the bitter, now-lukewarm coffee out of the disintegrating Styrofoam cup and sticking close to the buildings to keep dry.

At 75th, I turned left. In daylight, the vestibule looked unfamiliar. I pushed the button next to her name. The intercom was broken, but she buzzed me in.

And then I started climbing the stairs that I had climbed while looking up at her torn tights, her pale dancer's legs, her incongruously pigeon-toed walk; the landing where I had pinned her against the wall and had kissed her hard and deep; the landing on the second floor, where I had torn at the torn tights and had put my fingers against her and inside her; the landing where I had dropped to my knees, hungry to taste her; the stairs I had stumbled up as she unbuckled my belt, as I tore at the last remnants of the torn tights, telling her I was sorry and promising to pay for a new pair—both of us laughing. Beyond the door where she'd fumbled for her keys as I kissed her neck and ran my fingers along the delicate bones of her rib cage was the room with the high ceilings and the picture window that framed the hackberry tree that grew from the courtyard below and the spider web cracks on the walls; in the center of that room, the worn, brownish couch with its nubby couch covers—the couch where she'd knelt before me like a hungry supplicant as I awkwardly kicked off a shoe or tried to wrestle off a pant leg; the couch that she stood on, legs spread, so I could stare up at her swollen parts before she lowered herself with great concentration onto my dumb thickness; behind that couch, the doorway that led to the bedroom and the bed she had lain face down, because she wanted, she told me later, to be hurt by me; and the bathroom and shower where she had washed me so that Lily wouldn't smell our sex.

"I could fuck you forever," she'd once said.

I hadn't answered.

What would it be like to live here? With her?

I was standing, now, in front of her door. She didn't know I was coming. She hadn't heard my voice. I could have been a UPS guy or somebody with a wrong apartment number. If I wanted, I could turn and leave. She wouldn't know I'd come.

What would it really be like to live with her?

I thought about the baby. I imagined a little girl. A girl like the one I had just seen dancing down Amsterdam Avenue. A little girl stomping in rain puddles. A little girl whom I could scoop up and cover with kisses. A little red-haired ballerina looking up at me.

I knocked.

The Comic answered.

If he wasn't sixty, he looked it. He had just pulled on a pair of pants but not a shirt. He had a sagging gut, a sour face, unruly hair, and tortoise shell glasses.

He put his arm up on the doorframe. He hadn't washed.

I started to introduce myself.

"I know who you are," he said, scratching the back of his neck like an ape in a zoo. "Looking for your girlfriend?"

I had gotten accustomed to telling half-truths and telling them quickly.

"She's not my girlfriend."

"She's not here."

"Do you know where she is?"

"She said she had something she had to take care of."

"What?"

"A problem."

"What problem?"

"She didn't say. She doesn't tell me everything. Like what douche bag bartender she's fucking at work."

"I'm not fucking her."

"Oh. Sorry. I must have gotten it wrong."

"Where did she go?"

"Why do you care where she went?"

"I care."

"You didn't seem to care when your friend was calling every night and bullying her on the phone, trying to convince her to have an abortion, when what she really wanted was to have a kid. I use the word *wanted*, because once she found out how seriously fucking depraved you and your friend were, I don't think she wanted it as much. Pretty disgusting to have your friend do your dirty work. But I guess that's how the world is: a big bowl of shit."

"How do you know what my friend was doing?"

"How? I heard her crying. I was worried about her. I picked up the fucking phone and I listened. That's how."

I was feeling very, very hung-over, and I couldn't say anything, so I just stood there taking his shit.

"You know, I think I can put the pieces together," the comic continued. "You were fucking her. She got pregnant. You got scared. Wanted her to have the abortion, so your wife wouldn't find out. But your wife found out anyway and kicked you out. That's why you look like a piece of wet dogshit. So now you come over here thinking maybe you want her to have it after all. That about right, you fucking coward?"

"It's not right. It's not that simple. And I have a kid who's depending on me."

"If you have a kid who's depending on you, maybe you shouldn't have been fucking her. Maybe you should have used a condom. Or maybe you should have come in her ass."

"I did."

He dropped his arm from the doorway and took a step toward me. I knew that if it came to a physical fight I could beat him badly. But for some reason, I was scared of him.

"You know," he said, putting his face six inches from mine, "there's a guy I see walking around the Village whenever I'm down there in the daytime. He's probably about sixty-five, I would guess. Bartends somewhere on Bleecker. Dresses like it's 1970. Still in pretty good shape for an old guy. I see him walking his dog, getting coffee, reading the paper. That's his life. Sleep late. Get yourself breakfast. Get some air in the park. Go back to work. Serve drinks until four in the morning and listen to assholes until your body gives out, and then you may as well go die in the park because you can't do anything else.

"She told me about you. She's kind of an open book. She tells all the men in her life about all the others. You want to know what she said about you? She said you were smart and talented and a little bit lost. She said you'd been a part-time professor, or part-time theater director, or something like that? But she told me you don't really do much about it. And then about month ago she told me she was wrong. Maybe you weren't so smart or talented after all. She said you were a loser. A coward. Too scared to try to get what you really wanted. I'm sure she told you about me. I'm an old, fat alcoholic. I piss in the bed. My dick doesn't work without Viagra. And even then, it doesn't always work. But guess what? I have talent, I have a career, and I have a life. I'm not a bartender. I'm not waiting on people. So have a nice fucking day, asshole."

He slammed the door in my face. I left. I walked down the hallway and down the stairs, running my fingers along the banister. Outside, it was still raining.

I only knew one clinic off the top of my head—Planned Parenthood on Bleecker. I couldn't get a cab, so I ran over to 72nd and got the express train downtown. At 14th I switched to the local and got off at Christopher. It seemed like there was nobody on the street. When I got to Bleecker and Lafayette I saw two figures under a black umbrella. One of the figures was Annabel. She was with Lenore, the songwriter. She was leaning on her for support. She looked up and saw me. She froze.

The only sound was the sound of the rain and a few cars passing.

"What the fuck is he doing here?" said Lenore.

"Did you just come from my apartment?" Annabel asked.

The rain was so loud I could barely hear her.

"Yes," I said.

"Did you talk to him?"

"Yes."

"Oh God. Why?"

"I was looking for you."

"Why didn't you call me?"

"I did. You didn't answer."

"Does he know?"

"Know what?"

"Does he know where I went? Does he know what I'm doing?"

I guessed that he would take her back and that he wouldn't let on that he knew.

"No," I lied. "He doesn't."

"Did you tell him we were fucking? Did you admit it?"

"No."

"Because I need someone there for me."

"I didn't tell him anything. He's waiting for you."

"If you fucked it up for me, I'll call your fucking wife."

"You should call his wife anyway," said Lenore. "Why is he the only one who doesn't have to face any fucking consequences?"

"Because," said Annabel, throwing her hands in the air, "because, because…"

"That's not your fucking problem," said Lenore.

"Oh God," she said, doubling over. "It hurts."

She grabbed the railing of the subway station. I went toward her.

"Don't you fucking touch her," said Lenore, moving to cover her under the umbrella.

"Oh God," said Annabel, looking down. "I'm bleeding all over the place. And these fucking cramps."

Lenore looked at me with hatred.

"I'm sorry," I said, not sure whom I was apologizing to.

"Why are you still here?" asked Lenore.

I slumped against the railing. Annabel, huddled under the umbrella, her hand on her gut, looked up at me.

"Please don't tell me you left her. Please don't tell me she threw you out. Please don't tell me you wanted it."

"Don't talk to him," said Lenore.

"Please don't tell me that, okay? Please don't tell me anything. Just go. Please. Go."

I didn't move.

Lenore took her by the arm and led her out to Lafayette. A minute later they hailed a cab heading uptown.

I watched it disappear in the rain.

Annabel didn't look back.

The Tombs

In September, Sparrow turned eighteen.

He was still seeing the social worker and was an outpatient at Bellevue. He took his SATs. He did well. We began the process of applying to schools. Some days he was lucid; other days the paranoia was too much and he retreated to his room.

He spent more and more time on the Internet.

Seven times he had signed up for the service; seven times we had refused to give our consent. Eventually, the seven different recruiting officers connected the dots, conferred, and decided in concert to block any more attempts at his enlisting. This was interpreted as further proof that the government was against him. He lost touch with his other friends and began spending more time with the Rossmans.

He would come home from their townhouse, sit down to dinner, and launch into long jeremiads on the evils of the federal government, the loss of state's rights, the long-term dangers of going off the gold standard, and the evils of the big city.

"*Those people*," he said, righteously waving a fork in Lily's face, "don't know how to take care of their basic needs—how to grow food, how to hunt, how to build a house. I'm sorry, but they're parasites."

"What do you mean when you say '*those people*?'" asked Lily.

"The people who go to my school, their parents, the people who live on the Upper West Side."

"Okay," said Lily, "so you mean me."

"Well, I think we're all hypocrites. We city-folk hate guns and slaughterhouses, but then we go the supermarket to buy our carefully trimmed and packaged meat."

"Just because I hate guns and want animals treated humanely and shop in a supermarket doesn't make me a useless parasite," said Lily.

"It's not just you. I didn't mean to single you out. I think we're all parasites, me included," he said, looking glumly down at his dinner.

"But you did just single me out."

"Well, I'm sorry. But to be honest, I've sat here night after night and listened to you ridiculing the rural population."

"I never ridiculed the rural population!"

"Yes, you have! 'They're so stupid.' 'If you're not a Democrat, you're an idiot.' 'If you're not pro-choice, you must be a moron.' 'If you didn't vote for Al Gore, you must be an idiot.'"

"If you voted for Bush, you *are* an idiot."

"Jefferson was right," said the boy, pushing his plate away. "We should have stayed an agrarian republic. Cities are corrupt, and their citizens are a bunch of effete snobs."

"What do you think?" asked Lily, turning toward me.

"I'm just impressed that the kid uses words like *agrarian* and *effete*."

"Thanks so much for defending me," she said, before bolting toward the bedroom and slamming the door.

The boy had stopped eating but kept talking. He was getting manic.

The United States was a Democratic theocracy. Corporate elites were planning on taking over the world. This was a natural outgrowth of the great joint-stock trading companies, royal charters, and monopolies. Some of it sounded like his language; some of it didn't—what teenager talks about joint-stock trading companies and royal charters?

I suspected Karl Rossman's influence, and I didn't like it. I wanted him to spend more time with Asma's family, but he refused because he thought the feds were monitoring all Muslims. Then he decided that the feds were monitoring the Rossmans. I couldn't keep track of the competing conspiracy theories. The walrus psychiatrist tried different antidepressants. They dulled him, so he didn't like it. In my ignorance, I told him he didn't have to take them. He got more depressed, more manic, more paranoid.

Everything in my life felt like it was getting darker.

Annabel had quit the bar. I went up to Vincent's more often. I needed the escape. The winter came.

By January, it was clear that the country was gearing up for war with Iraq, seeking to destroy weapons of mass destruction that didn't exist. On the fifteenth there was a big protest in New York City. In February, there was an even bigger one.

Lily went with a friend. I went alone.

A half an hour after I got home, the phone was ringing.

It was the boy. He'd been arrested. They were holding him at the Tombs.

Thirty minutes later I was downtown.

The courtroom had a high ceiling and lots of wood paneling. The predominant tones were depressing: the institutional-green walls, the attorneys in gray suits, the cops in dark blue, and the sickly yellow-green tiles of the holding cell.

Under a banner that read, *In God We Trust*, sat the judge, a black woman who exuded royalty. In front of her, at the tilted wooden podium, a short, balding public defender stood with his hand gently placed on the elbow of a handcuffed young black woman. Surrounding them were a horseshoe-shaped series of desks occupied by clerks, a photographer, a stenographer, and other public defenders. One of the court officers had a long, blow-dried mane of gray hair and a well-kept beard and moustache. I thought he looked like Serpico. The other cops were big muscular guys with shaved heads, tattoos, and goatees.

I found a spot on one of the worn wooden benches and settled in.

On the judge's left hand, the mousy prosecutor—her slight, pale figure barely visible behind her stacks of files, her thin voice barely audible over the disorienting echoes of murmured conversation—began the proceedings.

"Your Honor, the people are requesting bail in the amount of one thousand dollars in cash. Your Honor, on February fifth at approximately twenty-two hundred hours, the defendant was seen stealing an ice cream bar from the Pathmark on one fifty East One Hundred and Twenty-Fifth Street—"

"You Honor," interrupted the defender, his hand still on his client's trembling arm, "the defendant has a child in college."

"A child?" asked the judge. "How could this child have a child?

"And she is trying to address her treatment issues," continued the defender. "She would like to plead guilty."

"Is it true you took an ice cream bar without paying for it?" asked the judge.

"Yes, Your Honor," answered the woman.

"And are you pleading guilty because you are, in fact, guilty?"

After an inaudible, quick conference, the woman answered yes.

The judge offered five days of community service or thirty in jail.

"Take the community service!" shouted a man who was sitting behind me.

The woman took the community service. When she turned to leave the courtroom, I saw that her face was black and blue with a bruise under the left eye that looked like it was the result of repeated beatings—like the permanent swelling, I thought, that I'd seen under the eyes of boxers who'd fought long past their prime. The defender, his brown corduroy jacket stained and dirty, walked her to the door, never taking his hand from her arm.

The next defendant was a tough-looking Eastern European in his late thirties.

"Your Honor," began the prosecutor, "the people are requesting bail in the amount of five thousand dollars. The defendant was seen punching and choking the witness. The attack left deep scratches on her neck and chest. He has a history of domestic abuse. There's an outstanding warrant in Kings County from 1999 and in Duchess County from 2001."

"Your Honor," said the defender, "they live together. His girlfriend is in the courtroom. She sought me out. She persisted in wanting to speak to me. They have a five-year-old child together. She has no job. She doesn't want an order of protection."

The judge looked at the defendant. She wasn't buying it. "I'm issuing an order of protection," she said.

More defendants emerged from the Tombs below.

"Your Honor, the people are requesting bail in the amount of twenty-five thousand dollars."

"Your Honor, the defendant attempted to take the victim's cell phone and then punched the victim in the face."

"Your Honor, this man kicked a stroller with a four-year-old kid in it."

The boy still hadn't appeared.

And then, without warning, the courtroom became very quiet. A phalanx of ten court officers stepped forward.

A very muscular black man with a shaved head was led in. Craning his neck, he strained toward the court photographer, contorting his face like some strange sea creature peering into the mask of an intrepid deep-sea diver.

Then he was led to the judge.

"Your honor," began the prosecutor, "the people are requesting that the defendant be held without bail. The charge is murder in the first degree. The defendant shot his pregnant girlfriend five years ago. There was an order of protection against him at that time. He has a long juvenile record. Detective Moth states that the defendant admitted to the shooting. Apparently a neighborhood drug dealer gave him a thousand dollars and a gun, and told him to clear the doorstep at Lenox and One Hundred and Fortieth Street. He killed one person and wounded three others."

Bail was not granted. Handcuffed, the still-grimacing man was led back down into the honeycombed underground labyrinth of cells.

I went up to the rail and got the court clerk's attention.

"That guy they just took away isn't down there in the general population, is he?" I asked. "My kid is down there, and I don't want him in a cell with that guy."

The clerk assured me that he wasn't and told me to sit back down. I did.

The next guy in was wearing gray sweatpants and a blue fleece. On the seat of his sweatpants was a brownish splotch. He had obviously soiled himself. The blue fleece was partly covered in dried vomit.

"Your Honor," began the public defender. "They found a bag of heroin. Seems to me it's a personal-use amount. My client is fifty-six. He's legally blind. Lives in an apartment with his brother, who's also legally blind, and his ninety-seven-year-old mother. Judge, can we just clear him for medical attention? Can we get him cleaned up and straightened out enough so that he can go back and

Seth Kanor

help his brother take care of his mother?"

The judge agreed.

As he walked by I saw that the cops had used two pairs of handcuffs on him so that his hands wouldn't be held so tightly behind his back.

He was the last man they arraigned that night. The boy hadn't been brought out.

I spoke again with the court clerk, the one who looked like Serpico.

He told me they'd been too busy to get to everyone. He checked for the boy's name and told me to come back in the morning.

I told him the boy had psychological problems, that he was an outpatient at Bellevue being treated for paranoia, and that I didn't think he should be down there overnight.

The clerk told me he would make sure that he was segregated from the general population. He said he'd give him his own cell with a pay phone and that the boy could call collect and talk as long as he wanted. Other than having the guards keep a close watch on him, that was the best he could do.

When I got home after midnight, Lily was hysterical.

The phone rang.

It was a collect call.

"Are you okay?" I asked.

There was no answer. I could hear him breathing, but he wouldn't talk. I kept calling his name. Lily sat close, her hand in mine. Her body felt as if it had hardened to me, or maybe it was my flesh that had hardened to hers, but still, she held to me. I kept talking into the void, calling his name and telling him that I was there and that I would be there all night if need be, if he wanted. Finally, he said something.

"They're listening," he whispered. "I know they're listening."

"They probably are, but we can still talk. Is there anybody in there with you?"

"No. This guy with a beard and moustache came down and moved me to my own cell. He said you asked him to."

"I did."

236

"You came? You were up in the courtroom?"

"Yes."

"So you saw who I was in with?"

"Some of them."

"It's pretty grim down here. Everybody was making fun of the guy who shit himself."

"In the gray sweatpants?"

"Yeah. There's some pretty rough guys in here."

"I saw him. It was sad."

He was silent for a minute and then spoke.

"I'm scared I'll end up like that," he said.

"You won't."

"You don't know that."

"You won't."

I could hear his voice go hollow. That's what it did when he was having a breakdown. I told him he had to keep talking to me.

"I'll stay on the phone until you get tired, and I'll come get you in the morning. Okay?

"Okay…"

I asked him what had happened.

"I was at the rally," he answered.

Lily, still next to me, heard and smiled.

"You just made Lily very happy."

"Can she hear me?"

"She's right here."

I chuckled a little. It started to feel like one of our dinners.

"I thought you didn't like the antiwar movement," she called into the phone.

"I hate it when they disrespect the president. But I don't want people dying. I don't want them dying for nothing."

"I don't either," said Lily.

"Tell us what happened?" I asked.

"I walked over through the park. It was cold. One guy, he was dressed as the Statue of Liberty, and he was in a cage. I guess he had a good point, right?"

"I guess so," I answered. "And then what happened?"

"Everyone was chanting that chant, you know?"

"Which chant?" asked Lily.

"What do we want? Peace. When do we want it?"

"Now," said Lily.

"I think it was making me a little crazy."

His voice started to sound more normal. He told me that the cops, the helicopters, the crowds, and the barricades had freaked him out.

"And then they came through on the horses. They were wearing leather jackets. They started pushing people. There was a pretty blonde girl in a red knit hat who was standing next to me, and one of the cops told her to move, but she couldn't because we were penned in. When one of them threatened her with a nightstick, I jumped in to defend her. And that was when they put me in those white plastic handcuffs."

I asked if he'd heard any of the music.

"I heard Richie Havens. He was singing that song "Freedom." It was pretty beautiful, I thought. I didn't know there were any voices like that left in the world."

"There are," I said.

"But fewer?"

"Maybe. But there are still some."

Lily was still next to me, but she was exhausted. I told her to go to bed. She got on the line and told him she loved him. Then she kissed me and gently closed the door and went to bed.

I kept talking to him. He spoke more about how he loved Richie Havens and asked me about other musicians, but at some point—I don't know when—we got back on the topic of the war and the Middle East and terrorism, and it sounded like he was getting manic. I think it was starting to get light out.

And then, as the city traffic slowly began its flow and the sounds of horns began to echo through the still empty streets, and that particular shade of pale blue began to flood across the still-dark sky, I felt myself exhausted and slipping away. But I could still hear his voice, echoing in the cell, sounding more high-pitched than usual, as if he were a bird in a cage, but I wasn't sure if I was dreaming or if he was still talking to me, and then everything went black.

I had a dream concerning the moon.

The River

Suddenly the city was awake and the subways were rumbling, the taxis swerving, the workmen shouting, the passing sirens crying. And underneath the rumble, swerve, shout, and cry, the never-ending hum of the grid was humming its never-ending hum.

The sun, shaking off the salt and brine of the ocean, had climbed quickly, like a goat, up the steeply stepped buildings, its lengthening rays flooding the cross streets and lifting the curtain on the city at work: the jackhammers jack-hammering, the erectors erecting erector-set scaffolding—the endlessly multiplying crisscrosses of pipe chasing after the sun.

It was past ten o'clock.

In a panic, I grabbed my coat and ran out the door.

By the time I got to the courtroom at 100 Centre Street, the boy was gone.

The clerk told me the judge had given him an ACD.

"What's that?" I asked.

"Adjudication in contemplation of dismissal," he explained.

Back outside, the sun had disappeared.

Snow was starting to fall, and the city was closing in on itself.

I called the school; he wasn't there. Nobody was. It was Sunday. I called his friends. They hadn't seen or heard from him. He wasn't at Bellevue, and he wasn't with his social worker. Late in the afternoon, I went to the precinct to file a missing persons report. The wind was blowing strangely from the south. By ten o'clock, the temperature had dropped into the single digits, the fire hydrants and garbage pails had disappeared, the cars had turned into white burial mounds, and I could hear the scraping of the plows—the sound of the city grinding to a halt. Lily was in a trance. Her face had hardened into a mask, and she was pacing around the apartment as if she were an actor in a Greek tragedy waiting backstage for her cue.

At midnight, Laroche called. Apparently, the boy had taken the last bus out from the Port Authority to Monticello and had called from a pay phone. Laroche had picked him up at the station. He was exhausted but safely in bed. Lily started crying and clapping her hands. I told Laroche we'd be up the next day.

By morning, the Port Authority had been shut down, but the Croton–Harmon line was still running.

I called Pierce and asked if I could come up and borrow his car. As I was getting ready to leave, Laroche called back. The boy had flown the coop.

"He said he wanted to go for a walk in the woods. I told him to wait until you got up here. A few minutes ago I heard the door slam. He took one of my guns."

"What did he take?"

"A twenty-gauge pump shotgun."

I hung up.

"What happened?" asked Lily.

"He bolted. Into the woods, apparently."

"Oh God. Should I go with you?"

"No. You stay here in case he calls."

I went into the bedroom and called Vincent to let him know I wouldn't be in that night.

I told him what had happened.

"Why are you talking so quiet?"

"Because if my wife hears that the kid is wandering around in the woods with a shotgun, she'll fucking go berserk."

"All right. You gotta piece?"

"A gun?"

"Yeah."

"No."

"You should."

"Why?"

"My man, you just told me he's walking around in the woods up there in Cally-fucking-coon with a twenty-gauge shotgun."

"I'm not going to shoot him."

"I know that, but he might need backup. You don't know how it is up there. A lot of it is off the grid. No electricity, no law enforcement, no law, no nothing. It's all mobile homes, run-down shacks and trailers. It's dogpatch. It's Clorox-and-Wonderbread-white-supremacist-mountain-motherfuckers, and they're armed to the teeth. They got a grand-fucking-Kleagle living up there, and if you walk deep enough into those woods, you'll hear machine-gun fire. Okay, my man? And let me tell you something: if your boy's fucking around up there in the wrong place or with the wrong guys, he could get caught in the middle of some serious shit. And so could you."

"If somebody has a gun, I'll call the cops."

"I don't think you understand, shit-steen. You're gonna be in the boonies with two feet of snow on the ground. There's no cops to call. Especially if he went across the river into the Pennsylvania side. I know that country. I'm from there. It's a no-man's land, and I wouldn't go without something. Come over here, and I'll hook you up."

I looked at the clock on the dresser. I wanted to catch the ten-twenty out of Grand Central.

I could hear Lily's footsteps. She was coming toward the door.

"Vincent," I said quietly, "I'm not going up with a gun."

"Listen, Rab. You're going into enemy territory, so don't give me that left-wing-liberal shit about how you're safer without one."

"No. Thank you."

"You get your motherfucking ass over here, and you get it over here right now. You don't got to use it, but it's a nice thing to wave in someone's face if you have to."

I told him I'd come, stuffed a change of clothes into a bag and told Lily everything would be okay. She looked up and put both hands on my cheeks but didn't say anything. Then I stumbled out into the snow.

I needed coffee. The Spanish bodega was closed, but the Arabs were open.

The streets hadn't been plowed, and there were no cabs out. It took thirty minutes to get to 79th.

Vincent was waiting at the door. The table was set—this time, not with wineglasses.

"I think you should take the forty-five. Hit someone with a nine-millimeter, they'll keep on running, but with the forty-five, the round goes out real slow, and when it hits you it spreads out and knocks you right the fuck down. It's a bad motherfucker. Your dick doesn't exist with this. This is your new best friend. You know how to load it?"

"No."

"You ever shoot a gun?"

"No."

"It's all right, my man. It ain't your fault you were brought up by liberals. What time's your train?"

"Ten twenty."

He looked at his watch. "Okay. Let's do this fast."

He showed me how to load the magazine, how to slide the magazine into the gun, how to rack the slide, and how to put a bullet in the chamber. He emptied the gun and had me dry fire it just to get the feel. Then he reloaded the weapon and handed it to me, barrel pointed down.

"When you come back from Donkeyville, I'll teach you how to take it apart, how to lubricate it properly. You got an inside pocket in your leather jacket?"

"Yeah."

"Put it in there."

"I'm not gonna carry a loaded gun in my jacket."

"Take it with the magazine separate if you're worried about it going off."

My hands were shaking as I fumbled with the weapon. He took it.

"Just pop it out like this, my man."

I didn't have time to argue. I figured I'd just take it and leave it in the car.

"There's nothing in the chamber?" I asked.

He racked the slide.

It was so quick I couldn't tell what he was doing.

"Don't worry, my man," he said, smiling, "you're good."

I put the gun in my right pocket, the magazine in my left.

"Listen to me, Rabbi. I want you to load it when you get up there. You can shoot it in the air if you want. But load it. Scare the fuck out of somebody."

"I will."

I rushed down the dark stairs, worried I would miss the train out of Grand Central. At the first landing, he called out to me.

"Hey, Rabbi?"

"Yeah?"

"You want me to go with you?"

"No. Thank you."

I got down another flight when he called again.

"My, man?"

"Yes?"

"Let the target pull you in."

The tunnel and a slight rise, and then Spanish Harlem—the gray light of snow and fog, and the monochrome brown of the buildings.

125th Street, housing projects, the bridge over the East River, the Bronx.

The currents calm, the tides slack, the gun heavy in my jacket pocket.

At Spuyten Duyvil, a few hunched figures waiting for a train. Some steps to nowhere. A bend. The Hudson.

Low brush along the river. Power lines sagging—the poles passing by the window as if viewed through a kinescope or flipped through on a deck of cards.

An abandoned factory, an open flame, a sewage treatment plant.

Falling snow dissolving into open chemical pools, mist rising.

Low-slung brick buildings, yellow school busses sitting on a lot.

Twisted strands of pipes like intestines, storage silos like stomachs, a belching-burping sugar refinery surrounded by barbed wire.

Ludlow.

Yonkers. Getty Square. Grand mansions up on the hill with their red clay tennis courts and blue cement swimming pools, housing projects and slums on the twisting streets below. Years ago there was a bar here that catered mostly to midgets. One night, Pierce and I, wearing dark sunglasses, searched for it in his Mustang convertible, cruising like characters in a Fellini film, looking for sex and the grotesque.

On the Manhattan-bound side, advertisements for the Broadway shows. Civilization is south; the woods are north.

A boatyard with boats on blocks for the winter.

Hastings. I walk up the hill. I take the keys. I scrape the windshield.

The engine turns over.

Like a snake, the Tappan Zee winds across the river.

The roads are barely passable.

When I get to Goshen, I overtake two school busses with Hebrew lettering on the side. Tilting their black hats up, the bespectacled, bearded drivers peer down as I pass.

Monticello; the raceway; the Orthodox enclaves; Bethel Woods; Fernwood Assault Weapons; Johnny's Sports TV and Topless—closed, shuttered for good.

Winding roads, snow-covered fields, farms, fog in the gullies, red barns, coal silos, stars on the sides of the houses to denote military service, and gold stars for those wounded in battle.

The Delaware River with its tributaries and feeders.

Birch trees, rock walls.

Creamery Road, Seminary Road, Conklin Hill Road, Baker Hill Road, Rock Run Road, Galilee Road.

Callicoon. Two hotels, both haunted.

I take the small road that runs along the river until I come to a mobile home that sits on cinderblocks. Laroche is distraught. He's called the police. He doesn't know what else to do. He thinks the boy has gone north. Into the woods.

Blindly, I follow.

So much snow had fallen that it was almost impossible to know where the banks of the Delaware ended and the river began. The branches of the evergreens, pines, and firs were straining under the weight of the snow. The birch trees looked like Japanese drawings, as if their outlines had been brushed in with the least possible ink, and the hills were buried in a ghost fog that seemed to be covering the entire northeast. Where the sun was, I couldn't tell. Snow was still falling. All light and sound was diffused; the source impossible to locate.

I thought I heard something. The sounds were weak and indistinct but human. Backsliding in the snow, I labored up a hill, toward the voices. Halfway up, I stopped. The frozen river was below me and, on the other side, what I thought might be the rolling hills of Pennsylvania.

When I got near the ridge, I saw three figures: a man in his fifties with a moustache, dressed in camouflage; an old man wearing wool pants, an oversized parka, and a Russian winter hat; and a teenage boy with thick eyeglasses and what looked like a military uniform. All three were carrying rifles. When I was ten yards away, they turned toward me.

The old man had a large piss stain on his left pant leg. I think he was saying something to me because I saw his mouth moving, but all I could hear were the piercing warbles of a flock of turkeys foraging about fifty yards in the distance. Above us, the sky was darkening.

I came closer to talk to them. I described the boy and asked if they'd seen him. They seemed suspicious. They said they hadn't seen anyone. They told me they were hunting.

"I thought turkeys went south for winter," I said.

"Nope. They stay right here," said the man with the moustache, talking quietly so as not to scare off the birds. "They eat from seeps," he continued. "The groundwater keeps the snow melted, and they can eat around that. They'll walk under the hemlock and white pine. Gives 'em a break from the wind, and the snow's not so deep there. But not today."

"Nope. Not today," echoed the teenager.

The old man's mouth was still moving, but no sound came out.

I looked out at the frozen tundra.

"They'll eat bugs, trees, slugs…whatever they can forage," said the man.

"Crickets," added the kid.

"Yup. They'll eat a cricket. Or they'll go to the farms around here and forage for leftover corn and grain. They do need a lot of water. Probably see more up by the quarry."

I was about to go when one of the turkeys wandered from the flock. The bird had the red face, long nose, wattled neck, and sad eyes of a rich old aristocrat.

The man with the moustache turned and crouched in the snow. We were all quiet, like we were in church. The man brought the shotgun to his shoulder and had the bird in his sights. He wasn't wearing gloves, and I could see that his hands were red and blue from the cold, but they weren't shaking. A shot rang out as the rifle kicked back. Suddenly there was a mad fluttering, and the air was filled with feathers and confusion. The bird that had been hit flapped with its one good wing, which only drove it closer to the ground. Another bird, oblivious to the danger, stood near him, dumbly watching. Somehow, the bird that had been hit managed to get airborne momentarily, but it quickly fell again, the one working wing propelling it into a small series of dying pirouettes. When it finally became still, two other birds came back to it. It revived for a moment, startling its mourners. Then it made a last few, feeble circles and fell alone to the ground.

The teenager dug his fingers into the snow and pulled up the empty shell casing.

"Ammo's really expensive these days," he explained.

"You can reuse those?" I asked.

"Oh yeah," said the guy with the rifle.

Together, we walked toward the dead bird. The man put his rifle aside and knelt down in the snow. He put his ungloved finger in the bloody hole where the eye had been and pushed it right through the head.

"That's where it exited," he said.

The animal's legs twitched, startling me.

"Reflexes," said the teenager.

It was getting colder and darker. The man picked the bird off the ground by its shank. He turned to me before he left.

"Come to think of it," he said, "I did see someone heading toward the quarry."

"Which way?" I asked.

"That way," said the man, pointing to what I thought was northeast. "But I wouldn't go looking around there."

"Why not?"

"Just wouldn't."

The old man was starting to shake pretty badly, and the teenager helped him as all three walked away from me and slowly down the hillside.

I stood alone in the snow, thinking.

I thought about the first time I'd seen the boy after his father's death, swinging a pickax into a piece of shale. I thought about rocks and quarries.

With the winter darkness now descending, I began walking in the direction the man had pointed.

I walked where the turkeys had been, through a grove of white birches shrouded in the white fog and then made my way up another hill. The river had vanished, and all was quiet. I climbed in the snow for a quarter of a mile and came to another ridge and then to a clearing. Below me in the distance was a massive wall of sheer rock, a great mist rising from the depths below.

That was when I heard the machine-gun fire, like a string of Chinese firecrackers, echoing in the hills.

The Quarry

Snow was falling and fog crawling up the great face of rock before drifting back, like the ebbing tides of the ocean, toward the depthless bottom. For a moment, before descending, I turned back, thinking there was someone behind, but all I could see was an amorphous mass of still more fog and still more snow.

All was white, blurring. And then I was walking downward, and the ground was angling away from me, and I felt my boots sliding and felt the snow cold against my ankles, and then wet and cold in the bottoms of my boots.

I put my right foot forward and kept the left behind, as a kind of anchor, but I was sliding down faster and faster.

I was losing my bearings.

The darkness was falling, the day departing. The little light that remained, reflected by the all-encompassing white, had a peculiar intensity.

Nothing seemed real.

Occasionally, if I was close enough, I would see the trunk of a pine or a birch. And then there were no trees. Nothing. Just a smooth, slow slope, and I was carried gently to the bottom of the bottom, where the fog and snow had cleared just enough so that the great mass of rock that I had seen below me was now towering above.

Ahead, the slope gave way to flatness, and a structure appeared, the gray mass of what looked like a large barn made from unfinished timber and roofed with wide wooden slats. On the right side of the barn a roughly built passageway led to a large shed.

As I got closer, about fifty yards away, I saw footprints. It looked like there were two sets. I couldn't tell if they'd been made at the same time, but both led to the rough-hewn front door. I followed them.

The whole thing seemed as though it were something out of a Grimm's fairy tale.

I thought again of the crackle of gunfire I'd heard earlier and remembered the turkey, driving itself into the ground with its one good wing and remembered the hunter, sticking his finger through the socket where the eye had been and through the back of the head to show me where the bullet had exited.

I was sick with dread.

I knocked. There was no answer.

And then I decided that I was not going to walk into some hellhole-shack at the bottom of a quarry in upstate New York with a fucking .45 in my jacket that I didn't know how to use and that made me nauseous to feel next to my shivering flesh. I corkscrewed in the snow, away from the door, clutched at my guts, and threw up a foul-smelling, watery, reddish liquid. I thought I'd been shot. Taking my gloves off, I ran my fingers along my ribs. I hadn't been. I heaved again; more came. When it finally stopped, I wiped the stuff from my lips with one of my gloves, turned back toward the door, and pushed it open.

Inside, I heard the hum of what I thought was a generator, but I couldn't see much, so I ran my hand along the side of the doorframe, searching for a switch.

A dim light came from above. Nobody was there.

In the middle of the room there was a fire pit and a long wooden beam laid across two barrels. Above, animal skins hung from hooks that had been dropped from the ceiling.

Despite the bitter cold, the place smelled of rotting meat and ammonia.

I felt acid in my throat, felt my guts contract, but there was nothing left in my stomach.

My eyes adjusted.

Against the far wall, past the pit, the beam, the barrels, and the skins, there was a workbench with tools: a knife with downturned handles on both sides, a curved knife with a serrated blade, a curved awl, and what looked like a steel haircomb. Next to the workbench was a metal rack stocked with boxes of oatmeal and bran, and bottles of soaps and oils. On the top shelf were five glass jars. In the dim light, I could barely make out the labels: nitric acid, potassium oxide, copper sulfate, sodium chloride, and grape sugar.

On the floor were ten big red cans with the word *gasoline* stenciled in white.

When the world ended, whoever lived in this shack was going to be just fine.

I called out again, but there was still no answer, so I decided to try the narrow passage that led to the shed. Halfway down, I saw a dim, greenish light coming from the far end and thought I could hear someone breathing, but I wasn't sure. Instinctively, my hand went to the gun. I'd forgotten it wasn't loaded.

Something brushed against my face.

I came closer. The door was half-open. I could see only a sliver of the room.

I could hear breathing.

Cautiously, I moved to the middle of the doorway. I could see more of the room now but not everything: a gun rack with three rifles and the same metal shelving I'd seen in the barn, stocked with gallons of water and canned goods.

The sound of the breathing had stopped. I took a small step to my right, and there, sitting on a green army cot, with a green blanket swathed around his shoulders was the boy. It seemed like he was in a trance. Even in the dim, greenish light, I could see that his skin was pale, white, and oily, and acne had broken out across his forehead.

I couldn't see to my immediate right, but I sensed there might be somebody else in the room.

I stayed in the doorway. Without turning to look at me, he spoke.

"Don't come in here," he whispered.

"I won't," I said. "I'll just stay right here. Okay?"

"How did you find me?"

"Claude called last night. He said you'd gone into the woods. I went looking for you. I ran into some hunters. They said they'd seen someone heading toward the quarry. I thought it might be you. I figured you'd need shelter. So I came in. Saw a light on. And I came down the passage, hoping you might be here."

He was still staring at the floor.

"Champ," I asked, "is it okay if I come in now?"

"No. I don't think you should."

"Do you want to come to me?"

"No."

"Okay.

He was still looking down at the floor intently. I looked down too, I think because I didn't know what to say or do next. And then I saw a thin shadow, about a foot and a half long, wavering slightly like the needle on a compass. It was the shadow of the barrel of a shotgun. And someone was pointing it at him.

I needed him to talk. I needed him to talk because I didn't want whoever was holding that shotgun to hear me take the .45 out of my jacket. And I needed him to talk because I didn't want them to hear me slap the magazine in.

But my mind was blank. I couldn't think of anything to say.

He still hadn't looked at me, but at that moment, he turned. His eyes had dark circles underneath and looked unfocussed.

"Why did you leave New York?" I asked.

He didn't answer. I had to keep talking.

"I'm so sorry I didn't get to you down at Centre Street," I said, fumbling with the gun. "I came, but I was too late. I just missed you...Why did you leave Claude's?"

"I think this is where I'm supposed to be," he said.

"Why?"

"I think it's probably the safest place to be when the government comes to get you."

From my vantage point, it didn't look very safe at all, but I didn't say anything as I finally managed to silently pull the weapon from my jacket.

"It's pretty hard to find someone up here," he continued. "Mostly, they leave you alone. And if you can hunt and grow things and keep to yourself and keep basic supplies on hand, maybe you can survive."

His voice sounded dulled, disembodied, but it occurred to me he might be spouting his antigovernment stuff to pacify whoever was in the room with him.

"I can see why you like it," I said, as I tried to fish the magazine out of the other pocket. My hands were shaking badly.

"You can?" he asked.

"I can," I said, terrified I was going to drop the bullets on the floor.

He looked at me. "So you don't think I'm crazy?" he asked.

"No. I don't," I said, stopping all my movement so as not to alarm him.

His eyes went back to the floor; I went back to work.

"You think our government is really messed up?"

"I've never liked our government," I said, which was the truth. "They're not really worthy of our trust, are they?"

"No. I think the founding fathers would be pretty upset if they saw what was going on."

"I do too," I said. "Very upset."

I couldn't see a damn thing, and I couldn't feel if the round was seated properly.

"You know, the Department of Defense has been doing gaming studies on unrest."

"I didn't know that," I said, still struggling.

"We have the lowest food stocks on record, this year."

"I didn't know that."

"It's because there's a fungus in Africa that's attacking the wheat."

"Oh..."

It felt like the rounds were seated in the magazine, and I'd lined it up with the well, but I didn't want to make any noise that would tip off whoever was holding the shotgun, so I just stood there with the gun in one hand and the magazine in the other. The boy had gone back into his shell. He was staring at the floor like a scared animal.

I couldn't wait any longer.

It happened fast.

I slapped at the magazine, missed, and dropped it.

The magazine and metal bullets clattered on the cement. An old, hard-looking man in a battered Stetson stepped suddenly into the doorway. The man had a full beard, and he was talking very fast in a heavily twanged drawl that made his voice sound like an old banjo. I couldn't understand a word of what he was saying, but he had a hard squint in his eyes and a shotgun in his hand.

He was dangerous.

I think he was telling me to drop my gun.

I told him to drop his, but he wouldn't. When I told him again, he just grinned and kicked the fallen magazine out of reach while keeping his shotgun trained right on me.

He said something else, but I couldn't understand him. His right hand tensed on the trigger. I was backing up. Sparrow had started screaming, but I couldn't see him. All I saw was the black hole in the middle of the barrel and the bony hand that held it. And then I remembered how Vincent had taken the magazine out of the gun he'd given me, how he'd said, "You're good, my man," and how he'd smiled when he racked the slide faster than I could follow.

"Six of my bullets are on the floor," I said, holding my ground, "but there's one in the chamber, and if you don't take that shotgun out of my face, I'm going to shoot you straight through the heart. The boy was cold and lost. He didn't come here to rob you or spy on you. So you just put that gun down right now, and you let us walk out of here. You understand?"

He hesitated. Looked me in the eye. Slowly, he let the rifle drop.

I kept the .45 trained on him and told the boy to walk out, then went out backward, still keeping my gun trained on the man. We ran past the fire pit and the hanging skins and through the rough-hewn door, back into the night, and climbed up the hill together. He stayed close to me. He seemed not to remember what had just happened.

For a long while, we said nothing.

When we were halfway up the hill, he dropped to his knees in the deep snow and started sobbing. He said he was sorry. He said he didn't know how he'd ended up in the barn. He said he was scared that he wouldn't be able to fight the madness that ran in his family, in his blood. Schizophrenia, paranoia—whatever the doctors wanted to call it—would eventually descend on him. He was sure of it. He would end up like the old man in the quarry, crazy and alone, living in the woods with nothing but guns and gas cans and animal skins, and there was nothing I, or anyone else, could do about it.

I let his sobbing come to an end and then pulled him to his feet.

I didn't have a handkerchief, so I took my fingers and wiped the tears from his eyes.

I thought of his father, and his father's father, and of all the sad poets that populate this world.

I wanted to tell him how hard I'd wept when his father died. And how the shock was still with me. I wanted to tell him how I wept when I found out he would be coming to live with me. I wanted to use Lily's words to tell him that I thought he was the most "beautiful boy in the world." The most sensitive, beautiful boy. And I wanted to tell him that even if he never thought of me as his father, I would always think of him as my son. Even now. Always. Ever.

But I couldn't find the words. The moment passed, and we started walking again.

After a bit, we began talking almost as if nothing had happened.

"I don't think I fit in the city. I don't fit in with the kids in my school," he told me.

"I'm sure a lot of kids feel that way."

"Maybe it's because I'm so ugly."

"You are not ugly. You're a very handsome bird. You only look funny when I cut your hair."

"Not that it matters."

"Why doesn't it matter?"

"In a billion years the sun will burn out, and that will be the end of us. No one will know we ever existed."

We were talking like we always had.

"Maybe we won't end," I said. "Maybe we'll download ourselves into our computers, or integrate with machines, or go to another planet."

"I don't think I'd want that," he said.

"I wouldn't want that either," I admitted. "But maybe the world will end, and then it will start all over again in a great Vedic cycle, like in your book on Hindu myth."

"I don't know if I believe that. I think we're a rock in space. And I think once the sun goes out, we'll be a floating dead rock and no one will ever know we

255

were here, and everything will be erased forever."

"You're a very philosophical bird."

"You mean a weirdo?"

"No. I mean you're a deep and serious thinker."

"I don't think so. But you know how it gets really quiet right when the snow starts to fall. I don't know why it gets so quiet. It just does. And when I got up here and listened to how quiet it was, I felt like maybe I could understand how the snow had a spirit. And when I got to thinking about it more, I thought that maybe it was a good idea to think of the world that way—the way the Indians who lived here believed in all different kinds of gods and spirits. They had a god of the sun and a god of the moon and a god of the sea. They believed that there was a spirit of the river and a spirit of the woods. And they had other spirits for waterfalls and mountains."

We were nearing the first ridge I'd climbed, not far from the Delaware River.

The boy was still talking about the Indians, telling me about how they'd taught the Pilgrims to fertilize their crops with fish carcasses.

"The fish would swim upstream," he said, "just when you needed fertilizer for planting. Which I think is kind of amazing. The way nature gives you things that you need. But even though the Indians taught them that stuff, the Pilgrims still thought they were savages."

"We're the savages. Aren't we?" I asked.

"I think so. Everything we make is ugly and plastic and destroys our environment, and everything they made was amazing. It's not like they were simpletons. You try to make a flint knife. It's not easy. When I was at archeology camp it took me all summer just to learn how to do flint knapping. And remember the fishing nets we saw at the Museum of Natural History? To me those are as beautiful as any piece of European art in any museum, anywhere."

"What about the great canoe? That was my favorite when I was a kid."

"The one they hung from the ceiling?"

"Yes. It looks like you could kill a monster with that canoe. Or cross an ocean."

"It is incredible. I think it's from the Pacific Indians. Right?"

I leaned against a birch tree to catch my breath.

"It is Pacific."

"I like that stuff," he said, "but I really like the Eastern Woodlands. Maybe because it's where I'm from. You know, if we were Algonquin or Cherokee, we'd have snowshoes, and we could really use those right now," he said, as he went tromping through the deep snow. "Or we could go ice fishing with spears at night by torchlight."

I followed behind him and switched to monosyllabic answers.

"We could," I said.

"But I think I'd like to be a Sioux Indian the best."

"Why?"

"I like their ceremonies."

"Which one?" I said, struggling to keep up with him, watching my breath make clouds in the cold air.

He stopped and looked back at me.

"The one where an older member of the tribe adopts a young male," he said.

And then he started off again. I followed close behind.

"Do you remember how they do it?" I asked.

"Most of it. They make this altar out of a buffalo skull and reeds with eagle feathers and a stalk of corn. I think the kernels are supposed to be the people and all the things of the universe, or something like that. And then the older tribesman waves the reed with the eagle feathers over the boy's head and then he kneels and paints the symbol of the tribe on the boy's face. The boy is bound to him with woven rope to show that their bond is as strong as father and son."

We were back on top of the ridge. We were breathless. And the moon, which had just started rising, was at our feet. It was full, and there was light everywhere, and the birch trees were all around us, light and dark and mysterious.

The snow had stopped falling, and the clouds had cleared. I pulled him as close to me as I could and pointed toward the constellations that had just appeared in the winter sky.

Something had just occurred to him.

"Was there really a bullet in the chamber?" he asked.

I looked at him, took the gun out, aimed at the moon, and fired.

About the Author

Seth Kanor was born in New York City and raised in Hastings-on-Hudson where he studied English Literature with Charles Aschman while working as a stonemason's assistant, lifeguard, housecleaner, and on an assembly line at a local soap factory. After dropping out of both Boston University and Berklee School of Music, he studied jazz guitar privately while driving a taxicab. He then enrolled at UMASS/Boston as a political science major, and subsequently attended the Graduate Acting Program at NYU's Tisch School of the Arts. A ten-year detour that included appearances off-Broadway, on film, and in television, led him back to literature. *Indian Leap* is his first novel.

CPSIA information can be obtained at www.ICGtesting.com
Printed in the USA
LVOW04s0539260215

428421LV00004B/293/P